HAIL, COLUMBIA!

HAIL, COLUMBIA!

AN ALPHONSO CLAY MYSTERY OF THE CIVIL WAR

BOOK FIVE

Jack Martin

OPEN ROAD

INTEGRATED MEDIA
NEW YORK

This edition published in 2022 by Open Road Integrated Media, Inc.
180 Maiden Lane
New York, NY 10038
www.openroadmedia.com

Dedicated to Justin Martin, my very favorite (and only) child; I am immensely proud of you, and of everything you do.

HAIL, COLUMBIA!

PROLOGUE

A MANSION IN GRAMERCY PARK, NEW YORK CITY—MAY 1869

"So, Gould, how would you like to be the richest man the world has ever seen?"

Jay Gould leaned back in his wingback chair before the fire, and looked with black expressionless eyes at Jim Fisk, saying nothing.

The visitor occupying the other wingback chair before the fire was a large, healthy-looking man, giving the appearance of being no more than forty. Gould had sharp eyes, and could see the intricate network of tiny wrinkles covering his visitor's face; Gould wondered just how much older than forty Fisk might be.

Fisk interpreted his host's silence as reluctance. "No, Gould, I am not exaggerating. My friends and I can literally make you the richest man in the world."

"Why would you assume I need more wealth?" Gould finally replied. He gestured at the sumptuous library where they were sitting, with bookcases containing hundreds of thousands of dollars worth of rare volumes. "I have enough to indulge my passion for collecting rare books. I have this mansion, and a country estate. I have a wife I adore, who has just given birth to our third child, my first daughter. I am already worth many millions of dollars. So why should I want even more money? More to the point, what would you expect me to do in return for such . . . philanthropy on your part?"

Gould's visitor took out a cigar, lit it, and spent some moments studying it before replying. "I will be very candid with you, Mr. Gould," Fisk finally replied. "I represent interests that wish a fundamental political change in the country, a change that would make the Government much more sympathetic to the goals and ambitions of those interests."

"You are certainly planning ahead," Gould responded. "Grant has just been inaugurated President. Nothing could be done before '72."

"I wouldn't say that," said Jim Fisk, still looking idly at his cigar. "When I said 'fundamental political change', I meant it. The interests I represent wish elections to become irrelevant."

Jay Gould did not play cards, which was a pity: he would have been superb at poker. Not a single expression showed on his dark-visaged, bearded face. Nevertheless, the brain behind the face was racing frantically. He knew his visitor's reputation, and had expected to hear an illegal proposal; whether or not he would accept the proposal would depend upon whether the profit would justify any risk. Still, even Jay Gould hesitated at the thought of treason. Not because of patriotism, of which he had none; nor even of possible punishment, for he had enough money to buy any judge who was even slightly corrupt, and had . . . other means for dealing with those who were not. He was very well aware that should he be connected with a treasonous plot—an unsuccessful treasonous plot—his carefully constructed railway and banking empire would come tumbling down like a house of cards. Even a capitalist as rich as himself depended to some degree on the tolerance, if not good will, of the American public; and that tolerance could evaporate overnight. Gould cared for only three things in the world: his family, his books, and his fortune. He would risk much for even greater wealth, but the risk to those three things must be minimal before he would embark on a project such as his visitor was discussing.

"So, what would you want from me? Financing for your plot?" asked Gould.

His visitor expelled a cloud of cigar-smoke toward the ceiling and chuckled. "No, Mr. Gould, we have no need of your money, at least until the final phase. Rather, what we need is for you to simply make money for yourself, money on a scale undreamed of in human history, money obtained in the manner we direct. The way you will make it will aid the plans of my associates."

Gould did not believe in something for nothing. "Just what do you propose?"

Fisk chuckled again. Then, he leaned forward and began to speak softly.

Two hours later, Jay Gould staggered out his front door, dizzy with anticipation and lust for money. His visitor had departed only minutes before, after describing a plan on a monumental scale; describing the resources that would come together to make it succeed. Gould knew the reputation of his visitor, and was not even slightly inclined to treat his proposal as fantastic nonsense. Of course, there was some risk, but the titanic scale of the gains to be made caused Gould to consider the risks acceptable. *Still,* thought Gould, *some measures should be taken to minimize the risk.* He took it as a favorable omen that he had already scheduled a meeting with one of his most valuable agents for this very evening. He paused at the bottom of his steps, and nodded approvingly at the last vestiges of the sunset; the dusk would conceal his movements from observation, despite the pools of illumination around the occasional gas light post. With quick steps he crossed the largely-deserted street to the gated park that gave his neighborhood its name. He strolled along the sidewalk that ringed the park, turning left at the street that formed its northern boundary. Soon he was in the shadow of a large elm tree that overhung the sidewalk. The tree was far from the nearest gaslight, and he could barely see his own feet.

"Good evening, Mr. Gould."

Despite having received such greetings in the past, Gould nearly cried out in alarm.

"Damn it, Duval, try to give me a little warning! I am not as young as I was."

A silvery, chilling laugh came from the darkness. Silent as a ghost, a form glided out of the deepest shadow. With difficulty, Gould could make out a lithe, black-haired, attractive woman, her eyes glittering with amusement, her smile predatory.

"You are the one who wants our meetings to be discreet, so you can hardly complain that I remain out of sight until you are here," replied Teresa Duval. "Of course, this skulking about would not be necessary, if you would simply let me into your home."

"You know the reasons why that is not possible. Our meetings often involve matters of . . . debatable legality, and I have a strict rule that such matters never enter my home."

Again came the silvery laugh. "Besides, the beautiful Mrs. Gould might misunderstand our relationship."

Indeed she might, thought Gould, who had never given his wife any cause for jealousy, with Duval or any other woman. "You may be right, which is all the more reason for you to never set foot in my home."

Duval smiled broadly. She almost told Gould about the time she had broken into his house without detection, and spent some minutes at the foot of the bed Gould shared with his wife, watching their sleeping forms, toying with the idea of slashing their throats while they slept. She resisted the temptation; certain that Jay Gould would not see the humor in the revelation.

"Indeed, Mr. Gould. She might well misinterpret your giving me an envelope stuffed with banknotes." Gould took the hint. He drew a thick envelope from the side pocket of his frock coat and tossed it to Duval, who deftly caught it and made it disappear. She did not bother to count it; Gould was scrupulously honest—in certain things. Instead, she asked, "Any trouble with the family?"

"No. The widow was quite broken up over her husband's death. Unlike the late Mr. Trelawney, Mrs. Trelawney had no objection to selling her shares in the railway to me. In fact, she seemed quite grateful to make a quick sale. It is a pity; if only her husband had not been so stubborn."

Gould paused, and then went on, "You accomplished your assignment with your usual . . . discretion. You have been doing quite well because of me, these last few years."

Duval shrugged. "I have no cause for complaint."

"I am well aware that you have long wished to leave my service. With what I have paid you, supplemented by your salary from the Pinkerton Agency, your dreams of a luxurious retirement are almost within reach. I am in a position to help you fulfill that dream sooner than you had expected. I am going to need you in the coming months to perform a number of delicate tasks."

"What kind of tasks, Mr. Gould? Their nature will of course affect the price."

"The transaction is still maturing, so I am not entirely certain of the nature of the tasks. I am prepared to offer you $75,000 to be on retainer, $25,000 in advance, $50,000 upon completion."

Duval nearly gasped in surprise. With the more than $60,000 she had on deposit under various false names, such a sum would put her well over the goal she had set years previously for her "retirement" of $100,000. Duval careful concealed her eagerness, replying in a dubious voice, "Such a fee implies considerable risks."

"That is why the fee is so generous, Miss Duval. If you agree, I will be here tomorrow night at the same time with $25,000 in Federal banknotes."

"Very well, Mr. Gould. We will meet tomorrow night."

"One final thing, Miss Duval. I seldom interfere in the private lives of my associates, but it is well known in certain quarters that you have established a long-term liaison with Major Alphonso Clay."

Normally, Teresa Duval had nerves of ice. At the mention of Clay's name, her stomach took an uncomfortable lurch. "What of it?"

"Major Clay is not well known to the general public; if they hear of him at all, they only hear he is an obscure officer in the Army's Inspector General Directorate. Washington insiders have picked up hints that he is unusually well connected with the President, who uses Clay as his trouble-shooter in the most delicate political cases. I will not insult your intelligence. The scale of the fee I have offered you must have caused you to guess that my . . . enterprise will be on a massive scale, and may trigger interference by Washington. That interference will almost certainly involve Major Clay. I have a terrible feeling that any involvement in my affairs by Clay would prove unlucky for him. He might very well have the same fate that was suffered by Mr. Trelawney."

Duval was silent for a long moment, and then glided up to Gould until her face was only inches from his. Gould heard rather than saw a straight razor snick open in her hand. "Do you remember how we first met, back in '61, not far from this very spot?" she murmured softly, dangerously.

Gould was unafraid. "Indeed I do. A Mick guttersnipe clutching bloody money she had just taken from a dead banker. I could have sent you to the gallows. Instead, I gave you a path out of the street, a path to security and independence. Now you threaten me. Many things you may be, but stupid is not among them. Do you honestly think that if something happened to me, you would live very long? You are only one of my agents; my most valued and highest paid, but still only one. Should I have an accident, those agents will be informed of who caused it. You made your choice back in '61. It is unfortunate that you have become involved with someone who stands in my way, but life is full of tragedy." Gould coughed briefly, thinking of the tuberculosis that was slowly killing him. "Trust me in this, Miss Duval, I never have anyone removed unnecessarily. Contrary to what you may think, I am not an animal. There is only a possibility of Clay becoming an impediment, but should he do so, you are in the best position to remove that impediment. That is why your fee will be so huge; to assuage any grief that you may feel."

Gould faced the silent Duval for some moments, without fear, genuinely curious as to whether he had judged her rightly. Finally, he heard the snick of the straight-razor closing.

"Very well, Mr. Gould, we have a deal. However, Major Clay is left strictly alone unless there is no other way to save your plans. Is that clear?"

"Perfectly. I will be here tomorrow night with your money. Good evening, Miss Duval." With that, Gould turned and began to retrace his steps.

Duval stared after him for nearly a minute. Then without a sound she retreated deeper into the shadows of the elm until she seemed to completely disappear.

CHAPTER 1

"AND WHEN THE STORM OF WAR WAS GONE . . ."

"Good morning, Mr. President," said Major Alphonso Clay to Ulysses Grant as he entered the second floor library of the Executive Mansion that functioned as Grant's office. The short, slight, blonde officer snapped a formal salute while taking in the President's appearance. He did not like what he saw.

Grant sat behind a large mahogany desk cluttered with papers, gazing out the window toward the unfinished Washington Monument. He turned to Clay and nodded; a sad yet determined look on his face. Clay could see that the President's civilian clothes were tight on him, revealing an unhealthy gain in weight. The right arm holding the ever-present cigar was encircled by a black mourning band. Clay hesitated, but despite his cold nature, he decided to give Grant what comfort he could.

"Sir, may I offer you my condolences on the death of Secretary Rawlins? I realize that he was very close to you. You must think on his release from the sufferings of the consumption. The last time I met him he could barely breathe."

Grant nodded again. "Thank you, Major. John was one of the best friends I ever had, and gave me more than I could ever give him. I knew when I made him Secretary of War that he didn't have long to live, but I wanted to show the world what I thought of him." Grant sighed, then continued. "I suppose I should get onto finding a new Secretary of War, but I can't make myself do it right today. Sherman can hold the fort until . . . a proper interlude has passed. Anyway, that is not why I called you. Take a seat."

Clay drew an upholstered armchair up to the front of the President's desk and sat formally, his back not touching the chair at any point. Grant continued speaking.

"First, I wanted to personally thank you for resolving that matter out in the Plains so discretely. That Indian agent you found selling Winchesters to the redskins was brother to a Senator. The settlers, not to mention the army and the newspapers, would have started a new civil war if they found the guns used in bushwackings were being sold by an employee of the Department of the Interior. It was a lucky chance that the Indian agent seemed to have met with a fatal accident, so that no public trial that would embarrass an important Senator is necessary." Grant stared hard at Clay, who as usual displayed a bland countenance, the blue eyes behind the wire-rimmed spectacles giving nothing away.

"I thank you, Mr. President. With respect, I must mention that the untimely passing of the agent solves only the smallest part of the problem. So long as the Indians have grievances—and they do—and so long as there are some Americans so depraved as to sell them rifles superior to those issued to the Army, there will be violence on the frontier."

"Don't I know it," responded Grant, taking a long pull on his cigar. "If I could, I would leave them half of the West to do with as they will. Trouble is, settlers ignore the treaties and keep crowding onto their best land, trampling their holy sites, killing the buffalo the Indians need to survive, sometimes even violating their women. And when the Indians respond as you or I would and take a few scalps, the newspapers scream for the Army to come in and wipe them out. I will do what I can for the Indians, but I fear that in the end they will be reduced to pitiable survivors on the least desirable land, if any are allowed to survive at all. All I can do is try to keep the injustice from becoming flat genocide.

"Anyway, that is a problem I have to deal with on my own, and it does not require your . . . unique skills and discretion. What do you know of the Ku Klux Klan?"

Clay nodded slightly at the abrupt change of subject; he had known that it would only be a matter of time before Grant would call for his help on the Klan. "Only what I read in the newspapers, sir. It is a loose organization of Confederate veterans devoted to resisting the occupation authorities in the South, and in driving the liberated slaves into a state of impotent serfdom. The members don silly disguises and ride forth to terrorize officers and agents of the Reconstruction governments and the Freedman's Bureau. It seems that they are instituting a campaign of murder against selected pro-Union leaders, especially in the black community."

Grant took another puff on his cigar. "It is getting out of hand, Clay. The generals in all five occupation districts are reporting they are beginning to lose control of the situation. They are crying for more troops, but thanks to the doggone Congress's budget cuts, I don't have any more to send them, or at least not enough. At the rate the Klan's campaign of terror is stepping up, it will soon be impossible to govern any part of the South where a soldier isn't standing. The Klan will in effect become the government of the South; they may even effectively reinstate slavery for the blacks."

Clay frowned slightly. "Sir, I am not being modest when I say I am but one man. What difference could I make?"

Grant turned back to the window and gazed at the unfinished monument. Without looking at Clay, he said, "There is one course of action within our resources. It has been proposed to me by General Sheridan. I think you know what he proposes."

Clay nodded. "'The only good Indian is a dead Indian.' That is what General Sheridan said when he was sent to subdue the Plains Indians two years ago. For what it is worth, it has worked, in the areas where he has campaigned. The Indian troubles only continue where they face troops commanded by more . . . civilized officers."

"Don't get me wrong, Clay. Sheridan is a great general; he was next only to Sherman as my strongest supporter in the war. And I take full responsibility for turning him loose on the Shenandoah Valley; just as I take full responsibility for Sherman's March. Still, I thought we had seen the end of such . . . extreme measures in the South. When I told Lee at Appomattox 'Let us have peace' I doggone meant it. It takes far fewer troops to destroy than to occupy and police. If it is necessary, I will put Sheridan in command with orders to create a vast silence and call it peace."

Grant suddenly swiveled in his chair to face Clay, eyes hard and implacable. "I didn't send three hundred thousand young boys to their deaths only to see all they fought for slip away. I intend to break the power of the Klan, and insure that the Federal writ runs everywhere in the South. Without turning Sheridan loose if at all possible, but turning him loose if it is the only way. I am going get Congress to pass a law allowing me to suspend the writ of habeas corpus in areas of the South where public order has broken down, and permitting trial by military court martial of anyone trying to destroy Federal authority."

Clay arched his eyebrows slightly. "An ambitious design, sir. Are you sure that Congress will grant you such power?"

"I think they will. Senator Sumner and Cump Sherman's brother will push things in the Senate, James Garfield in the House. Between them, I should get the authority. Although it won't be enough if the Klan remains strong and unified. Then I will have no choice but to unloose Sheridan on them. He will kill and burn until the survivors beg for mercy; until they know there is only a choice between submission and death. I don't want to do that, Clay. Give me a reason not to do it. Give me something that will allow me to break up the Klan into a manageable problem. I know we'll never be rid of all the diehards and bigots; but if they are scattered and disorganized, the army I have can control them without resorting to . . . extreme measures. I don't want to make the South another Poland or Ireland."

Grant paused to take a deep draw on his stogie and slowly expel the smoke, never taking his eyes off Clay.

"Of course I've put the Provost on the case, but they've proved useless; they're good only for rounding up drunks and deserters. I don't expect miracles, Clay. All I am asking is, will you do what you can?"

Clay paused only briefly. "Sir, I have never refused a request from you and I will not create a precedent now. I cannot guarantee success; I can only guarantee my best efforts."

"That is all I ask. Of course, you are free to draw on the War Department for whatever supplies and money you may need. Quartermaster General Meigs has already been advised." Grant rose from his chair, automatically followed by Clay. Grant gave him a letter, saying, "This is an order over my signature for all Government and Army personnel to give you any assistance you request, without question." Then the President stuck out his hand, saying, "Keep me informed. Good luck, Major Clay."

Clay took the President's hand and shook it firmly, then saluted smartly, turned on his heel, and strode out of Grant's office.

Grant stared at the door for nearly a minute, his conscience bothering him. He well knew that unleashing Clay on a target was not something to do lightly; that people he had never met were likely to die. Yet the alternative could be carnage on as massive a scale as the War. He did not want to see that come again, but he would make it come if it were the only way to preserve the Union. If people died and wanted to haunt him, they would have to get in line behind the ghosts of Shiloh, the Wilderness, the Crater, and a dozen other horrific battles. He shrugged his shoulders slightly, and stubbed out his cigar in an ashtray. Grant decided he needed to see Julia; she could always lift his burdens. He strolled out of the library and descended the stairs in search of the love of his life.

Grant found Julia in the Blue Room, entertaining his sister Virginia and her new husband, Abel Corbin, the two women sharing a sofa while Corbin leaned on the mantelpiece. He was nearly as glad to see his homely younger sister as he was his wife; the two women got along famously, and never caused him any grief. He was somewhat less happy to see his brother-in-law. Corbin was a successful financier, handsome enough, but considerably older than Virginia. Grant could not understand what such a man saw in his sister save a connection with the President's family, and could not rid himself of a hidden dislike for the man. Seeing how his sister glowed in Corbin's presence, Grant guiltily suppressed his dislike.

"Sam!" exclaimed Julia Grant, her cross-eyed face lighting up with delight. "I was just telling Virginia and Abel that we couldn't expect to see you before lunch."

"Decided I needed a break, my love." He proceeded to give his wife a long, tender kiss, then leaned over to his sister and gave her a chaste peck on the cheek. "Virginia, you look more radiant every time I see you. Marriage must agree with you."

"It surely does, Hiram, just as it does with you." The middle-aged sister of the President giggled like a schoolgirl.

The lean Abel Corbin frowned slightly. "Sir, I've always been puzzled why your wife calls you Sam while Mrs. Corbin calls you Hiram."

Grant shrugged. "No secret there. I was christened Hiram Ulysses Grant, and that's how my sister knew me while we were growing up. When I went away to West Point, the doggone army made a mistake, and put me down as Ulysses Simpson Grant; never could find out exactly why. Well, I was new at the Point, and didn't want to draw attention to myself, so I let the new name stand. Didn't seem to matter much."

"But how did they get Sam out of that name?"

Grant gave another of his negligent shrugs. "My classmates noted my initials were U. S. Grant, and decided to nickname me Uncle Sam Grant. After awhile they shortened it to Sam, and it has stuck with me ever since. That's how Julia first came to know me in Missouri. Anyway Julia, I thought since the weather seems so fine, we might harness up a carriage and go for a ride."

The smile suddenly left Julia's face. "Oh dear. We can't leave Daddy here alone. He always gets in trouble with the servants. Besides, I haven't had a chance to tell you—Father Jesse has shown up without warning, as usual. You know that those two cannot get along if left to themselves."

"My father has shown up?" asked Grant. He could already feel one of his sick headaches beginning. As if on cue, the sound of quarreling voices became audible, shortly followed by the arrival of two old men, one short and fat, and the other lean and bearded. Suppressing a sigh, Grant stepped forward and grabbed the hand of the lean man.

"Father, what an unexpected surprise!" exclaimed Grant, smoothly slipping between the two oldsters. "What brings you to Washington?"

Jesse Grant favored his son with one of his born salesman's smiles. "Why, to see my son, the President. Why shouldn't I? After all, you have Julia's old Rebel of a father staying with you all the time. Surely you can put me up for a few days."

"Why shouldn't I live with my daughter?" replied the portly Frederick Dent. "When your son courted my Julia, I was a man of substance in Missouri, with thousands of acres and dozens of slaves, and he was a penniless scrub lieutenant. Then he got lucky, got control of the army, and destroyed everything that decent white people had built in the South. My slaves are all runaways; the land gone to rack and ruin . . ."

"Now Daddy, enough of that," said Julia Grant smoothly as she rose, crossed the room, and took her father's arm. "You've been arguing with Father Grant again, haven't you?"

"Why shouldn't I?" repeated Dent. "Every time I see that damn abolitionist he needles me about his great son, who destroyed the best civilization the world has ever seen."

"A civilization based on enforced labor of human beings," replied Jesse Grant. "Yep, my boy did more to end slavery than anyone except Lincoln, and I'm proud of that."

"Father, are you going to be doing anything else while you visit?" asked the President, knowing full well what was coming.

"Well, Hiram, thought I might mosey over to the War Department. They buy things for the cavalry there, and Lord knows the family business has a powerful lot of leather goods fit for reins and tackle."

Not again, the President thought to himself. Twice during the war he had been forced to have his own father escorted out of the war zone for trying to use his famous son's name to get business for the Grant tannery. Ulysses Grant had complicated feelings about his father. The old man had been an indulgent and loving parent, who had never so much as raised a hand to him or any of his siblings; as contrasted to Grant's cold and distant mother, still alive, still refusing to visit her son in the Executive Mansion. When Ulysses had entered his darkest days, just before the war, it was his father who had a made a job for him in the family business—a job for which he knew his son was ill-suited—with nary a complaint. His father had filled him with a hatred for slavery and a love for his country, and had made him the man he was. As an adult, Ulysses had come to realize that his father's business ethics were flexible—so flexible as to break at the first hint of gain. He knew that his father viewed his son's sudden rise to fame and power as an opportunity to get special consideration in government contracts, with an almost childish disregard of the ethical issues involved. Ulysses sighed, he supposed he would have to pass the word to Sherman and to Meigs that under no circumstances were they to see his father, much less consider giving the old reprobate any government business. Yes, a sick headache was definitely on the way.

"Well, dear, a carriage ride for all of us is a bit out of the question," interposed Julia Grant smoothly. "Sam, why don't you go meet that gentleman at Willard's while I have the servants serve up luncheon for the rest of us."

Grant almost said "What gentleman?" but stopped himself when he saw Julia wink one of her crossed eyes slightly. His dear wife knew how in their different ways the two old men got on his nerves, especially when they got to arguing, and was giving him a chance to avoid a social event with the two of them. Julia loved her now-penniless father, and was grateful for her husband tolerating the old man in their home. As much as she loved Frederick Dent, she was well aware of how insufferable he could be, and loved her husband even more for putting up with him. Creating an imaginary "appointment" was her way of allowing the President to gracefully have a break from the commotion generated by parent and in-law.

"Thank you for reminding me, love. I should be back in an hour or so." He kissed Julia, bowed slightly to the others, and left the Executive Mansion as quickly as dignity allowed, nodding slightly to the impassive doorman as he departed the building.

He was already looking forward to dropping into the lobby of Willard's and ordering one of their delightfully frosty concoctions they had named "milkshakes;" not as destructive as whiskey, he reflected, and far tastier. Of course, he might have to put up with a stream of favor-seekers. His patronage of Willard's lobby was so well known to the pestering crowd of influence peddlers that wits had taken to calling them "lobbyists." Well, he could put up with them, he thought, if it was the price of getting away from father and father-in-law for awhile—and of course the milkshakes did not hurt.

Three floors above the Willard's lobby, Alphonso Clay sat in his suite's overstuffed armchair. An observer would have looked upon him, motionless as a statute, and have concluded he was in some sort of trance. In fact, his unusual brain—more unusual than any doctor would have suspected—was rapidly evaluating numerous courses of actions, discarding some, modifying others, relegating still more to a "back-up" status.

"Well, Alphonso, woolgathering? That is not like you."

At the sound of the voice Clay came as close to being startled as his nervous system allowed. Surging out of his chair, he had half-drawn his massive Smith & Wesson revolver from its holster before he recognized the intruder as Teresa Duval. As he reholstered his weapon, he said, "Damnation, Teresa, I might have shot you. How did you unlock the door and enter the room without my hearing you?" Although his voice was angry, a small smile tugged at the corners of his mouth. He was in fact delighted to see her, and delighted to see she had not lost her skillful touch.

"You must allow a working woman her secrets," she replied with a silvery, unearthly laugh. "Why else would Mr. Pinkerton pay me as much as he does?"

"And why else would Mr. Gould pay you even more."

Duval froze. She had never mentioned her arrangement with Jay Gould to her lover. She respected Clay's intelligence too much to deny the connection. In a voice charged with the promise of violence, she replied, "You have been spying upon me."

"Not intentionally. The President does keep me busy these days. He wanted me to look into the matter of a Mr. Augustus Trelawney as soon as I was finished with my last assignment, out on the Great Plains. There was some reason to believe that Mr. Trelawney was acting as an agent for Napoleon III. The French Emperor seems to have learned little from the fate of Maximilian in Mexico, and is considering sending an army to re-establish French influence south of the border. Imagine my surprise when upon my arrival in New York, I find that Trelawney's body had been fished out of the East River, his throat apparently slashed by a straight razor. Since I knew that you had gone to New York on business, I will not insult your intelligence by describing the thoughts that this method of murder gave me. My surprise turned to interest when I found that shortly after his death, his widow had sold controlling interest in a railroad to Jay Gould, who had long coveted the property."

"What do you intend to do?" asked Duval, with enforced casualness.

"Nothing. I had already confirmed Trelawney was in the pay of a foreign power, and plotting with the French to overthrown a government allied with our own. The gallows was his destination in any event; you simply saved the Republic time and money in putting him there. It is your motive that concerns me. I have long suspected you had professional interests beyond Mr. Pinkerton's Agency. I knew I had no right to demand information of you that you were disinclined to reveal. Nonetheless, I can no longer ignore the fact that the . . . habits you revealed during the War continue."

"Habits?" replied Duval.

A pained expression appeared on Clay's face. "Here in this room, let it be said, the pleasure you take in the act of killing, the . . . carnal pleasure, I had thought that our relationship had weaned you of the need for that pleasure. It would seem that I was mistaken."

"Do not tell me you are any different," said Duval with a frown. "You forget what I know of your actions in the war. You forget what I know about your ancestry. You derive the same sort of pleasure as do I."

"I do not forget. I am many unpleasant things, but I am not a hypocrite, and I will not presume to take the moral high ground with you. What disturbs me is that you do not even try to control your urges; while I struggle mightily to unleash them only upon this nation's enemies."

Duval glided close to Clay and placed her hand on his deceptively thin bicep. To her own amazement, she found herself telling her lover the absolute truth. "There was a time when I would take a man's life with no more concern than that caused by wringing a chicken's neck. Since I have known you, that has changed. I will take a life, and will enjoy it, but only if the one I kill has shown that he does not deserve to live. What you said about Trelawney was not news to me. Before I agreed to do this thing for . . . my employer, I had satisfied myself that Trelawney was a traitor. I killed him for that reason, not because I was paid to do so. Did I enjoy it? Yes, as well you know. Just as you have enjoyed killing. The Indian agent you were sent to investigate died in an 'accident,' I understand. That was convenient."

Clay's face was taut with the effort to contain conflicting, powerful emotions. "It had to be done. Soldiers and civilians had died by the dozens because of the sales he made to warring tribes. The man's brother is a key supporter of the President in the Senate. Even though the Senator was not involved in his brother's corruption, a public trial would have ruined his career, and eliminated a key political supporter of the President. I confess it was dishonorable, but it was necessary for the good of the nation."

Duval edged even closer to Clay. With slow, erotic movement she removed the heavy revolver from Clay's holster. "This is new," she murmured. "The Smith and Wesson .44? It must have a more devastating effect than the modest little .32 you favored during the war." Gently she placed it on an end table. Then with equally sinuous movements, she divested herself of her small Remington derringer and her beloved straight razor, placing them beside the massive revolver.

Then with the speed of a striking rattler, Duval punched Clay in the stomach. He staggered backward, and a strange, inhuman look came over his features. He lunged forward and locked his hands around her throat. Gasping for air while weirdly smiling, Duval wrenched herself free of his grasp, snaked her leg behind one of his, and pushed him onto the room's bed. Before he could rise, she pounced on him, where the fight quickly became something else.

The rail-thin, grim-looking man stood on the veranda of his hilltop mansion, looking over Memphis toward the distant Mississippi. His dark visage combined with his black goatee and swept-back hair to make him look vaguely satanic. He had many things on his mind; the slow progress of consumption through his lungs was one, the need to preserve his beloved South from the rule of black Republicans another, the methods used to achieve that goal a third. His reverie was interrupted by a cheerful, piping voice from behind him.

"There you are, Granda. I bet Mr. Hampton I would find you here. Guess I win my bet."

Nathan Bedford Forrest turned to look at his nine-year-old granddaughter, and something like a smile came over his features.

"And why were you so certain I would be on this veranda?" he asked her in a mock-serious voice.

With the innocent gravity of the very young, she replied, "This was Grandma's favorite place in the evenings. Ever since she died, you come out here whenever you can."

Early in the war, Forrest had been shot through the stomach, not only surviving but killing the man who had shot him with a Bowie knife. The pain that now arced through him was not unlike that caused by the long-ago bullet. "I feel close to your Grandma out here, pumpkin," he replied, forcing himself to smile. "Will you ask General Hampton to join me out here? After that, please go upstairs and do your lessons." Forrest had not learned to read until he was an adult, and still could only write in a childish scrawl. He was determined that his granddaughter would be well-educated.

"Yes, Granda." Impulsively the child rushed forward to hug him, then skipped off to do as she had been told. A smile tugged at the corners of his grim mouth. The smile instantly disappeared as he saw the burly, bearded figure of Wade Hampton emerge onto the veranda. "Welcome, General Hampton," Forrest said coldly. He gestured to one of the two chairs on the veranda. "Please be seated."

The chair creaked as the bearded visitor settled in with a grunt. "It's been a Goddamn awful trip, Forrest. The railroads are still pretty broken up between here and Charleston. This better be important."

"It is, General," replied Forrest softly, smoothly setting himself into the other chair. "We must discuss the progress of the Cause."

Hampton emitted a wheezy chuckle. "Progress is Goddamn fine, far as I can see. Carpetbag government is breaking up pretty much throughout the South. The blue bellies are scared to leave their camps in groups of less than a company. Yankee politicians are learning it can be mighty unhealthy—even fatal—to do too much for the darkies. As for the niggers themselves, any who show a sign of wanting an education, much less of wanting to vote or hold office, well . . ." Hampton drew a finger across his throat in an unambiguous gesture.

"Yes, we are doing well, and stand fair to throwing off the North's yoke; but I'm not pleased with what I've been hearing about what goes on in areas controlled by your men. There's too much violence."

"Too much violence?" Hampton emitted a belly laugh. "That's rich, Forrest. You of all people to complain about violence. The slave-trader who ordered the Fort Pillow Massacre?"

Forrest's dark eyes narrowed; the expression on his face would have frightened someone more perceptive than Wade Hampton. "Let me remind you, sir, that this movement is mine. I have sunk my own fortune into it."

"As have I, and have brought in the enormous resources of my East Coast friends" growled Hampton.

"And that is why you are my right hand. You best never forget than you will answer to *me*!" Forrest leaned forward, as tense as a spring. "The papers are full of our men burning darkie churches, sometimes with Christians in them; of hanging darkie women, even of shooting picanninies. These are not our enemies! The blue belly soldiers and their carpetbagger allies are the enemy. I said we were only to frighten the darkies, make them scared to help the enemy."

"When they're on the end of a rope, they look pretty scared to me. My Eastern friends are very pleased with how things are developing, and want us to keep the pot boiling."

"Just who in the Hell are these friends of yours, who are pleased when churches burn and women hang?"

"I've told you before, General Forrest. They do not want knowledge of their involvement to spread beyond me. In fact, it would be doing you no favor to bring you in on the secret, believe you me. Besides, no one is impressed with your current delicacy. The man who ordered the Fort Pillow Massacre—who ordered the slaughtering of an entire surrendered regiment, black men and white officers together, is in no position to get high and mighty about a few excesses here and there."

"I gave no order for a massacre," replied Forrest softly in a voice charged with the menace of violence. "Major Ward gave the order, directly contradicting my instructions. He was captured, and died in Federal captivity shortly afterwards. If he hadn't, he surely would have died at my hand the moment I could get to him."

"Then it is just as well he was captured," replied Hampton, affecting not to notice Forrest's threatening tone. "My friends thought highly of Major Ward, and would have been angry at anyone responsible for his death. Let me assure you, you do not wish to incur their anger. And that is enough of them. Let us put the past behind us and speak of the future. How is the Klan fairing in your area of operations?"

Forrest relaxed slightly. "Well enough. We keep Memphis, Little Rock and New Orleans stirred up with demonstrations, cross-burnings and riots, so the carpetbaggers and their black allies mostly stay holed up in the city halls and forts. Things are even better in the countryside than the cities. Out away from the towns, just a handful of men can keep a whole county in an uproar. If the blue bellies send out a patrol of four or eight men, we lay an ambush and put them all in the ground. If they send out more troops, they never find us. Union officers are pretty much finding excuses to stay huddled together close to their barracks. That gives our boys the run of the countryside."

Hampton looked at Wade intently. "People are starting to talk. They suspect you may be running the Klan out here. It does my Eastern friends no good if the army scoops you up."

Forrest snorted. "Let them talk, let them think what they want. There's no proof, and there won't ever be any. I keep myself out of the raids. Hell, only a handful of my top men know I run the show. I made them swear not to let their own men know who the ultimate boss is."

Hampton frowned. "What if one of your 'top men' talks to the Federals, or even just gets drunk and spills the beans in some bar or fancy house? Federals no longer view what we do as war, but treason and murder. The gallows awaits you and me, if mistakes are made."

"General Hampton, we have both commanded men in battle; both been pretty good at it, even though the Cause was lost. A good commander knows how to pick good men. I am trusting my boys with my life, and they are trusting their lives to me. I don't expect any of us will have cause to regret our trust. I would stake my life on my men."

"That's fortunate, for it is exactly what you will be doing," replied Hampton dryly. "In any event, I am glad you asked me to come. My friends in the East are so pleased with how things are going that they want us to take it to the next level, and we need to co-ordinate our efforts. In short, they believe it is time to make a move for Southern independence; in fact by this September."

Forrest's eyes narrowed. "That is Goddamn soon, Hampton. I thought the idea was to wear down the blue bellies with several years of costly hit-and-run attacks. We're not in a position to take on the Federals in a stand-up fight."

"My friends think that it won't come to that. They are planning actions for this September, actions that will leave Washington in a state of paralysis. Combined with stepped-up disorder in the South, the blue bellies will be in no position to resist when we raise the Stars and Bars throughout the South."

"If they think Grant will just stand aside and let the South go, they don't know their man. I never met him personally, but I faced his armies and learned the hard way that he never stops, never gives up. No matter what your friends have cooking, Grant will just lower his head and . . ." Forrest trailed off, realization having hit him like a brick. "I see. I don't like that sort of thing. An enemy should be faced like a man; you owe it to him to look him in the eye."

"There's no other way, Forrest. Don't worry your tender conscience about it. My friends will handle that end of the business. Our job is to keep the pot boiling down South."

"I suppose there is no other way to gain our freedom," said Forrest in a surprisingly soft voice.

"None. Now General Forrest, shall we go in to your library? It is not long until September, and we need to decide the details of the coming campaign."

Jay Gould sat in a wing chair to the left of his library's fireplace, looking with some displeasure at James Fisk, who once again occupied the chair to the right of the ornate fixture. Fisk was cheerfully puffing on a large cigar, the fumes from which were irritating Gould's delicate lungs. The large, extroverted Fisk was such a cheering presence Gould tolerated his smoking. Besides, Gould knew he would need Fisk's help in becoming, quite possibly, the richest man in the world. Coughing delicately, Gould broke what had been a long silence.

"I am amazed at how simple it will be, and am astonished that no one has seen the opportunity before us. It is there for anyone to see—so obvious that no one sees it."

Fisk expelled a large puff of smoke toward the ceiling and grinned. "It is so damn obvious. The key is the fact that people do not trust banknotes as much as gold, and pay a premium for the former. I checked the market before I came over, and gold is near a twenty-five percent premium; a \$20 gold piece will get you \$25 in greenbacks. Just imagine what will happen when we start buying up the gold futures, and reducing the supply! That premium will go to fifty percent, seventy-five percent . . . one hundred percent. People will be paying anything we have the guts to ask for gold, because we will control the future supply."

"Don't forget the New York Subtreasury," replied Gould. "They have tons of gold in coin and bullion in their vault, kept there to back up international financial transactions. All Grant has to do is order the Treasury to release gold, the price will plummet, and our plan falls to pieces. In fact, we would be left penniless. The cost of buying up enough contracts for the future delivery of gold is enormous! It will take everything you and I have."

Fisk laughed heartily and took another drag on his cigar. "Gould, don't tell me you're getting cold feet. Of course we have to put everything we have in . . . but think of the rewards! We buy contracts through anonymous operatives to receive gold at a set price of, say, $25 dollars an ounce. No one will know until too late it is just the two of us. As the contracts start to come due, imagine the panic of the suckers when they find that we control all the available gold, and that they have to buy it from us at $70 or $100 an ounce, then turn right around and deliver it back to us for $25 in greenbacks. They have to take the paper money. After all, it is 'legal tender for all debts, public and private.' We will control the money supply, soon we will control the stock market; and once that is done, we are close to controlling the economy." Fisk laughed jovially at the prospect.

"Providing we can keep the Subtreasury from selling the Government's gold," replied Gould solemnly.

"Goddamn it, Gould, you are such a worrier. Aren't you the one who told me you had that in hand?"

Gould turned his head and stared out the window. "Yes. The Washington end has been squared. There will be no intervention in the gold market by the Treasury." He turned his gaze back to Fisk. "Do you realize that if we pull this off, you, I and our friends will control the United States? Gold is the foundation for all economic activity, and we will control the price of gold. It is not just a matter of becoming rich beyond the dreams of avarice. We will have control—political control—of this country. The prospect gives me pause."

Fisk laughed again. "Don't be such an old woman! You should be reveling in the prospect of such power. With such power come all the good things in life: mansions, yachts, country estates, women . . ."

"My wife is quite enough for me," interrupted Gould. "Speaking of which, the newspapers are full of your 'association' with the showgirl Josie Mansfield, and the public rows that you've been having with her other admirer. It would be scandalous enough if you were single, but you have a wife! The newspapers will have you on their front pages from now through September, the very time when we should draw as little attention to ourselves as possible."

"Don't you see, Gould, that actually works in our favor? Who will suspect what we are up to when I am seen every day cavorting with my paramour, and having public scenes involving her other would-be lovers? The public in general, and Wall Street in particular, will just make clucking sounds and say, 'That damn fool Fisk, it's a wonder he hasn't driven himself to the poorhouse with his wild living and expensive tastes.' It will never occur to them in a thousand years what you and I will be up to out of the public eye."

Fisk laughed, but almost immediately sobered. "There is one thing that does bother me. My sources tell me that Grant has a troubleshooter, a major named Clay. This Clay is supposed to be very good at protecting Grant's flanks. Rumor has it he has derailed major problems for the President in the past, with his role never suspected by the public at large. If Grant begins to smell something, Clay is who he would put on our trail. Normally, I would just buy him off, but it seems that he has quite a fortune of his own. We should have some plan in place to . . . remove Major Clay, should we find he is becoming a nuisance."

"There is no need to worry about that," responded Gould. "I am well aware of the potential threat from Alphonso Clay, and have taken action that will guarantee he does not become a roadblock to our plans."

Teresa Duval found the train ride to New Orleans tedious. Were it not for the company of Alphonso Clay, she would have found it intolerable. Many would have been excited at the prospect of seeing the wide-open spaces of the burgeoning Republic. In the last four years, she had seen much of the country; both in the service of Jay Gould and of the Pinkerton Agency. She now viewed travel as an unavoidable interval between assignments, not a source of pleasure. It had taken her only an hour of skillful argument to persuade Clay that she could be of great use on his quest, and had no pressing business that could not be deferred. Frankly, it had surprised her that he finally acceded to her demand so relatively quickly; he must feel indeed the need for someone to cover his back.

It was Clay who broke the silence that had lasted for almost an hour. "Look out there," he said somberly, gesturing at the scraggly farms and crumbling farmhouses visible through the window of their first-class compartment. "The war has been over for four years, and yet the countryside looks in most places like an army had marched through just yesterday. I remember the South before the war; a land of plenty, even if its prosperity did depend on the labor of slaves. Alas, that dreadful poverty out there was not caused by the end of slave labor. The South suffered demoralizing defeat, and many of its people have lost the will to better their lives. Also, the Klan has caused disorder throughout the land, inhibiting the planning and development that would allow these people to have better lives, and depriving them of the unfettered contribution the freed slaves could make to the region's prosperity."

"You sound actually sorry for them," replied Duval. "Remember, these are the English-loving traitors who started the war in the first place. I would have never expected you, of all people, to feel pity for them."

"I would not have expected it of myself. During the war, I would have been happy to see the leaders hanged from gallows by the thousands, and the ground sowed with salt. Yet in the last eight years, I have seen so much suffering I tire of it; even though many of those suffering deserve their fate. I would rather build than tear down. I would rather see construction instead of destruction." He shook his head as if to clear it of such thoughts. "The Ku Klux Klan is an obstacle to that construction. So long as it is powerful, not much can be done to lift up the South. It is hard to know what our humble selves can do to check such a large and ruthless organization. Still, I promised the President I would try, so try we shall."

"So my dear knight errant, why is your quest starting in New Orleans?"

Clay shrugged negligently. "We have to start somewhere, and Louisiana is a better starting place than most. The Klan is very powerful there. You undoubtedly remember the election riots of last November. The Klan organized mobs of former Rebel soldiers to attack black men at random. Over two hundred, many Federal veterans, were killed, and several times that number seriously injured. It would stand to reason that clues as to the Klan's organization and leadership would be easiest to obtain where they have been the most active."

Duval was increasingly feeling the heat and humidity of a Louisiana summer, despite the fact she was wearing the lightest of her silk frocks. She also knew that despite his lack of complaint, Clay must feel even more uncomfortable than she. Although he had left behind his woolen major's uniform in the interest of anonymity, he had replaced it with what looked to be an even heavier black frock coat, tightly buttoned. He even refused to remove the wide-brimmed planter's hat that completed his civilian attire. Duval rose, and as she opened the compartment's window said, "Well, where do we start? With the Governor or the state attorney general?"

"Neither, I think," Clay replied as Duval resumed her seat across from him. "The state officials under Reconstruction are sadly corrupt. Further, they are undoubtedly intimidated by the Klan, and hence will be reluctant to help. No, I believe that it may be best to start with the army's Commander of the Department of Louisiana, Colonel Robert Buchanan. He is reputed to be a brave soldier and believer in rights for former slaves, and as an army officer would be less subject to intimidation by the Klan."

"Do you have an appointment with him? I only ask because it might be best to take him by surprise. He might be a brave and worthy officer, but trust me, Alphonso, many a brave and worthy officer has had things needing hiding in his background before this."

"Sad, but true," replied Clay. "That is why he does not know we are coming." A thoughtful expression on his bland face, Clay turned his attention to the poverty-stricken countryside passing by the now-open window.

Although Duval struggled to conceal it, she was impressed by the Chateau Dupre Hotel, the most luxurious establishment in the French Quarter.

After arriving at the train station, Clay had loaded their bags into the coach, telling the black cabman without hesitation, "Chateau Dupre." The cabman nodded, and with a flick of his whip urged his roan mare into the confusing, dangerous tangle of traffic, cabs, carts, horsemen and pedestrians darting about with no apparent rhyme or reason to their movements. Much to Duval's amazement, the cabbie skillfully navigated through the crowded, narrow streets of the French Quarter without incident, until he pulled up in front of a tasteful stone building. Handing the driver a dollar greenback, Clay took both of their large carpetbags himself and led Duval through a massive entryway into a large room decorated with plush furniture and Tiffany lamps.

He strode over to the mahogany counter that occupied one wall, placed the bags on the floor, and then told the narrow-shouldered young man behind the counter, "Two adjoining rooms, if you please."

The young man nodded and placed a register in front of him, Clay swiftly signed in as Mr. A. Clay of Louisville, then signed in for his companion as Miss T. Duval of Dublin. The clerk cocked an eyebrow at Clay, subtly expressing his opinion of a single man and a single woman traveling together, but he apparently decided that since the niceties had been observed by the renting of two rooms, he would not have to worry about the reputation of his hotel.

Duval had caught the clerk's look and almost laughed aloud. She knew full well that before the night was over they would both be in one of the two rooms. She briefly wondered why Clay was going through this charade. As rich as he was, the extra room at a place like Chateau Dupre was obviously going to cost him a pretty penny. Then she shook her head with fond wonderment at her lover's behavior; he was too honest to falsely claim that they were married. To her own surprise, she found that the thought was suddenly filling her with desire, and was now anxious to get upstairs with him.

"Well damn me to Hell for a Dutchman!" came a voice from

behind her. "Alphonso and Teresa! What in the name of the Holy Reconstruction are you doing in New Orleans?"

Both Clay and Duval whirled with a speed that shocked the desk clerk. Clay had half-drawn his massive Smith & Wesson from under his frock coat, and Duval and almost flicked open the straight razor that had appeared in her hand like magic, before they recognized the speaker and simultaneously relaxed.

Before them, dressed in flashy clothes, ginger moustache waxed to points, stood Ambrose Bierce.

CHAPTER 2

"LET NO RUDE FOE, WITH IMPIOUS HAND, INVADE THE SHRINE . . ."

Ambrose Bierce grinned with delight at the half-revealed weapons; he had several flaws of character, but physical cowardice was not among them. "Damnation, I know we have had our differences over the years, but they have usually stopped short of violence."

Clay and Duval had restored the weapons to their hiding places before the desk clerk could obtain a clear view of them. "Come over here before we talk more," whispered Clay fiercely, gesturing to a deserted corner of the lobby where a couple of settees displayed their plush velvet finery. The smile swiftly disappeared from Bierce's face, and he nodded his agreement. Clay then addressed the desk clerk in a loud, clear voice.

"Please have our bags taken to our rooms. We need to chat with our old friend here." The three then went to the corner and settled themselves, where it was clear that they could not be overheard. As soon as they were seated, Bierce offered an apology, a rare event for him.

"Damn it Clay, Miss Duval, I made an ass of myself, and I beg your pardon. The moment I saw you in civilian clothes, I should have realized that you were on some sort of mission, and did not want to attract attention. Damn it, I was just too pleased to see the both of you."

"Apology accepted," replied Clay dryly.

"So, are you making any progress on emasculating the Klan?" asked Bierce casually. Clay started; he had forgotten just how intelligent Ambrose Bierce could be.

"How came you to know of our business?" asked Duval in her sweetest voice, a bare hint of unspeakable violence detectable in her tone.

"I assure you both I had no idea until I saw the two of you at the reception desk in civilian clothes. I asked myself what could bring the two of you to New Orleans. Could it be routine Army business? Not with Alphonso out of uniform. Could you two have finally tied the knot, and come here on a honeymoon? Neither of you wore wedding rings. Therefore, you were here on some confidential business for Grant. Such business was most likely to have something to do with the latest Klan depredations."

Clay nodded approvingly. "You were always clever, Bierce. I only wish you showed a bit more discretion in how you use your cleverness. Given what you have deduced, may we count on that?"

"Of course. I know you wouldn't be here except to break the Klan's back, and you have my most hearty support in such an endeavor. In fact, that is what brings me here."

"The Klan?" asked Duval curiously.

Bierce shrugged. "The sale of fiction is not providing enough to live on, so I have accepted employment with a San Francisco newspaper. The folks out in California get a vicarious thrill reading about the Klan atrocities. They should be more concerned with how they treat their own Chinamen. Anyway, the editor sent me out to do some digging and come up with some first-hand articles about the evils of the Klan; the more degenerate and cruel they make Southerners appear, the better. The editor even cut loose with a handsome sum for expenses. Usually he is a cheap so-and-so, I hope this generosity doesn't give him a stroke. Why else do you think I am putting up in a place such as this?"

"So, how has your investigation been progressing?" asked Clay.

"Not as well as I had hoped," admitted Bierce. "I'm sure lots of people know juicy things about the Klan, but they are well and truly clammed up. You shall see, the boys in the white sheets have folks so terrified that I can't get any of the inhabitants of the bars, fancy-houses and such to give me anything useful. About all I could get out of them is that the carpetbagger officials hide behind army bayonets, trembling with fear; and the army doesn't do much more than act as bodyguards to the politicians. The Klan goes where it pleases and does what it pleases."

"It does not sound like much of a story," commented Duval.

Bierce grimaced. "True enough, Miss Duval. That is why I decided to change my approach and beard the army in its lair—specifically Colonel Robert Buchanan, the army's boss for all of Louisiana. I especially would enjoy hearing him explain why he isn't able to do more to protect the freedman and Union sympathizers."

Clay arched an eyebrow. "Indeed? We, ourselves, have an appointment to meet the Colonel tomorrow."

"Damnation!" exclaimed Bierce. "I have been trying to get in to see Buchanan for more than a week, without success. How did you swing an audience with his august majesty?"

Clay shrugged. "I have a letter from Grant directing all army personnel to co-operate with me in any way. Buchanan had little choice."

Bierce hesitated, then spoke almost apologetically. "Look Clay, I hate asking for favors, especially from friends, but surely I must ask. Could you take me in with you when you go to see Buchanan? I will be up front with you. I have been fired off two newspapers in the last year. The one I'm now working for now is the last major one in San Francisco that would have me. My own damn fault! My pride caused me to insult the boneheaded editors who presumed to edit my prose when they themselves could not push a noun against a verb without doing injury to the English language. Seeing as my personal funds are almost gone, this is make-or-break for me as a journalist."

Clay paused for only a few seconds before replying. "Ambrose, I want to be of service, but you must know that anything we discover relating to our assignment cannot be disclosed in a newspaper, ever."

"I am a patriot, Alphonso. You saw that in the war. I give you my word as a gentleman that you may see whatever I intend to send my editor, and delete anything harmful to Grant or the country. After all, I cannot imagine any journalist, much less myself, publishing a story that would harm his country."

Clay pondered for just a moment, cast a glance at Duval, and gave Bierce his answer.

The headquarters of the Department of Louisiana was located in a barracks to the south of New Orleans. Clay noted approvingly that that there were clear fields of fire in all directions, and the wooden stockade looked well-maintained. A pair of alert sentries stopped visitors at the main gate. They checked the identities of Clay and Duval, confirming that the Colonel was expecting them. Ever cautious, they were puzzled by the third visitor; not only had they received no word to admit Ambrose Bierce, but the journalist had been turned away twice in the recent past. A mute display of Clay's letter from Grant silenced their objections, and the trio was admitted inside the barracks complex.

The parade ground within the stockade was immaculate; the grass cut short, the pathways well graveled. The few soldiers in sight moved hurriedly and with purpose; obvious that Colonel Buchanan ran a tight ship. The three friends strode up to the stone building, a flagpole with a limply hanging Old Glory indicating it was the headquarters of the United States Army in Louisiana. Rapidly ascending the short flight of steps, they crossed the broad veranda and passed through the door that had been left open in a vain attempt to catch a cooling breeze. The door to the Colonel's office was also open; they could see a grey-bearded officer talking gruffly to a portly, nervous young lieutenant. The Colonel shifted his dark, fierce eyes to the new arrivals, then indicated with a jerk of his head that the lieutenant should take his leave. Colonel Buchanan rose slowly to his feet, placing his arms behind his back. Although dressed in civilian clothes, Clay touched the wide brim of his planter's hat in salute. The colonel did not return the salute. He stood glaring at his visitors without speaking, until Clay broke the silence.

"Colonel Buchanan, I do appreciate you taking the time to meet with us."

"I had no choice; the President's order was clear," responded Buchanan in a gruff monotone. "Nothing was said about two companions."

"Allow me to introduce Miss Teresa Duval, an employee of the Pinkerton Agency, and Mr. Ambrose Bierce of San Francisco. They are providing discrete assistance in my inquiries."

The Colonel's dark eyes shifted toward Bierce. "So it has come to this, then. I cannot keep gossiping newspapermen out of my own headquarters. Still, my orders were to assist you in any way I can, and I follow my orders."

"May we be seated, Colonel?" said Duval in a fair approximation of a Southern belle's simper. "The heat is dreadful, and I have come some distance."

Buchanan had a choleric temperament, but he was still an officer and a gentleman. Still scowling, he wordlessly came from behind his desk and moved one of the room's heavy wooden chairs to where Duval could seat herself with a minimum of movement. Clay and Bierce, left to their own devices, drew up chairs on either side of her. Buchanan then returned to his own chair, placed his forearms on the desk, and looked at them intently.

"Well, what does the President want? It must be damn important to be handled in such an irregular fashion."

Clay sat ramrod-straight, enunciating clearly. "The depredations of the Ku Klux Klan have intensified to the point that the President's entire Reconstruction policy is threatened. He has sent me to gather information on why the Army has not been able to control the Klan, and to suggest ways and means by which he can restore peace and order throughout the South." This was not exactly true, but Clay had decided this was how he would represent his mission to Buchanan.

Buchanan slowly leaned back in his chair, his face reddening. "I see. So Grant has decided he will finally drive me out of the service in disgrace; his revenge will be complete. Well, God damn him, and God damn you! I have done the best that can be done. I have less than two thousand troops to maintain order in the entire state of Louisiana! With the Klan so numerous and so secretive, it is flat impossible to protect all points. Hell, it is hard enough just to police New Orleans and Baton Rouge with what I've got. Yes, the Klan is running rampant, and as things stand there is not much that either I or that drunken bastard Grant can do about it!"

Clay's eyes narrowed slightly. "Colonel Buchanan, I am a serving officer, as are you. Furthermore, there is a lady present. I would strongly advise you not to speak of the President in such a manner in my presence, or hers."

Buchanan took a deep breath. "I do apologize for my language. However, I make no apology for the sentiment."

"Why do you have such hatred for Grant?" asked Duval with genuine curiosity.

"It is about that business in Northern California, before the war, isn't it, Colonel?" replied Bierce unexpectedly.

Buchanan's hostile stare snapped over to Bierce. "What do you know about that?"

Apparently perfectly at ease, Bierce slouched deeper into his chair. "Oh, the story is still told all around California. Grant's meteoric rise will not let it die." Bierce ostentatiously turned in his chair to address Clay and Duval. "It seems that in the mid '50's a young, troubled officer was transferred from Oregon Territory down to an isolated coastal fort some distance north of San Francisco. The young officer had a sterling record for bravery during the Mexican war. He did not pay much attention to his appearance, and missed his family which he had refused to subject to the dangers of the frontier, and had left in Missouri. Most officers who leave their families behind console themselves by shacking up with some half-breed squaw, but our young officer would not do that, and instead consoled himself with John Barleycorn. The fort was commanded by a major, a stern disciplinarian with no sympathy for any weakness. I hear that he harassed the young officer continuously, which of course just drove him deeper into the bottle. Then he gave the young officer a choice: resign, or face a court-martial for drunkenness on duty. Of course, he took the former course."

Buchanan glared at the nonchalant Bierce. "Yes, I drove Grant out of the service. He was a disgrace! Uniform askew, boots unpolished, stupid with drink more often than not. The army could not afford the luxury of such an officer; especially not at that fort, at that time, with the Modoc always on the verge of taking the warpath."

Duval smiled unpleasantly. "I see. You ran out of the army the greatest general of our time. Speaks well for your perception."

"And I have paid for it, Miss Duval! Who could have foreseen the War, or where his career would go once it started? As for being a great general, I am afraid I must contradict you. Luck, good political connections, overwhelming numbers explained his success. I am ten years older than him, and have been a far better officer than he ever dreamed of being. I should have had a major role in saving our country. Thanks to Grant, I only received a volunteer commission as general; never commanding more than a division, and at the end of the war I reverted to the rank of colonel, where I have stayed ever since. So don't go feeling sorry for Grant! If I was hard on him, he has been doubly hard on me."

Clay's features had settled into a thoughtful expression. "It would seem to me, Colonel, you overestimate the hostility the President entertains concerning you. With the demobilization of the Volunteers at the end of the war, many professional soldiers reverted to lower ranks. I know of one case where a major general of the Volunteers became a mere captain. You have done better than many. In fact, if the President wished you gone from the Army, he would have no more trouble than you had yourself back in the 1850's.

"Be that as it may, what would be your recommendations for enhancing the Army's ability to combat the Klan in Louisiana?"

"Send more troops; many thousands of more troops. But Grant hardly needs me to tell him that."

"Perhaps not. I will see to it your advice is forwarded to him. As it is, I fear that we have taken up too much of your valuable time." Clay astonished Bierce and Duval by smoothly rising and saluting Colonel Buchanan, then turning and marching out the door. Wordlessly, they hurried to follow him, leaving Buchanan with a look of furious bafflement on his face. Clay refused to speak, and it was only after they had left the fort and were halfway to the streetcar terminus leading to New Orleans proper that Duval broke the silence.

"Alphonso, was it wise to leave so abruptly? We had hardly begun to interview Buchanan."

Clay answered without looking backwards. "It is possible that I made a serious error by approaching Buchanan directly. In fact, I have to thank Bierce from saving me from even greater error."

The lean journalist frowned as he matched Clay's rapid walk. "I am always glad to be of help, but damned if I know how I helped."

"My pride, my arrogant belief that I knew all that needed to be known kept me from properly researching Buchanan before I arranged for a meeting. I had no idea that he was responsible for driving Grant from the Army in disgrace before the war."

"I do not imagine either of them would be anxious to publicize the incident," commented Duval. "It reflects badly on both of them."

"Still, I should have prepared properly. If Bierce could learn of it in saloon banter, I could have learned of it with ease."

They had reached the bench that marked the end of the streetcar line that led into the city. A hundred yards off, a lone horse pulled a tired-looking car along narrow iron rails toward them.

Duval frowned and said, "I still do not understand why it was a mistake to talk to Buchanan."

Clay turned to face his companions. "I am surprised that you do not. Then let me be explicit. The Klan has enjoyed considerable success throughout the South, but no where more than in Louisiana. Imagine how much easier such success would be if the commander of the Union forces was your secret ally."

"Come on, Clay, I am as cynical about human motives as the next man," exclaimed Bierce with considerable understatement. "But to imagine a colonel in the United States Army actively supporting the Klan, simply because a subordinate got promoted over his head, is going a bit far."

"Not just a subordinate being promoted over him," responded Clay. "A man Buchanan views as a worthless drunk. Buchanan is clearly a man proud to the point of arrogance. We must consider the possibility that wounded pride has driven him to treason, and adjust our plans accordingly."

The streetcar had reached them, the tired horse obviously grateful for a short break. Wordlessly, thoughtful expressions on their faces, the three companions boarded the vehicle.

Ulysses Grant strolled the lawn of the Executive Mansion with General Daniel Butterfield; the pair quietly smoking cigars. They paused to contemplate the golden sunset as the blazing orb touched the Potomac. The President sighed, and turned to face Butterfield.

"General, you are probably wondering why I invited you for this little walk."

"Indeed I am," responded the short, compact Butterfield, who in fact knew precisely what was on the President's mind. Butterfield exhaled a mouthful of smoke, and then stroked his carefully-groomed handlebar moustache, silently reminding himself to act surprised.

"I need a good man at the New York Subtreasury," continued Grant. "Next to the Secretary himself, it is the most important job in the Treasury Department. It controls the bulk of the government's gold reserves, and is vital for maintaining stability in international transactions. You have had great experience, not only in the War but in running your family's Butterfield Stage Company. I need someone I can trust, someone not totally beholden to Wall Street, to take charge there."

"You surprise me sir," replied Butterfield carefully. "Why is the job suddenly so delicate? And if it is so delicate, why not appoint one of the experienced Wall Street insiders?"

"It is delicate because of the harvest season. The early word is that our crops are going to be enormously successful, producing far more than we can consume."

"How can bumper crops be a problem?"

The President sighed. "That will mean enormous sales to European countries at unpredictable prices, during a very short period of time. That means payments crossing the Atlantic in a variety of currencies, with unprecedented exchange rates. That means various banks will end up with the currencies and will want to immediately unload them for American gold. And that means the supply of gold specie on the open market will fluctuate haphazardly. If it fluctuates too much, a panic can start on Wall Street, and Lord knows what that might lead to. I usually don't hold with the Government intervening in business; the business of America is business, and the Government should let business take its course. This must be an exception. Gold underlies our currency, our financial structure. We have an obligation, a duty, to make sure that the supply of gold, and therefore the value of money, remains stable. As the Subtreasury in New York possesses most of the government's reserves of gold, I need a good man there, a military man, who can act decisively and on his own initiative; by instantly selling gold if the price starts to rise, buying it if it starts to go down."

Butterfield pretended to consider what Grant had said. "I still do not see why you have chosen me," he finally replied.

"That much power over that much gold could be too much temptation for a civilian businessman; too many different ways he could dip his hands in the till. I prefer someone with unquestioned devotion to the country, someone with military experience. I've met an impressive businessman during a trip to New York named Jay Gould. I asked him if he could think of someone with a military background who had the experience to handle such a responsibility; yours was the only name he could suggest. I also talked to Corbin, my sister's husband, to see if he could think of anyone since he has also had quite a lot of dealings on Wall Street. You may be as amazed as I was to hear that he came up with your name as well. That was good enough for me. Well, General, will you take the job?"

"I fear I must," said Butterfield slowly. "I can hardly turn my country and my President down when the call comes."

"Good!" replied Grant with emphasis. "I will send your name to the Senate tomorrow, but that is just a formality. Senators Sumner and Sherman will see you confirmed before the end of the week. Well, that is a load off my mind. Shall we go back? Julia should have the dinner ready by now."

The two men began to stroll back to the White House in silence. Grant was thinking that at least one of the burdens on him was lessened. Butterfield was thinking of the wealth beyond imagining that would soon be his.

Teresa Duval awoke with a start, and was astonished to find herself alone in Alphonso Clay's bed. Clay had apparently dressed and gone out without waking her. Normally, she slept as lightly as a cat, but she realized that the energetic exercises of the previous night had left her more exhausted than usual. She inspected several developing bruises on her limbs and torso, and remembered similar wounds she had left on Clay. She smiled chillingly with remembered pleasure.

Deciding that Clay must have gone down for an early breakfast, she quickly dressed and hurried down the stairs to the dining room. She could see no sign of her lover, but spotted Ambrose Bierce sitting alone at a table, reading a newspaper over the ruins of his breakfast. He spotted her as she glided up to his table.

"Good morning, Miss Duval," he said in greeting, folding up his paper. "May I order you some breakfast?"

"Not at the present," she replied, eyes searchingly around the room. "Have you seen Alphonso?"

"Yes, he left just minutes ago. He told me to tell you that he had some personal business to which he must attend, and that I should let you know he would not be back until this afternoon."

The chill wind of jealousy began to creep through Duval. Clay had left without telling her where he was going, and New Orleans was a city notorious for its houses of carnal pleasure. The cold, logical part of her brain told her that after the previous night, Clay would not feel the need to seek feminine company, but to her own amused amazement, she realized that she was not feeling logical. An overwhelming urge to find out where her lover was and what he was doing coursed through her. Nodding briefly to Bierce, she strode out of the dining room and out onto the busy street, leaving the young journalist frowning with surprise.

She immediately encountered a stroke of luck. Just as she emerged from the hotel, she spotted Clay in the traffic, riding a black mare that he must have rented from the nearby livery stable. Clay seemed preoccupied, and did not see her. Duval frantically motioned to a passing two-wheeled cab, which shuddered to an unexpectedly sudden stop as the driver jerked back on the reins. Duval swiftly entered the cab, handing a greenback up to the cabbie on his perch behind the passenger compartment.

"Stay within view of the man on that black mare, but do not let him see you following him," she said briskly. The dusky cabbie saw that the denomination on the bill was five dollars; shrugging, he flicked his whip lightly onto the back of the horse, and proceeded to do as he had been told.

They followed Clay for some ten minutes, easily threading the bustling traffic until Clay suddenly turned into a quiet side-street near the beginning of the French Quarter. Clay stopped before a large stone building with graceful ironwork shutters.

Smoothly dismounting, he tied his horse to the hitching post under a massive cypress, and strode in through the front door, passing several young people being escorted by an ascetic-looking man in priestly garb.

Duval lightly jumped from the two-wheeler, and silently glided into the building. The driver, well-paid in advance, shrugged incuriously as he turned his cab back toward the main thorough-fare; having lived in New Orleans all of his life, he had seen stranger things.

Duval found herself in a long marble-floored corridor, just in time to see Clay knock on a door halfway down the hall, entering after the briefest of pauses. There was a half-open closet door to her left, through which she spotted cleaning supplies and the shapeless smock left by some charwoman. After a quick glance revealed no one in her immediate vicinity, she slipped into the closet, silently closing the door behind her. In less than half a minute the door opened and a woman emerged from the room; not the vibrant, elegantly-dressed Teresa Duval, but a middle-aged drudge, shoulders slumped from years of heavy lifting, shuffling along with the weight of a bucket filled with soapy water, dull eyes focused on the floor before her. When she reached the door Clay had used, she lowered herself to her knees with a sigh, then took out the soapy brush and began to scrub a slight discoloration on the floor. She slightly opened the door, giving the impression she wanted to be sure the stain was scrubbed away on both sides.

Out of the corner of her eye she saw Clay sitting in front of a plain desk, behind which a grey-haired cleric sat. The priest gave her a sour look, but immediately turned his attention back to Clay, who did not bother to look at the intruder. Duval scrubbed her way back into the hall, being careful to leave the door partly ajar. Through the opening, she could clearly hear what was being said. The priest spoke with a deep, disapproving baritone.

"Dr. Mudd, it has been a long time since you graced us with your presence."

"Father, I have business obligations throughout the country, and can seldom come to New Orleans," answered Clay. "My principal is confident that the Society of Jesus is taking good care of the Devereaux children. He only desires me to visit in order to make the payments for their support in person. Transmitting money via the post is problematic, given the unrest throughout the South." Duval heard a slight rustling, as if Clay had removed a paper from his coat pocket.

"A five-thousand dollar bearer bond on the United States Treasury," murmured the Jesuit. "Frankly, this is far more than is needed for their immediate support. In fact, it will go some distance toward paying for the college education that both Jerome and Marie seem to desire. I wonder why your . . . principal chose to make payment in this fashion. The buyer's name appears nowhere on the bond, and anyone with physical possession can present it for payment, no questions asked. This is a somewhat dangerous document to have on your person; men are killed for far less in New Orleans."

"That is my concern, not yours," answered Clay. "My principal feels this guarantees him anonymity. All he requires is a receipt from you acknowledging payment."

Duval heard the priest sigh, then the light scraping of a pen against paper. "There you are, sir. Now, would you like to meet Jerome and Marie, so you can report to your . . . principal on their health and condition?"

There was a long pause. "No thank you, Father; I would rather they not know of my connection with their support; they might mistake me for their benefactor."

"I felt that might be your position," Duval heard the Jesuit say dryly. "Nevertheless, I have arranged it so you can observe them from a distance without being seen. When you sent the message asking for a meeting at this time, I arranged for their mathematics instructor, Father Albert, to have them on the bench under the tree just outside this window. Come, Dr. Mudd, they are undoubtedly still there."

Through the open door Duval heard the scraping of chairs. There was a long pause before she heard the priest again speak to Clay.

"Both of the Devereaux children show a strong liking for mathematics and the natural sciences. Look how they hang on Father Albert's every word. Our other charges are good children, but are sadly bored by the more abstract subjects. I have no doubt that the scientific world may come to hear much of Jerome Devereaux in the years to come. Even Marie may come to leave her mark, although of course it is much harder for a woman."

Duval heard a long pause, finally broken by Clay in a strained voice. "Their ages are now fourteen and fifteen. A difficult age for young people; they are often beset by gawkiness and even surliness, yet those two show no signs of that. It is often a mistake to judge by one impression, especially at a distance, but they seem to have sunny characters and to be quite fond of each other. Amazing, given their history. It pleases me."

"I would think it would . . . Major Clay."

A shocked silence burst from the office like a physical wave. Duval was stunned for a moment, but then her hand smoothly sought the straight razor concealed under her borrowed clothing, determined to aid her lover in silencing the meddlesome priest. Before she could spring into action, she heard Clay speak in a low voice.

"I must congratulate you, Father. I presume you guessed my identity from the various stories drifting around Louisiana."

"It was not hard. Do not underestimate how you have entered the local mythology. The stories usually describe your . . . distinctive appearance, down to the wire-rimmed spectacles. Your resemblance to the butcher of the Devereaux family, combined with the Kentucky accent I noticed on your previous visits, and the fact that 'Mudd' is a type of 'Clay', left me with little doubt."

"You have not told anyone of your surmises?"

"No, Major Clay. Although no charges were ever brought against you, there are some die-hard Rebels who would gun you down like a mad dog if they knew your identity. It is neither the purpose of the Church, nor my personal desire, to see yet more violence in this already too violent land. Besides, knowing that you are still in the Army, I suspect you are investigating the Ku Klux Klan with a view to curbing their outrages. Although the Church has no official opinion on that subject, as you know, Catholics remain a despised minority outside places such as New Orleans and New York, and can empathize with the plight of the freedmen. You have my personal best wishes in your task."

"Father, although I have no right to demand it, I have a favor I would require of you. I would ask that the Devereaux children never learn the identity of their . . . benefactor." Duval noted a hint of pleading in Clay's voice that she had never heard before.

"They will probably someday learn it, but it will not be from me."

"Then our business is concluded." Duval heard the scrape of chairs being drawn back, and then the Jesuit spoke.

"Son, before you go, would you care for me to hear your confession?"

Clay responded with a barking laugh. "I am not a member of your faith," he responded.

"It is a pity. I believe your soul needs unburdening."

"Clays bear responsibility for their actions. I do not wish to be unburdened of my responsibility."

"That must be a heavy burden indeed. You will permit me, at the appropriate time, to say a prayer for your soul."

Again came the barking laugh. "You may do as you wish. Good day, Father."

Duval quickly lowered her head and made a show of busily scrubbing just as Clay left the office, completely closing the door behind him.

He took a number of quick steps down the hall, then stopped, breathing heavily. He carefully adjusted his spectacles, which Duval had learned he tended to do when feeling extreme emotion. Then, without turning his head, he said, "Teresa, I will wait for you outside while you get out of those ridiculous rags." Then he strode toward the front entrance. Duval froze for an instant, and then responded with one of her silvery, chilling laughs.

Wade Hampton sat on the veranda of his favorite mansion, watching the blacks tending the cotton fields. Slavery may have ended, but he held many of his former slaves in his service by ties stronger than chains—ties much, much stronger. Actually, this mansion had once been his second favorite. The very favorite of his several homes had been burned to the ground back in 1864 during Sherman's March, torched by some unidentified Union officer. Of all that he had lost in the war, that was the hardest. He had kept his main library—his special library—in his incinerated mansion; a library filled with the rarest and most arcane of books, most of them impossible to replace.

Lost also were the special chambers where he could conduct peculiar 'studies' in complete privacy. The chambers were of less importance, as they could be, and had been, replaced with time. Time he could ill-afford to lose, time that could never be regained. Hampton began to fantasize about the unknown Union officer who had inconvenienced him so, and about the attentions he would wish to pay that officer should he learn the man's identity.

Hampton's reverie was interrupted by the sight of a lone rider cantering his horse up the graveled driveway. Hampton drew out his pocket watch and nodded approvingly; precisely on time. The stranger reached the hitching post to the side of the front entrance. As the man secured his stallion, Hampton rose to greet him.

"Dr. Tillinghast, thank you for agreeing to make the trip down here personally."

Tillinghast turned to greet his host, unbuttoning his long linen duster to reveal a well-cut Brooks Brothers suit, seemingly inappropriate for a horseback ride through a South Carolinian summer. He took off his wide brimmed hat, revealing a full head of raven-black hair, ascended the steps of the porch, and bowed slightly to Hampton. "Your New York associate indicated it would be financially well worth my while to make the trip. Even so, I was disinclined to come, but he mentioned the involvement of Starry Wisdom. That placed the matter in a different light."

"As it should, Dr. Tillinghast. The goals of the Order . . ."

"Are of absolutely no concern to me," interrupted Tillinghast smoothly. "I know enough about Starry Wisdom to wish to know nothing more, until they themselves tell me. I will do as they wish, providing the remuneration is appropriate, but I desire no knowledge of the reasons for the commission."

"Fair enough. Come join me in the library for some refreshment."

Hampton led his visitor to his new, richly furnished library, marred only by the absence of the ancient books he had spent so much time and money assembling. A sharp order from Hampton brought an obsequious, elderly black man into the library, with drinks and cigars on a silver platter. As Hampton and his guest settled into comfortable leather arm chairs, the old retainer left the room, closing the door behind him. Some might have lingered at the door to overhear the conversation, but the old man had been with Wade Hampton since long before the War, and knew well what could happen to a black man showing curiosity over

Hampton's affairs. He scurried to the pantry as quickly as his arthritic legs could take him.

Hampton and Tillinghast spent a few minutes enjoying their cigars. Finally, Hampton broke the silence.

"I propose to offer you the most money you have ever received for an assignment."

Tillinghast blew out a puff of smoke and favored Hampton with a tight smile. "I seriously doubt that, General Hampton. You can have little idea of the value placed on my services by the select community which knows of them."

"No disrespect, but I believe I do. I am prepared to offer you $200,000."

Tillinghast had been about to bring his cigar to his mouth. Instead he froze for a moment, then carefully returned it to the ashtray. "Yes, you are quite correct. I have never been offered anything approaching that sum. Since I presume you do not do so from philanthropic motives, there must be something very special about this . ... assignment."

"Of course there are conditions. You will be paid half in advance, with the remaining half to be paid only upon successful comple-tion of the assignment, which must take place before the second week in September. Further, even if the target is eliminated by that date, there must be no hint of my involvement or that of Starry Wisdom. If there is, forfeiture of the remaining fee will be the least of the consequences."

Tillinghast grimaced wryly. "Do not worry; I have not the slightest intention of incurring the wrath of the Order. Now, who is the target?"

"Ulysses Grant."

Tillinghast leaned back in the chair. "That explains the fee," he commented dryly.

"Will you do it?" asked Hampton impatiently.

"There is little difficulty in killing the President; Booth showed that. The challenge would be to avoid implicating your friends, and above all myself. It would not be enough to get away, if my identity became known. The Federal Government would never stop looking for me. I would rather enjoy the fruits of my success in peace and quiet, without looking over my shoulder continuously. If it were not that this is something the Order would want, I would decline the commission. Seeing as I have longed for admission to their formal ranks ever since they gave me my first assignment, when I learned something of their long-term goals, this is an assignment I will accept with pleasure; providing that you could assure my induction into Starry Wisdom."

"I will discuss the matter with the Elders. Should you accomplish your assignment successfully, there will be no opposition."

Tillinghast rose abruptly. "I think it would be better if we not meet again. I will shortly be in contact with you by post on how to pay the first $100,000. You will receive a similar message after the assignment is complete. Agreed?"

"Agreed," responded Wade Hampton, offering the thin man a firm handshake. First giving a slight bow, Dr. Tillinghast turned and strode out of the library. In mere moments, Hampton heard the crunching of hoofbeats down his gravel drive. Hampton reflected upon the fact that although the emotionless, machine-like nature of the killer for hire should have frightened him, it had not. After all, thought Hampton, someone who deals regularly with the Ku Klux Klan on the one hand and Starry Wisdom on the other could scarcely be frightened by a mere assassin.

Clay, Duval and Bierce had met in the hotel's small but excellent restaurant for an early dinner, each ordering one of the spicy, but appealing, seafood dishes for which New Orleans was justly famous. Bierce was the first to move beyond bland pleasantries and speak on the business at hand.

"While you two were doing . . . whatever it was you were doing, I made the rounds of several of the less exclusive drinking establishments in the French Quarter," he said around a mouthful of spicy catfish and rice. "At the cost of buying several rounds of drinks for everyone, I picked up a likely lead. A few denunciations of 'free niggers' convinced several of the disreputable denizens that I was a kindred spirit. A combination of bigoted comments and free liquor loosened some tongues. The barflies did a lot of complaining about how things are being run in New Orleans by darkies and Yankees. They complained even more that the Klan couldn't recruit as many as they like in New Orleans proper, and was having to import members from the sticks. It seems that despite the recent riots, hatred of the freedman is less here than almost anywhere else in the South."

"New Orleans had a thriving black business community before the War," commented Clay. "Some had become wealthy, even to the point of themselves owning slaves."

Bierce nodded. "I'd heard the same. Anyway, one of the old drunks mumbled that I should talk to Hiram Needham about joining. One of the drunk's friends jabbed him hard in the ribs, but I had been feigning increasing drunkenness for the last hour, and pretended not to hear. Out of the corner of my eye I saw the drunk's friend look real hard at me. For a moment I was worried I might not get out of that dive alive, but the suspicious one finally seemed convinced I was too far into my cups to understand what his friend had said."

"It is fortunate you have had extensive experience with inebriation," commented Duval dryly.

Bierce chuckled at her comment. "True enough. In any event, as soon as I could gracefully stagger out without raising too much suspicion, I made for police headquarters. It seemed likely that someone important in the Klan had been in trouble with the law in the past. As it was, I came up trumps. A sergeant I talked to was very aware of Hiram Needham; a gambler, sometime pimp, all the time scoundrel, suspected of being involved in a number of robberies, less reliably rumored to be important in the Klan. A few dollars procured me Needham's address. I took a stroll by it; a small, grimy warehouse in the worst part of the docks."

"If this Needham is such a scoundrel, why have the police not arrested him?" asked Clay.

"Ah, it's the connection with the Klan. My friend the police sergeant would not say as much, but you should have seen the look on his face when he mentioned the Klan."

"A coward," sniffed Duval, who feared nothing of this Earth save poverty.

"Some fears are reasonable," replied Clay unexpectedly. "The man may have a family, and the Klan has shown no hesitation in attacking the families of its enemies. Well, it sounds as if I must pay a visit to Mr. Needham tonight."

"When do we go?" asked Duval.

"You mistake me. I will be going alone."

Duval uttered one of her silvery, chilling laughs. "You have no idea if he will have friends, or how many of them. You think you can handle everything yourself. One day that will be the death of you, but not while I am there."

Bierce chuckled. "Well, I guess that makes it a threesome."

Clay looked appraisingly at his two companions. "Very well, Teresa will come with me. Ambrose, I must decline your offer. There is an urgent need for any information this Needham may possess. There is no time for the niceties of due process. This is a war, and must be fought like a war. I remember how you were disturbed at certain things that were done to procure the silence of Mrs. Surratt before her execution. I respect your scruples, and would spare you the pain of participating in such methods."

Bierce had stopped laughing; the smile on his face disappeared to be replaced by a look of intense unease. He remembered that hot summer day in 1865, and the confrontation in Surratt's cell. He remembered all too clearly Clay showing her a photographic plate of what Duval had done to a Confederate agent in Buffalo, and telling her that a similar fate awaited her son John unless she maintained her silence on the gallows. Despite the fact that she possessed knowledge that could have destroyed the Republican Party, the horror she had seen in that photograph convinced her to keep her silence. Bierce remembered how, veteran of the horrors of Chickamauga and Shiloh that he was, he had vomited at the sight of what Duval had done to a human being.

"I suppose I could do the rounds in the French Quarter, see if I can come up with something more on the Klan," Bierce said, his eyes not quite meeting those of his companions. He had especially not liked the sensual expression he had seen on Duval's face.

Hiram Needham looked at the small pile of jewels on the scuffed table in front of him, and frowned at the lumpish Rice brothers standing uneasily in front of him. He leaned back in his chair, and curled his mouth into a sneer. "This all? From a family as rich as the Penderghasts?"

"'Fraid so, Mr. Needham," said Sam Rice, nervously wiping his nose on the sleeve of this threadbare jacket.

"Mebbe sold some of them off during the War," added Joshua Rice, a smaller, burlier version of his brother. "Sam and me would never hold out on you."

Needham studied the brothers' faces closely, and saw no signs of guilt, only fear. He sighed to himself, rubbing the stubble on his unshaven chin. The Rices were skilled burglars, but otherwise as dumb as posts; too dumb to even think of cheating the man who used his connections with the Klan to keep the police away from them.

"All right," Needham said. "I believe you. God help you if I find out you ever cheated me. You might just end up on the next two crosses the Klan burns. You'll get your usual cut when I have these trinkets sold up river. Now get out!"

The Rice brothers scurried out the door, banging it hard behind them. Needham laughed quietly at his two minions. *Such cattle*, he thought. He looked down at the pile of jewels on the table before him and smiled, reflecting that the smartest thing he had ever done was to join up with Klan. It was not just keeping the uppity niggers in their places, although that mattered very much to Needham. As the underworld, and therefore the police, became aware that he had become something important in the Klan, his small criminal empire began to grow. He had gone from being a street pimp, to owning a high-end fancy house with a connected gambling parlor, one where the rules of chance played only a small role. He had gone from being a sneak thief and footpad to an employer of professional burglars who concentrated on easily portable jewels. The police knew about his activities, but never intervened; the knowledge of his position in the Klan made sure that they concentrated on criminals with less violent patrons. *At this rate*, thought Needham, *before long I will start becoming respectable*. He laughed at the thought.

His reverie was interrupted by a knocking at the door of the warehouse, accompanied by the sound of a drunken woman's laugh. Needham frowned. The riff-raff that constituted his neighbors knew better than to disturb him late at night, or any other time for that matter. He threw open the door, and saw an ill-assorted couple in front of him: a lithe, well-dressed woman who was nonetheless drunker than a fiddler's bitch, and a small, slightly built man, planter's hat cocked at an odd angle, wire-rimmed spectacles crooked on his face. He was used to the sight of drunken couples in this neighborhood, but not ones so obviously well-dressed. Needham grimaced; some rich young Creole buck taking his woman for a cheap thrill by showing her the docks.

The woman surprised him by asking: "Hiram Needham?"

Without thinking, he answered "Yes."

Moving faster than Needham would have thought possible, the small man punched Needham in the face, breaking his nose. Needham tried to pull out his gun, despite the pain and the blood streaming from his face, but with an economy of motion the small man had produced a massive Smith & Wesson, bringing it down on the wrist of his gun hand so hard that Needham could hear a bone in his wrist break. Meanwhile, the woman, now completely and obviously sober, had stepped inside the warehouse and swiftly closed the door, securing the lock in one smooth motion.

Coughing on the blood from his broken nose, Needham began to curse the visitors, but despite his pain and rage, he stopped immediately when the small man cocked the large revolver and pointed it in his face. "Mr. Needham, please sit in the chair at that table. My associate and I intend to ask you some questions."

With fear gripping his chest, Needham took only a moment to comply; the excruciating pain in his now-useless right hand was unbearable, and he was in no position to resist. The moment he was seated, the woman produced a length of rope from some-where under her dress, and with amazing speed deftly tied him securely to the chair.

"Mr. Needham, we need to know everything that you know concerning the activities of the Ku Klux Klan."

"Don't know nothin' about the night-riders," was Needham's surly response. This earned him an agonizing blow to the jaw as Clay struck him with the barrel of his revolver. Needham felt several teeth crack.

"We do not have time for foolish games," said Clay. "We need information on the Klan. We know you are important in its New Orleans operations. You will provide us with the information. How much pain will be involved in the process depends entirely upon you."

"Go to Hell, Yankee bastards!"

Clay sighed, and restored the Smith & Wesson to its holster under his frock coat. "I feared that might be your response. Well, we must do it the hard way." Clay now produced from under his coat a Bowie knife.

Needham's eyes widened when he saw the Bowie. He then looked at the woman who had produced a straight razor from somewhere. His eyes widened farther, but not at the sight of the razor; rather with dawning horror at the look of purest pleasure that was on her face.

Clay and Duval rose from the cold floor of the warehouse, stark naked. They quickly donned their clothes; Clay with some signs of embarrassment, Duval with a complete lack of self-consciousness.

As they had gotten more and more into the interrogation of Needham, as more and more blood flowed, Duval became more and more aroused. She was hardly able to contain herself until Clay had said he believed Needham had truly told them all he knew. At that point, she attacked Clay with a fury and intensity that had little to do with love. Clay resisted for only a moment, then they were tearing off each others clothes and committing acts on each other that had more to do with violence than affection. The noise they made would have drawn attention in most neighborhoods, but in this part of the riverfront it did not, nor more than had Needham's screams; which simply did not warrant attention in this part of New Orleans.

"So an Army officer is indeed involved," remarked Duval as she rolled on one of her stockings. "Do you believe him when he says he does not know the traitor's name?"

"I believe that I do," replied Clay, smoothly slipping on a boot. "If he knew, he would have told us." He spared a look to the chair, where a bloody figure whimpered incoherently.

"Do you think it is Buchanan?"

"Perhaps. I do not intend to make any assumptions."

"I still find it hard to believe he knows as few Klan officials as he does," mused Duval, primping her hair back into place.

"Actually, it makes sense," replied Clay, restoring his white planter's hat to its accustomed position.

Duval glanced over at the moaning figure. "I suppose it does not matter for your investigation, but I still find it interesting that mere membership in the Klan gave this filth such protection. You heard his list of crimes. He even raped a fourteen-year-old mulatto and placed her in his whorehouse."

"Yes, a man who seems hardly human," replied Clay.

Duval had a sudden flash of memory. Of a burning house, with a man hanging from a tree in the front yard. Of red-coated men bent over a woman on the ground, committing an obscenity. "One moment, I've forgotten something," she said.

She walked around behind Needham, then in a flash of movement the eye could hardly follow, she made her razor appear, flicked it open one-handed, and cut Needham's throat to the bone. A cascade a blood washed forward over the table, but it did not last long. Duval wiped the razor clean on the back of Needham's shirt, and restored it to its hiding place.

Clay looked at her disapprovingly. "Was that necessary? We obtained the information that he had."

Duval smiled weirdly. "That was for the mulatto he violated. Now, what will be our next step? Talk to some of the local Klansman he named?"

Clay shook his head. "Perhaps later. I think we should first meet with the man he claims to be the head of he Klan in the Mississippi Valley."

Duval nodded. "I suppose that means we take the cars to Memphis tomorrow to track down . . . Oh, Hell! What is the English-loving bastard's name?"

"I wish you would not swear, ever when we are alone. As for the name, it is Forrest. Nathan Bedford Forrest."

CHAPTER 3

". . . ONCE MORE TO SERVE HIS COUNTRY STANDS, THE ROCK ON WHICH THE STORM WILL BREAK . . ."

Ulysses Grant was seated in his usual armchair in the lobby of Willard's, enjoying his afternoon milkshake; the heat of late-summer Washington made this break from work especially necessary. People wandered in and out of Willard's' lobby as he relaxed; for once none of them were the dreaded "lobbyists." Of the non-lobbyists, those who recognized the President did a double-take, but did not presume to interrupt his privacy. All but one, that is.

"Mr. President! Good to see you!"

With an inward sigh Grant looked up to see Vice-President Schuyler Colfax bustling toward him with his usual air of aggressive friendliness.

"Mr. President, may I join you?" Without waiting for a response, Colfax drew up a chair and seated himself across from Grant with a bounce.

"Of course, Schuyler," replied Grant, placing his milkshake

on the small table beside his chair. "What brings you to Willard's this time of the day?"

"Why, a chance to talk to you in private," responded the Vice-President brightly. "No place so private as the lobby of a public hotel."

Grant realized the truth of what Colfax said; he generally found that people (excepting always the persistent lobbyists) respectfully left him alone when they saw him enjoying his afternoon milkshake. Colfax himself was an exception. "True enough. So what can I do for you?"

"It is what you can do for the country," responded Colfax with earnest sincerity. "Rumor has it that you have appointed General Butterfield to head the New York Subtreasury."

"No secret there. The Senate confirmed him yesterday."

"Rumor further has it that he has special orders from you to intervene in the gold market should there be fluctuations in the price of that metal."

Grant gave his Vice-President a hard look. "That *is* something of a secret. Just how did you learn that?"

Colfax laughed easily. "Mr. President, there are no secrets in this town. In any event, I am here to respectfully urge you to reconsider."

Frowning, Grant fished a cigar out of his coat pocket, then lit it with the curious mechanical device he had been given during the war.

"I do not intervene in the business of America lightly. I have good reason for having given General Butterfield his orders." Grant paused to take a long pull on his stogie. "Just what is your concern on this matter, Schuyler?"

"Smiler" Colfax lived up to his nickname, and favored the President with a wide grin. "I was Speaker of the House for six years, and keep in touch with my old friends at the other end of

Pennsylvania Avenue. My friends in turn have their own friends—bankers, industrialists, railroad men. They are deeply concerned with any move to keep the price of gold low in terms of greenbacks. Low gold means those who are owed money receive less value for the repayments than if the price was high."

"And the people repaying the debts want the value of gold to be high in relation to greenbacks, for that in effect means it will be easier to pay off their debts," responded Grant. "These people tend to be farmers, factory workers, fisherman—the backbone of the country."

"Do not forget that the bankers, industrialists, and railroad men are busy making this country great," responded Colfax in a friendly voice.

"In any event, it is not my intent to favor one part of our country over the other, Schuyler. My only goal is to keep the value of gold relatively stable within broad limits. You can tell your friends that they can tell their friends I have no intention of seeing the economy destabilized, or the value of our currency debased. They will have to be content with that."

"I believe that will be of some reassurance to them," responded Colfax in a voice syrupy with gratitude. Standing up, he bowed to Grant. "And now, I will leave you to enjoy your milkshake in peace. Forgive my intrusion, Mr. President." The Vice President turned on his heel and strode across the lobby, tunelessly humming a melody to himself.

Shaking his head and smiling ruefully, Grant turned his attention to his rapidly melting refreshment.

From the far side of the lobby, Dr. Crawford Tillinghast was comfortably seated in a wingchair, pretending to read a newspaper, but actually scrutinizing Grant closely. Although his lean, ascetic face gave no sign, inwardly he was trembling with joy, believing his task would be much easier to accomplish than he had dared to dream. He had spent nearly a week observing Grant, and was pleasurably astonished to see that aside from doorkeepers at the Executive Mansion, he was without armed protection of any kind. Tillinghast had been even more excited to see that, like most military men, Grant was largely predictable on his daily routine. Discrete inquiries revealed that except during brief trips to New York City, which were always publicly announced in advance, Grant almost always took an afternoon walk to Willard's for one of the newfangled milkshakes.

Tillinghast had considered entering the Executive Mansion at night to accomplish his task; the sleepy doorman would present little problem for someone as experienced as himself. Thinking on this a bit more deeply, he had decided that Grant's extended family living with him would present too many variables. They certainly could not prevent his killing the President, but Tillinghast knew full well an unpleasant fate awaited him if he did not make the death appear unquestionably "natural." A plan was forming in Tillinghast's cold, logical mind; a plan to murder the President in Willard's while making it appear to be a natural death.

He leaned back in his chair, closed his eyes, and allowed himself to daydream for a few moments. He remembered the promising start of his career on the faculty of Miskatonic College Medical School, shortly after returning from his stint as a Union army doctor. During the War he had learned surprising things in the concealing dark hours of the night concerning the reaction of bodies—and parts of bodies—to certain combinations of chemical and electrical stimulation. Scarcely months after Tillinghast arrived at Miskatonic, Dean Wilmarth had entered the college's operating theater unexpectedly late one night and had discovered Tillinghast experimenting on the remains of a recently deceased woman; in fact, a neighbor of Wilmarth's. Tillinghast had procured her for his studies via certain "resurrection men". Accepting none of

Tillinghast's attempts at explanation, Wilmarth demanded his instant resignation. And although the Dean had tried to keep the scandal quiet, somehow whispering had started, and Tillinghast found himself unemployable.

Tillinghast's eyes flew open, as he gripped the arms of his chair so hard all his knuckles turned white at the thought of how his life's work had been derailed before it had properly started by the pious old Puritan Wilmarth. He lessened his hold on the innocent chair and allowed himself a grim smile at the memory of how his rage at Wilmarth led him to place a subtle poison in a druggist's delivery to the old man. No one had detected his meddling with the medicine, and no one suspected a thing when the old man expired from an apparent stroke.

His success at undetected murder had given Tillinghast an idea. Using his contacts with the "resurrection men" who had supplied his research material, he came into contact with criminal leaders in the Arkham underworld, and offered to dispose of those they found inconvenient in a quiet, uncontroversial way. His reputation soon spread to Boston's criminal milieu, and from there to New York and points beyond; his fees escalating in proportion to his increasing notoriety in the criminal world. Still, it was not enough for Tillinghast. He wanted more than anything to return in triumph to Miskatonic College, and the resources of its medical school; superior to any in America save, perhaps, Harvard's. With Wilmarth dead, Tillinghast felt he could defy the rumors and regain his professorship, provided he had enough money to "donate" to the trustees. The payment promised for this assignment would provide him with sufficient funds, he estimated. Then he could abandon the criminal world he viewed with such contempt, and begin his real work.

Tillinghast rose swiftly and strode purposefully across the lobby, passing within feet of Grant on his way out the door. Grant, pursuing the last dregs of his milkshake, did not even notice the lean, well-dressed Tillinghast.

Once again, Teresa Duval and Alphonso Clay shared a first-class compartment on a train, this one chugging heavily northward through the thick Mississippi Valley summer air. Their window was wide open, but provided surprisingly little relief from the oppressive humidity. Still, neither of the compartment's occupants seemed particularly uncomfortable. Clay's face showed not the slightest trace of perspiration, despite his tightly-buttoned frock coat. Duval was visibly perspiring, despite the lightness of her silk frock. Regardless of her discomfort, she seemed happy enough; avidly taking in the countryside as it passed. Clay paid no attention to the countryside, lost deep in his own thoughts.

Duval was pleased that Clay had asked Bierce to stay behind in New Orleans; wiring sensational articles concerning the Klan to his newspaper, while surreptitiously researching their higher leadership and connections. Duval smiled at the thought of Clay's ludicrous "gentleman's standards". Although he did not say so, it was obvious to her that he was giving the financially strapped Bierce time to earn his keep with his publisher without embarrassing him by referring to those financial needs. *Ridiculous, but somehow an endearing sensitivity*, thought Duval. Be that as it may, she was looking forward to having Clay to herself.

She could not help but notice Clay's brooding melancholy, which was very likely to spoil their time together. Believing that the direct approach was sometimes best, she decided to broach the subject.

"I remember you mentioning this Nathan Bedford Forrest before. Isn't he the one who took your cousin Arabella to the plantation where she met her death?"

Clay was silent for near a minute before responding. "My father disapproved of my . . . 'relationship' with Arabella, a slave who was in fact my uncle's child. While I was absent in Europe, he sold her to Forrest, a notorious slave dealer, for one dollar, with instructions to remove her as far as possible from my home in Kentucky. To do my father justice, he demanded that she be placed with a family who would not put her in the fields or otherwise abuse her. Totally ignoring my father's request, Forrest did not exercise the care that my father had expected. She was abused, and being a proud woman, she took her own life." Clay's voice nearly broke on the last words, and he turned his attention to the scenery visible through the open compartment window.

Duval knew the rest of the story, of how Clay had joined the Union army specifically so he could get to Louisiana and rescue his love. Arriving too late, he found her dead and buried. Consumed with the mindless, inhuman rage, which she had witnessed on several occasions, he had killed the plantation owners, the Deverauxs, and their overseer, leaving only two children from the family alive. He had then set fire to the plantation house, unaware that a third child, an infant of six months, had been hidden in an upstairs closet. Since then, Clay had carried an unshakeable burden of guilt, as proven by his anonymous and extravagant charity toward the surviving children. Duval found herself puzzled by this guilt; she was without conscience and never felt the slightest twinge of remorse over her killings. And although she would never dare to tell Clay, she thought things had after all worked out for the best. For if Arabella had not died by her own hand, Duval would have killed her herself, once she decided she wanted Clay.

She leaned forward, and placed her hand lightly on her lover's arm. "Let us attend to Mr. Forrest, as we did that piece of offal in New Orleans. We can obtain what information he has, and then . . ." She moved her hand suggestively along her thigh; only Clay would have known she was gesturing to where she kept her straight-razor strapped to her leg.

"No, Teresa, that cannot be. The President made me swear to leave Forrest alive, unless there was incontrovertible proof he was violating his parole and engaging in new treasons."

"Then let me do it alone. You needn't be . . ."

"No!" exclaimed Clay in a commanding voice that seemed an octave lower than his normal speaking voice. "You are an extension of me in such matters. I have sacrificed far too much of my honor as is. You will not touch Nathan Forrest. Should we find evidence of treason, I, and only I, will dispatch him to Hell."

"Then we will just have to make certain we obtain evidence of his treason," replied Duval. She uttered one of her silvery, chilling laughs, and Clay looked at her closely, frowning but saying nothing.

Jay Gould looked expressionlessly at James Fisk, who was sitting in his favorite chair in Gould's library, merrily smoking a cigar and chuckling to himself. Gould had long ago learned to master his emotions to the point that no one could read them; he disliked the openness with which Fisk displayed his approval of the plot's progress.

"Things are going smoother than we had dreamed possible," said Fisk with another chuckle. "Our lackeys are buying up gold futures for us left and right, and no one seems to be noticing."

"Surely there must be some upward movement?" asked Gould.

"Obvious signs of change are being lost in the normal fluctuations that people expect around harvest time, what with all the transactions with Europe on grain sales. No, the sheep are lining up for the shearing, and suspect nothing. When our holdings in gold futures get above the point we discussed, we will make a final run. The value of the futures will skyrocket as the fools try to obtain gold to satisfy our calls on the futures. Except you and I will not sell, at any price. We will bankrupt the lot. Share prices will plummet, and we will use our gold to buy control of all the major publicly traded firms. We will control the economy of the United States, and therefore the Government. The only thing that could stop us is Butterfield releasing government bullion from the Subtreasury, And considering what he stands to make with us, that simply isn't going to happen."

"Of course, Grant could move fast, and either order Butterfield to release the gold, or fire him and appoint someone who would," commented Gould.

Fisk laughed as he stood to go. "Don't worry about that, Gould. Something tells me that Grant will not be removing Butterfield, no matter what. Anyway, I have to be going. It will not do to keep the delightful Miss Mansfield waiting."

"You should be spending more time with your wife and less with your actress," replied Gould with a frown.

"Gould, you are a constant surprise to me. With all the underhanded things you have done, you remain a Puritan at heart. Do not interfere in my private life, and I will return the favor." With a jaunty smile, Fisk left the room; in a few moments, a frowning Jay Gould heard the front door slam.

Nathan Bedford Forrest cantered his magnificent stallion along the road from Memphis toward his home, having completed some business with his cotton factor. He could have demanded that the man come to Forrest's estate; most people in Memphis were anxiously eager to do whatever Forrest said. Unfortunately, he was having one of his bad days, with fits of coughing and pains in his chest, and he thought that a ride through the fresh air would do him good. So it did. No matter how he felt out of the saddle, when he was in the saddle, he felt young and vibrant, capable of anything, with a wild and free future ahead of him.

His good mood suddenly deserted him when he spied a funeral procession approaching him on the road. A small group of blacks was leading a mule harnessed to a buckboard, in which there were two crude wooden coffins. They were obviously heading to the potter's field he had just passed, a place reserved for the burial of darkies only. He found it strange how a reminder of death made him uneasy these days. During the war, and for that matter before the war, he had been left unmoved by death in its ghastliest forms. As he reached the procession, he brought his horse to a stop and removed his hat respectfully. He in no sense thought the black man equal to the white, but he had always showed reverence in such solemn occasions. The men and women in the small procession studiously averted their eyes, and mumbled insincere words of respect as they came abreast of Forrest. They knew who he was, and knew, if the Yankee authorities did not, of his leadership in the Klan.

As the buckboard with the coffins reached Forrest, he suddenly wrinkled his nose at a foul, remembered smell; the burnt pork smell of roasted human flesh. "Stop!" he commanded in the voice that had ordered thousands to their deaths. "What happened to these people?"

No one seemed inclined to answer Forrest's question; the mourners shuffled their feet and looked anywhere but at the aging Confederate cavalryman. Then a lean man of about thirty spoke, without raising his eyes from the ground.

"There was a fire in the schoolhouse, Mistah Forrest. The teacher, Miss Luella Waite, was keeping a boy after school, to help him in his lessons. Seems the fire spread too quick. They were killed trying to get out of the schoolhouse."

Forrest frowned. The story seemed improbable. He knew Waite, a meddling Northern carpetbagger from a fine Boston family who had come to Tennessee to teach young blacks and give them ideas above their station. Forrest's people had tried to frighten her off several times, without results. He also knew the darkie schoolhouse; a flimsy one-story wooden structure with two doors and half a dozen large windows. It seemed impossible for anyone to be trapped and burned alive in such a building. Something was wrong about this story.

"Open the coffins!" commanded Forrest. There were several gasps of shock from the mourners, but initially none of them moved to obey. Finally, the man who had addressed Forrest did as ordered, still not looking the old Rebel in the face. Grabbing a hammer from the bed of the buckboard, he quickly pried the lids off the two coffins. The stench intensified; many of the mourners recoiled away, but Forrest cantered his mount forward for a closer look.

Forrest remembered the stubborn Luella Waite as a proud, haughty woman with a handsome face. There was no handsomeness in the coffin. The body was clothed in scorched rags; apparently there had been no undamaged clothes in which to dress the remains. Her face was seared into a parody of a human visage. Seeing the evidence, Forrest realized she had not died in the fire; his expert eye saw the clear signs of a bullet-hole in the woman's forehead, and the signs of at least one other such wound in her chest. He then leaned over to examine the other body closely, and saw something that touched his stony heart. The remains were those of a painfully thin black boy, who could not have been more than ten years old; the same age as his granddaughter. Although the flesh was badly burned, Forrest again saw the clear signs of a gunshot wound to the head.

"Who committed this outrage!" demanded Forrest, without thinking.

The young black man responded, but again without looking Forrest in the eye. "It weren't no outrage, suh. It was a fire. That's what the men in white said, and said anyone holding otherwise might have trouble with a fire too." Finally the black man raised his eyes and looked steadily at the old Rebel. There was no deference in his look, only a chilling combination of grief and rage held barely in check. "Now suh, with your permission we would like to bury mah son and the fine woman who died trying to save his life."

Normally Nathan Bedford Forrest would have shot on the spot any black man showing him such insolence. Instead, his hand was stayed by an unfamiliar emotion. With some surprise, he realized it was guilt. The Klan he had helped create had done this thing— not to enemies with guns, not even to men, but to a woman and a child. This was not the way he meant his war against the blue bellies to be fought, he realized.

From horseback he bowed solemnly to the mourners, replaced his hat, and set his horse on the path to his home, a grim expression on his face.

The lunch had turned into a trial of Ulysses Grant's patience.

"You've got to give up using the army to make white folk down South treat darkies as equals," commented Old Man Dent to the President, talking around a mouthful of potatoes and gravy, ignoring the shushing motions of his beloved daughter Julia.

"You leave Hiram alone," responded Jesse Grant, who had only picked at the meal; in his old age, the appetite of the stringy merchant had declined. "He's doing the right thing, and shouldn't be bothered in his own house about it." Having delivered this rebuke, Jesse turned to his son and compounded the offense. "Hiram, I have been meaning to talk to you about the trouble I've been having trying to get leather contracts over at the War Department. Something strange is going on there. The cavalry still needs leather, yet the President's own father can't seem to get any of the business."

Ulysses Grant poked at the beef on his plate, his normally healthy appetite killed by the conversation around the luncheon table. Someone not knowing him would think he was repulsed by the overdone nature of the beef, burned until it contained not the slightest trace of red. Understanding what others did not, Julia looked with concern at her husband, knowing that he could stand no trace of blood in his meat ever since the Civil War, and that it was the badgering by the two old men that was affecting him.

"I don't know, Father," said Grant deceitfully. "Sherman runs a pretty tight operation, and never allows any favoritism." Silently Grant blessed Sherman for doing as he had been told.

"Well, doesn't seem right that the kin of the man who saved the Union can't benefit by providing good material," grumped Jesse.

At that moment, Grant's brother-in-law, Abel Corbin, directed the conversation in a more pleasant direction. "Sir, I've been talking to Virginia, and we think you could use some relief from the stresses of politics," the elegant Corbin said smoothly between sips of wine. "We have received an invitation from my good friend, Mr. Jay Gould, to spend some time with him at the Grand Union Hotel, in Saratoga Springs, where he maintains a number of suites. He also extended an invitation to yourself and sister Julia. We would be honored if you would accompany us."

"Oh, let's go!" said the First Lady excitedly. "It will get us away from the Hellish heat and humidity in Washington. And the Goulds are leaders of the society people in New York, who all go to Saratoga Springs. Think of it, we would be dining and visiting with the Vanderbuilts, the Morgans, the Roosevelts, the Penderghasts—it would be such a grand time!"

For a moment Grant was silent. "I suppose a small vacation would hurt nothing," he finally said. "Congress is not in session, and most of the Cabinet has fled to cooler climes for the next few weeks. The telegraph would keep me in touch with Washington, should there be an emergency. Yes, why not?" What Grant did not say is that it would provide a diplomatic excuse to get away from his father and father-in-law. Hopefully Jesse would have gone to his own home by the time the vacation was over, and he could truly relax in the Executive Mansion. Well, not completely relaxed; Old Man Dent would still be there.

"I will wire Mr. Gould, and make the travel arrangements," said the smiling Corbin. His cheerful face concealed the immense relief he felt. It had been difficult to secretly persuade the bickering old men to stay on despite their mutual loathing, but it was worth the effort. Nothing was more certain to persuade Grant to accept Gould's offer than the continuing presence of both Old Man Dent and Jesse Grant in the President's home.

A huge bonfire cast a flickering light upon the trees that surrounded the clearing. Despite being deep in the second-growth woods lying to the east of Memphis, and the nearness of midnight, the clearing was crowded with about a dozen men, dressed in outlandish costumes that all involved some variation of white. They conversed with raucous cheerfulness, disturbing the horses that had been tied to various trees at the edge of the clearing, causing most to whinny with unease. Suddenly the men went silent, as they heard the pounding hoof beats of a rapidly approaching horse. A magnificent animal bounded into the clearing and came to a smooth stop by the fire; Nathan Bedford Forrest had retained perfect control of his animal. He did not dismount, but studied the dozen men in silence. These were not ordinary Klansman, but the local leadership, the Kleagles and Dragons, who alone knew of his involvement with the Klan, the men he depended upon to enforce his will at long distance. Forrest addressed them without preamble.

"Men, the day we've prayed for since April of '65 is near at hand. Soon the order will go out through the South—some places in the North as well. Then we will start taking our home back from the blue bellies."

Several of the men threw back their heads and cried out the blood-chilling Rebel yell. Forrest glared at them stonily, and the men subsided into silence.

"You must be ready to spring into action when the word comes," continued Forrest, his dead-black eyes slowly sweeping across his audience. "You will never be given the entire plan, never be given explanations; that way there will be nothing for the Yankees to beat out of you, should you be taken alive. You will be given your orders, and will follow them to the letter; not the slightest change or hesitation will be tolerated. Failure to follow orders is treason to the Cause."

A chill entered the listeners; they glanced at each other uneasily. Forrest slid off his mount and secured it to a nearby branch. Then he faced his men, the flickering light from the bonfire giving his saturnine features a near-demonic cast.

"A darky school has been burned. A woman and a child were killed. I recall giving no order for that to be done." The color drained from most of the men's faces. For a few moments, the only sound that could be heard was the crackling of the bonfire.

Finally one of the men spoke, a burly blacksmith named Ryan. "Hell, General, fires happen all the time. Don't mean nothing to us, especially since it was a nigger school."

Forrest's piecing eyes locked onto Ryan. "Fires do not shoot a woman and a child through the head." His voice was even, but murderous rage built inside him. He remembered all too well that although it had been a subordinate who had ordered the massacre of unarmed prisoners at Fort Pillow, Forrest was now and forever damned in the eyes of the world for that atrocity. Now a smaller but no less tragic atrocity could be laid at his feet.

"Mr. Ryan, you led the party that burned the schoolhouse, that killed Miss Waite and the child." It was a statement, not an answer.

"Ah, General, everyone hereabouts knows about that Yankee

bitch and her school, about how she was trying to raise up pickaninnies so they didn't know their places. 'Sides, almost all of them got out and lit out for the woods. Then she shows up at the door, with the kid hanging on her, waving a small Colt and calling us all kinds of names, and well, one thing led to another . . ." Ryan's voice trailed off; he was becoming unnerved by Forrest's unwavering stare.

Ryan started speaking again. "Anyways, they were just a Yankee whore and a nigger kid, no loss to the world . . ." Again Ryan trailed off; beads of sweat appeared on his face.

Forrest finally spoke in a calm but violence-charged voice. "They were a woman and a child. I have repeatedly instructed that our weapons are to be used only against men bearing arms, or against carpetbagger officials. We are Southerners, and we do not fight women and children. Even nigger women and children. More important than that, you defied my orders." Forrest drew a Colt Navy from beneath his coat and pointed it at Ryan. "Seize him," he commanded.

The men hesitated for a few moments, but then did as they were told, pinning Ryan's arms behind his back and relieving him of his revolver. It never occurred to the men to resist Forrest's direct order. Too well they remember how during the war Forrest had been shot in the belly by a mutinous officer. Forrest had knocked the gun out of the man's hand and proceeded to gut him with a Bowie knife.

"Tie his hands behind his back, and his legs together," commanded the old Rebel. This was done with nervous speed. Then Forrest asked a question.

"Which of the horses is his?" Several of the men pointed to a black stallion.

"Untie the animal and bring him here." Again several men hurried to do Forrest's bidding.

"Now, take a length of rope, tie one end to the pommel of the saddle, and the other securely around Ryan's lower legs."

The Klansmen all realized what was intended. They began murmuring, while Ryan blurted, "What the Hell, General, you cain't do this! Not to one of us!"

A distinctive click caused instant silence in the clearing; Forrest had drawn back the hammer of his Colt. "Anyone defying my orders is guilty of treason to the Cause, and will be immediately executed," said Forrest in a soul-chilling voice. "Now, do as I said."

It spoke volumes of the fear that Forrest could strike into men's hearts that although the dozen armed Klansmen could have easily overwhelmed him, none considered it. Amid Ryan's increasingly hysterical pleas and shrieks, his comrades knocked him to the ground, and did as their leader had commanded. When Forrest was satisfied that the man was secured, he strode up to the horse, which was already nervous from the commotion surrounding it. Softly he murmured soothing sounds into the animal's ear. Then, in a swift movement, he brought the Colt up to the horse's ear, turned the barrel skyward, and fired.

The startled creature reared, and then plunged straight into a gallop, dragging the screaming Ryan behind it. The men in the clearing could hear the screams for some time, could imagine the agony as Ryan was scraped along rocks, branches and other obstacles, unable to do anything but suffer. Then, far off in the distance there was a particularly agonized yelp, which was cut off suddenly; no further screams issued from Ryan's throat.

Forrest turned to face the men in the clearing, who refused to meet his intense gaze. Smoking revolver held loosely in his hand, he began to address them in a soft, low voice.

"Ryan may have been the leader of what happened at the schoolhouse, but I know most of you were in on it. Well, this is your warning. My orders are to be obeyed, without question or delay.

Understand that, and I will forget the involvement of the rest of you. Do you men understand me?" There were a few inaudible murmurs. In a voice that promised death, Forrest said, "I could not hear you. Do you understand me?"

"Yes, General," the men loudly replied, still refusing to meet his eyes.

"Very well. The day when we will reclaim our homeland is near at hand. Wait for my orders, and follow them to the letter." Forrest smoothly reholstered his Colt, mounted his horse in a single fluid motion, and cantered off into the darkness without another word.

It was some minutes before any of the men even began to think about mounting their own steeds and heading off into the dark.

It was late morning of the following day. Clay and Duval were in a one-horse gig bouncing over the dirt road leading toward Forrest's mansion. Duval turned her head to study her lover's face, to have some idea as to how the prospect of meeting Nathan Bedford Forrest for the first time was affecting him. He handled the reins with deft and skilled motions, his face showed nothing. Nothing, but she knew that behind that expressionless mask, an unearthly anger lurked.

Clay nodded his head toward a dirt road branching off to the right of the main road. "That looks to be the turn that was described to us." He set his jaw even more firmly than usual, and wordlessly directed the gig up the driveway leading to the mansion. Stopping to the side of the portico, Clay tied the horse to a convenient post, then formally handed Duval down. They ascended the steps, but before they reached the door it was opened by an elderly black servant in formal clothing. Clay addressed the servant with his usual quiet politeness.

"I am Major Alphonso Clay of the War Department, and this is Miss Teresa Duval of the Pinkerton Agency. I wired ahead to Mr. Forrest that we were arriving today."

"The General be expecting you," said the old man, eyes carefully averted from their faces. "He be in the library. If you will follow me." The old man, obviously beaten down by a lifetime of care-taking, turned and shuffled into the house, followed after a brief hesitation by Clay and Duval. The servant showed them into the library, then silently departed, closing the door behind him.

Clay and Duval saw a rail-thin figure dressed in white, standing by an open window. Nathan Bedford Forrest coughed softly, a deep dry cough, then turned to view his visitors. He nodded slightly to Duval, but made no gesture of greeting to Clay. Instead, he spoke abruptly.

"Major Alphonso Clay and Miss Teresa Duval. You are prompt; arriving when your telegram said you would, to the minute. I understand you need to speak to me on some matter of interest to Washington, which is of little concern to me. Please be brief. I have affairs to attend to."

"This should not take long," replied Clay in the softest of voices. "You were paroled four years ago on the condition that you obey the laws of the United States. I will come directly to the point. There are rumors circulating in Washington that you are involved with the terrorist organization, the Ku Klux Klan. We are here to inquire about the truth of those rumors."

Forrest locked eyes with Clay. "Major Clay, may I know the names of the . . . gentlemen who are making such accusations against me?"

"You may not. I am sure that you appreciate the fact that the persons making those allegations would be at considerable risk, should the charges be true and you learn their identities."

Forrest paused for a few moments before an ugly smile crept over his features. "You are not much of a poker-player, Major. If you had multiple witnesses, if you had any kind of evidence that would stand up in court, a squad of cavalry would be handcuffing me at this moment. No, this is a laughable attempt to get me to incriminate myself. I have co-operated as much as my parole requires. You and your lady-friend can now take your leave. I have scheduled a tutoring session with my granddaughter, and that must take precedence over entertaining a pair of Grant's spies. My man will show you out." Forrest gave a shallow bow in Duval's direction, then turned on his heal, threw open the door to the library, and strode quickly out of the room and up the main staircase.

Duval turned to say something to Clay, but the words caught in her throat. Clay was visibly trembling; trembling in a way she had only seen when he was in the grip of the deepest physical passion. She touched his arm lightly. Clay started, and the trembling ceased. The black servant appeared in the doorway, bowed to them, and wordlessly led them to the front door, which he softly closed behind them.

"He is a leader of the Klan," said Clay in a controlled, soft voice. "Note that he never actually denied involvement, but only sneered at my lack of proof. I am released from my promise to President Grant. Nathan Bedford Forrest's life belongs to me."

"Shall we kill him now?" asked Duval, a trace of husky eagerness in her voice.

"No. I still must have proof that I can present to the President. I care little what happens to me, but to take his life now would have repercussions for you that I would rather avoid. We will take our knowledge of his certain guilt back to New Orleans, and plan with Bierce how best to destroy him in a way that also destroys the Klan." Behind his wire-rimmed spectacles, Clay's eyes glowed with a sinister light.

"Oh, Sam, this is so wonderful," said Julia Grant, her eyes drinking in the ornate exterior of the Grand Union Hotel. "Thank you for bringing me."

"Thank brother Corbin," responded Grant, himself impressed against his will at the magnificence of Saratoga Springs' finest resort hotel.

"You should rather thank Jay Gould," responded Able Corbin, giving an affectionate squeeze to the arm of Grant's sister. "He is a true man of the world, and never settles for anything but the best. Like the Grand Union; it is the largest hotel in the world, with eight hundred twenty-four rooms, covering seven acres. He maintains a permanent set of rooms here, whether he is present or not, so that he and his friends can come at any time, even the height of the summer season, and not have to worry about being turned away. And wait until you see the ballrooms and public assembly areas. Ah, there is Gould himself."

The Presidential party spotted three figures coming down the marble steps of the hotel's entrance. Corbin bounded forward and vigorously shook the hand of the thin, bearded man in the party.

"Jay, so good to see you! I believe you have already met the President."

Grant stepped forward and shook the hand of the financier. "Thank you for the invitation, Mr. Gould. Mrs. Grant and I would do anything to get out of Washington in the summer."

"Let me introduce my business partner," responded Gould. "James Fisk."

"A pleasure to meet you and Mrs. Fisk," responded Grant. Corbin snorted and Fisk chuckled, while Gould glanced crossly at his partner. To his embarrassment, Grant realized he had made a serious error. The brazen Fisk attempted to put him at his ease.

"My apologies, sir, but this is my friend, Miss Josie Mansfield. Mrs. Fisk is ill, and could not join us." Grant caught a faint sneer of disapproval on Gould's face, and instantly understood the situation, deciding with equal swiftness that he would not add to the party's discomfort by raising an eyebrow at Fisk's lie.

"I have arranged for your luggage to be taken directly to your rooms," said Gould, gesturing to a group of servants who scurried toward the carriage. "In the meantime, let me take you in for some refreshments."

Gould led the President and his party up the steps and into the marble-floored lobby of the Grand Union Hotel. Ignoring the front desk, he then escorted them across the lobby into an elegant, well-lighted dining room; to a reserved table next to a bay window overlooking one of the many springs that gave the resort town its name, personally seating them all at the elegantly-set table.

Grant looked at his wife; her eyes wide with wonder and happiness. This luxury was far beyond what she had ever experienced, even in the Executive Mansion, which was more a busy office building than a luxury home. Grant himself was less impressed. Yet, with a pang of guilt he remembered the hard times of the '50s', when his drinking and inability to succeed at civilian jobs had reduced her to poverty. He remembered how she had stuck by him, with nary a word of remonstrance. She deserved a life like this, he decided; she deserved every bit of it.

Gould gestured imperiously at a waiter, who approached humbly, retreating silently after a few whispered words from the financier. Gould then addressed the President.

"I have taken the liberty of ordering for the party, sir. Having dined here many times, I have a fair idea of the best dishes." He then gestured expansively to the entire party. "Just relax and enjoy. After we are done, I am then going to introduce you to the mineral spas for which this town is so famous. You will forget the Hellish Washington summer soon enough."

"This is extremely generous of you, Mr. Gould," responded Grant uneasily. "You must allow me to pay for our share of this."

"Nonsense!" boomed Fisk. "Jay and I are picking up all bills.

You have saved the country; a country which should be showing its gratitude in every way."

"The country has been generous enough," objected Grant. "My salary is $50,000 a year, more than I ever dreamed of seeing."

Gould waved a negligent hand. "Sir, your modesty does you credit. We well know that much of the expenses generated by the Executive Mansion must be met by that salary, which in any event ends when you return to private life. Further, you will have no pension from the Government. You must save what you can from your salary to obtain a gentleman's income when you leave public service."

"There is much truth in that," added Corbin smoothly. "You and sister Julia deserve the best the country has to offer."

"Well, I suppose it hurts nothing, if you insist," responded Grant with reluctance, thinking more of his wife than himself. "Still, I hate imposing on others."

"No imposition at all," responded Gould. "None whatever." Out of Grant's line of site, Corbin and Fisk exchanged winks.

"You took your time getting here," said Forrest in a darkly ominous voice to the blue-clad officer.

"The rail connections from New Orleans were awkward, sir. It would have been quicker if you had sent a coded telegram."

"What I have to say is never to be committed to paper, coded or uncoded. Never!"

The army officer visibly paled. Although he had found his dealings with Forrest financially satisfying, he was all too aware of the consequences of angering this dangerous man. "It must be important, sir."

"It is. I need you to start a race riot in New Orleans. Nothing too big. Target a few of the more uppity bucks, and as many carpetbaggers as you like." Forrest paused, and stared with such intensity at the officer that the latter visibly gulped. "No women or children are to be hurt under any circumstances. I want you to make that plain to the Klansmen you use. I just want a flare-up. Make sure it ends after a single night."

"I understand sir."

"One more thing. There is a Yankee major likely to be in New Orleans sometime in the near future. He will be in civilian clothes, but hard to miss. Alphonso Brutus Clay is his name."

The officer started. "The Butcher of the Deverauxs?"

"Yes. Time your little "demonstration" for when he is likely to be in New Orleans. He is a danger to the Cause. He is to be killed, not just for what he has done, but because of the threat he might pose when the true rising starts."

The officer cleared his throat slightly. "This is a bit more than you've required of me in the past. I think the, ah, compensation should reflect the risks."

"You will be paid when Clay is dead," replied Forrest. "Now, any questions?"

"No sir. It will be done just as you say."

"Then good night," the old Confederate responded with a dismissive wave of his hand. "Be sure to take the riverboat to New Orleans, it's quicker than the train."

After he was certain the traitorous officer was gone, Forrest strolled to the open window and breathed deeply of the fresh air; he always felt polluted when he had dealings with this particular visitor. He knew the feelings were purely in his mind, but his revulsion at a traitor for hire, even one that he himself had corrupted, was hard to contain.

Jay Gould and James Fisk, the latter with Josie Mansfield clinging to his arm, watched from a distance as the President and his wife strolled about the hotel's ornamented gardens. Fisk chuckled.

"Look at how content they are, Gould. Seems as if all their cares have just melted away. When the time comes, they will hardly disregard the advice of such good friends as we have proven to be."

Gould frowned. "We can't be sure."

"Can't be sure of what?" asked the Junoesque Josie Mansfield.

"Business dealings, dear," responded Fisk. "Boring matters that need not concern you. Why don't you go up to our room while I finish talking business with Jay. I'll be right up, and then you will have my complete attention."

Mansfield giggled lewdly, patted Fisk on the cheek, then began walking toward the entrance of the hotel, her bustle swaying provocatively. Fisk's piggish eyes lingered on her as long as she was in sight. A disapproving Gould decided he could hold his silence no longer.

"Fisk, this has got to stop! I accept that you don't care what this does to Mrs. Fisk—that is your personal life. With your outward public display of affection towards a woman you are not married to, you are drawing unnecessary attention to us."

Fisk laughed genially, showing no offense at the reproof. "I've told you before, this is the perfect cover for our actions. No one will suspect Jim Fisk of plotting to take over the economy of the United States, not while he is publicly making a fool of himself over a young actress."

"You might be a little too confident. What about Edward Stoker, Josie's last fancy man before you?"

"Stoker?" Fisk laughed. "A harmless, pitiable fool. Do you know the gossip columns say he abandoned his wife and children, and his business, to go in pursuit of Josie? You will never find me abandoning Mrs. Fisk, much less my business, for a pleasing liaison, no matter how attractive the doxie is."

"I've read the same columns as have you. They also say that Stoker has been making wild threats against you. He has even spent a weekend in jail for disturbing the peace after disturbing all Delmonico's with drunken, rambling threats."

Fisk laughed genially. "All the better. While everyone is focusing on the jealous lover, they will not be paying attention to what you and I are doing on the gold market—until too late."

"If you say so," replied Gould dourly. "In any event, we need to prepare Grant to support us at the key point in our run on gold. That bothers me . . . he is a simple man, but not a stupid one."

"All the more reason for us to concentrate our considerable charm upon him, and convince him we know far more about the markets than he."

"And if we cannot?"

"Don't worry about that, Gould," replied Fisk with a smile that had suddenly gotten very ugly.

"So tell me again Alphonso, why are we on a train to New Orleans when Forrest remains in Memphis?" Teresa Duval was hot and bothered; more by the prospect of a killing slipping from her grasp than the muggy night air puffing into their compartment.

Clay turned his head to look at her, the tiniest smile of fond amusement flitting across his face. "You know the reason, Teresa. I have only ever met one woman as intelligent as you, and never one more intelligent. Prove me right, and tell me my reasons."

Duval sighed with exasperation. "Very well. Forrest would be very careful near his home, where his family lives. His treasonous actions would take place far away. Since New Orleans is showing some of the strongest and most violent Klan activity, the evidence against him is most likely to be obtained there." She sighed again. "But Alphonso, why all this playing around? Let's kill Forrest on a dark road near his mansion with no witnesses about. Washington will not grieve his passing."

Clay took Duval's right hand and kissed it. "You will always have trouble seeing a point like this. Nevertheless, let me make it one more time. I have sworn to the President of the United States I would not take Forrest's life without proof of treason."

Duval waived her other hand dismissively. "Oh, I've seen you lie. If Grant were to ask you whether you did the deed, you could lie convincingly enough to persuade him."

"I suppose I could," replied Clay in a melancholy voice. "And that is why I never will." He leaned over and kissed Duval tenderly on the mouth.

Ambrose Bierce stepped out of the Western Union telegraph office feeling a rare wave of contentment sweep over him as he breathed the cooling air that had come with twilight. The long message he had just sent to his employer in San Francisco, expensive as it was, would please his editor mightily. Bierce had pulled out all the stops, producing a story that would make the stones weep for the oppressed former slaves of the South. He had even named some lower-level Klan leaders, something that few reporters would have dared to do. Bierce did not care; cowardice was not to be found among his many faults.

Bierce came to a sudden stop. He could sense something in the air. He saw nothing out of the ordinary in the streets, heard nothing out of the ordinary. Yet there was a heavy feeling of expectancy, similar to what he had felt in the moments before Johnstons's Confederates had come screaming out of the morning mist at Shiloh, before Bragg's hardened veterans had jumped Bierce's corps at Chickamauga. Like any true veteran, he had learned to trust such feelings. He could not explain how they were created, but he knew they were real. Swiftly he moved to the corner of the building containing the telegraph office; the side of the building would give him some cover from trouble coming down the main street, while the alley at his back gave him a path for a strategic retreat, if necessary.

He now became aware of a hum of many distant voices coming down the main street. Peering into the rapidly-deepening darkness, he saw three black people, a man, a woman and a teen-age girl, running for their lives in front of a small crowd of white sheeted figures, some holding torches, others various kinds of weapons; some on horses, others on foot He judged the relative speeds of pursuer and pursued, and estimated the three fugitives would be caught about the time they drew parallel to his hiding spot. Cursing himself for a fool, he stepped boldly into street, holding up his right hand in a command to stop.

"Leave these people be!" shouted Bierce in the commanding voice he had reserved only for combat during the War. Both groups skidded to a halt, the pursued in terror, and the pursuers in astonishment. Bierce took a dozen swift steps and placed himself between the two groups. He knew very well what was happening, but feigned ignorance as he addressed the sheeted figures. "What is going on here? Why are you pursuing these people?"

"An' jest who are you to stop the Klan from goin' about its business?" replied the burliest of the sheeted figures in a rough, uneducated voice.

"Ambrose G. Bierce, correspondent for the San Francisco Chronicle. My readers would dearly like to know why so many armed, disguised men were chasing a man, a woman and a child down a peaceful street in New Orleans."

"Suh, mah wife and daughter was jes' goin' home from church," said the black man. "Ah don' know why, but suddenly those fellahs there took after us ..."

"We are keeping niggers off the streets at night," growled the burly Klansman as he dismounted, strode over to Bierce, and stuck a Colt Navy in his face. "Lot's of us are out tonight, teaching the niggers that they cain't be out at nights, doin' their thefts and rapes, an' the blue bellies cain't do a thing to stop us, never mind no reporter."

Bierce now was hearing cries, crashes and the occasional gunshot from adjacent streets, showing that this was indeed a general Klan insurrection. He glanced briefly at the frightened family, then returned his attention to the Klansman, showing no fear of the pistol before his face. "You must be mistaken. I see no thieves and rapists here. Only a pious family returning from church." Without removing his eyes from the Klansman, Bierce called to the black family in a loud voice.

"Go home now, and stay off the streets."

The man looked uncertainly at Bierce. "Sir, will you be all right?"

"Of course. I have nothing to fear from bullies so cowardly they will not show their faces."

"You Yankee cur," growled the beefy man under the sheet, who swung the long barrel of the Colt at Bierce's head.

This was the move for which Bierce had hoped. He grabbed the pistol's barrel with his right hand and rabbit-punched the Klansman with his left, while shouting "Run!" to the black family behind him. Twisting the man off-balance, Bierce elbowed his opponent in the face, and heard the satisfying crunch of nose cartilage. With a howl of pain, the Klansman released his pistol, and while his followers hesitated on what to do, Bierce gained possession of the revolver, stuck it in the small of his opponent's back, and wrapped his left arm around the Klansman's throat in a choke-hold. The angry followers began to edge forward, some brandishing pistols. Before they could rush him, Bierce had raised the Colt Navy to their leader's head; a sharp cocking sound was audible to all.

"Go easy boys," said Bierce in a conversational voice. "If you make a wrong decision here, things could go South on us all very quickly. Now, let us have a look at your leader." Bierce deftly released his left arm from around his captive's neck, whisked the hood from his head, and reapplied the chokehold before the injured man could respond. Holding his captive between himself and the man's followers, he examined the features of his captive, who proved to be a surprisingly young man with a beefy face to match his beefy body. Bierce frowned. He felt there was something damnably familiar about the man, but he could not remember if he had ever actually seen the man before, or if so, where it had been. He decided that racking his brain on the matter could wait. He checked behind him; the would-be victims of these Rebel die-hards were gone, and Bierce decided he could now think of his own survival.

Dragging his prisoner with him, Bierce edged over to the alley. When he reached the corner, he suddenly shoved the man down onto the road, turned on his heels, and rabbited down the dark, narrow passage-way. Just as he reached the end of the building, several shots rang out. Not daring to look behind him, Bierce slid around the corner of the building, skidding to a stop. He stuck his gun arm around the corner of the building and let off two shots without aiming. To his amazement, he heard a yelp of pain along with various cries of surprise. Knowing that his pursuers would now follow more slowly, if they followed at all, Bierce resumed his flight. After dodging into alleys, jumping over fences, and darting across narrow streets, all in dim twilight, Bierce found himself thoroughly lost. Suddenly, he spotted a set of railway tracks between a pair of dilapidated shacks. He leaped onto the gravel right of way, looked both directions, and saw what had to be the lights of a station far down the tracks to his right. Quickly deciding he would be marginally safer in a railway station with officials and passengers as witnesses, he ran for all he was worth. Although an agonizing stitch had developed in his right side, he forced himself to keep running at top speed toward the lighted station. As he got closer to the station, the light seemed to divide in two. He suddenly realized that he was running head-on into an approaching train. Giving wheezy vent to a creative obscenity, he threw himself onto the platform and lay gasping for breath as the train slid noisily into the station, coming to a halt with a hissing expulsion of steam. He heard the sounds of several doors opening, but was too exhausted to even raise his head and look at the debarking passengers.

"Well Bierce, you seem to have seen the elephant," said a familiar voice. The still wheezing Bierce looked up to see Clay and Duval looking at him, unsympathetic smiles on their faces. "How came you to be lying prone on a railway platform, gasping like a fish out of water?" asked Clay.

"It would seem that I stuck my nose in where it didn't belong," muttered Bierce. "At least that is the opinion of some gentlemen of the Ku Klux Klan."

The smile disappeared from Clay's face, and he turned his head sharply, seeming to be listening intently. Bierce staggered to his feet, still clutching the revolver; the debarking passengers and the stationmaster looked at him uneasily. Bierce paid no attention to the glances of the bystanders; he was straining to hear what Clay was hearing. It took him a moment, but he finally heard the angry murmur of the approaching Klansmen.

"Time to redeploy to the rear," Bierce said urgently. "Those are the Johnnies I've seriously riled."

"I think not," replied Clay calmly, drawing his massive Smith & Wesson from under his frock coat. "A Clay does not flee danger, especially when it comes from a mob of traitorous crackers. Please be so good as to escort Miss Duval back to the hotel while I occupy the approaching gentlemen."

Bierce looked at Duval, and was surprised to see that a Remington derringer had appeared in her hand as if by magic.

"I think not, Alphonso," she said. "Do not insult me by treating me as one of those helpless, simpering Southern belles."

Clay looked toward the street entrance and frowned slightly as the mob came into view. "Clays may not run from danger; but they are not fools. Let us take some cover behind those solid-looking benches." All three swiftly crouched behind the sturdy platform benches and aimed their weapons at the approaching mob, leaving only their heads and shoulders exposed.

The pudgy leader of the mob had not recovered his hood, but his red-faced fury made him almost unrecognizable to Bierce. "There's the bastard!" he screamed. "Kill him!"

With no warning to his companions, Clay stood erect and pointed his large revolver at the man's head. "Stop there or I will kill you," announced Clay in a deep, penetrating voice, at odds with his normal soft-spokenness.

The Klansmen came to an almost comical, skidding halt. The leader had about a dozen followers, most brandishing firearms. "You and the missus should take off," blustered the leader. "This has nothing to do with you."

"Missus, indeed" said Duval in a low, feline voice. She ostentatiously aimed her two-shot derringer at the leader. "This man is our friend, and we are not leaving him to your tender mercies."

"Maybe you should do as they say," said Bierce uneasily. "They outnumber us considerably, and I would never think of asking you two to die alongside me to no purpose."

Clay pitched his voice so that he was certain the Klansmen would hear. "It really does not matter that this man is our friend. I would act the same were he a drunken hobo completely unknown to me. Now, surrender your weapons. You are all in violation of several statutes, and are under arrest."

"That's amusing," responded the mob's leader. "We outnumber you four to one. You would all die, and we would still have him.

Boys, kill that little pipsqueak so that the woman will know we are serious."

"They may very well kill me," responded Clay in his calm voice. "As for you, you would not live to see it, nor would several others of your followers. I am prepared to die. Are you?"

Suddenly, Clay narrowed his eyes. "I know you. I have seen you before." His narrowed eyes widened. "You are Colonel Buchanan's aide! You foul traitor! I will see that you hang higher than Haman!" Completely oblivious to the threat of death, consumed with rage at the idea of a Union officer leading a band of Klansmen, Clay vaulted the bench and began walking toward the bulky man, pistol held steadily before him. The man and several of his followers cocked their revolvers, but uncertain of whether Clay's two companions would shoot if they did, and intimidated by the yawning maw of Clay's Smith & Wesson .44, they hesitated in opening fire. At that moment, they heard from the street the sound of pounding hooves and orders yelled in a clear Yankee voice.

Colonel Robert Buchanan smoothly vaulted his horse over the low railing separating the train station from the street; right behind him jogged about sixty infantrymen, led by a puffing, overweight captain. Buchanan addressed the Klansmen from atop his steed.

"All right, you whoresons! Drop your weapons and surrender or I will have you murdering bastards shot down where you stand!"

The bulky leader's followers immediately complied; sixty to twelve represented unacceptable odds to them. Buchanan's soldiers moved in to secure the prisoners. Their leader hesitated, an irresolute look on his face. He suddenly darted toward the platform's edge, aiming to jump down and use the train as cover for an escape.

He never made the edge of the platform. Three shots rang out, throwing his now lifeless body forward on his face. A startled Clay looked at Colonel Buchanan, who was controlling his horse with one hand while holding a smoking Colt in the other. His voice dangerously quiet, Clay addressed Buchanan.

"Sir, that was not necessary. With the aid of your soldiers, I could have secured him alive. He could have provided valuable information on the leadership of the Klan. Especially, since he was your own military aide." Clay looked meaningfully at Buchanan.

Unperturbed, the colonel reholstered his revolver. "Oh, I recognized him all right. Lt. Talbot. My own aide a traitor and a Klansman! I'm glad he tried to run. It gave me a reason to put down the bastard myself. No need to waste the Government's time and money on a trial."

"He undoubtedly was a small player in such matters; he might have led us to more important leaders."

"Sorry, I didn't think about that," replied Buchanan, not looking sorry at all. "Still, we will get the other leaders with time." He turned his attention to his captain. "Take the prisoners to the stockade. We will turn them over to the civilian authorities after we have had a chance to 'encourage' them to talk."

"What about Talbot's body?" asked the captain, nervously licking his lips.

"Throw it in the Mississippi," replied Buchanan, who then sharply jerked his horse's head around, put his spurs to its flanks, and jumped the low railing back into the street.

Bierce and Duval came up beside Clay, still holding their pistols loosely.

"The aide to the military commander of Louisiana a traitor and a Klansman," muttered Bierce. "I don't like this, Clay. I don't like this one little bit."

"If the aide is involved, why not the commander," added Duval softly. "With all the soldiers Buchanan brought, it would have been easy to seize the lieutenant. Now we will never know what he might have revealed."

"Oh, we will learn what he knew," responded Clay. "It is now a much more difficult task, but we will learn. Then we will follow the trail of his masters, wherever that may lead." Clay looked at the darkness into which Buchanan had disappeared, a strangely avid look on his face. An uneasy Bierce could have sworn that his friend looked . . . hungry.

CHAPTER 4

"IMMORTAL PATRIOTS, RISE ONCE MORE . . ."

"I suppose it is possible that the lieutenant was acting on his own, and that Buchanan overreacted due to a sense of betrayal," muttered Bierce as he slouched deeply into the wing chair in Clay's luxurious suite. Duval occupied the only other chair, the slightest of frowns upon her deceptively angelic face. Clay stood by the open window, through which the faintest of muggy night breezes managed to barely disturb the curtains.

"It is possible," said Duval in a grudging voice. "It is *also* possible that he was acting on Buchanan's behalf, and that the colonel shot him in order to ensure his silence. What do you think, Alphonso?"

Clay only spoke after a long pause. "I would like very much for him to be a traitor. Therefore, it is essential that the evidence against him be unimpeachable."

"So where would you look for such evidence?" asked Bierce.

"Buchanan was born in Baltimore, and over the years has maintained a home there that he uses between postings. I believe the next step is to examine his career records at the War Department, and to make inquiries among his neighbors and associates. Bierce, could you stay on here and dig around? I know Buchanan has only been here a short time, but it is just possible that he has been indiscrete with some of the locals."

Bierce stifled a yawn. "Not a problem. My employer won't complain; right now they cannot get enough of Klan horror stories." He stood and stretched. "I will be off to my own quarters. I wish you both a good night." With the faintest of winks, he turned and started to exit the room. However, as he opened the door, he paused and looked seriously at Clay and Duval.

"We may be at some risk from Klan retaliation, even in such a fine luxury hotel. You should take especial precautions."

"Let the cowards try," said Clay in an oddly expressionless voice. Bierce could have sworn that Clay seemed anxious for an opportunity to take on Klan assassins.

"And I can take care of myself," added Duval with a smile. She made her derringer and straight razor appear with blinding speed, and then disappear in an instant. "Just make sure that you sleep lightly, and keep your revolver at your side."

Bierce shook his head in amusement. "Then I wish you all good evening." He exited, shutting the door behind him.

"You should go to your own room, at least for the next couple of hours, in order to maintain appearances," said Clay the moment Bierce was gone.

Duval stood, and glided over to Clay, looking the short officer directly in the face. With a doe-eyed expression, she said, "To Hell with appearances." Then her innocent-seeming face suddenly slumped into a mask of fierce arousal. She lunged at Clay, tumbling them both onto the room's large bed.

Sometime later, Duval and Clay lay naked beside each other, still gasping, numerous bruises and scratches ignored in post-coital bliss. Clay was gently stroking her long, glossy black hair while his face bore a strange, almost agonized look. Duval stared into his eyes with adoration she had never imagined she possessed.

Suddenly, Duval stiffened. Clay felt the change instantly, and looked into her face with deep concern. With a stifled moan she jackknifed out of the bed, staggered to the water-closet, and was noisily sick into the toilet.

Clay had jumped out of bed and entered the bathroom just as Duval finished her explosive vomiting. He knelt, drew her away from the toilet, and gently cradled her head against his chest.

"What is it?" he murmured. "Bad food? I had doubts about those oysters at dinner."

"Yes, it must have been the oysters. I will be all right in a moment." The undeniably haunted look in her eyes gave lie to that statement.

"Damn it, Hampton, these visits are becoming too common," said Forrest. "The blue bellies are not fools. They'll notice the connection, and start asking questions." He suddenly got up from the library wingchair, brought out a large handkerchief, and hacked wheezily into it for nearly a minute.

"You all right, General Forrest?"

Forrest looked at Hampton, and was surprised to see a look of genuine concern on his face. The old slaver put his handkerchief away. "Nothing, Hampton. Just having trouble recovering from the grippe." Forrest sat down slowly, treating his body as if it were made of glass.

"I do worry about you, Forrest. In more ways than one. Must be the night air. I apologize for keeping you up past midnight like this; but it is best that as few people as possible see me coming and going." Hampton paused, grimaced, then continued. "We are going to need you in the days to come. Too few men of ability are with us. Lee would not hear us out; God damned Longstreet has actually joined the Republican Party! For the most part our people are ignorant crackers with hardly a brain between them all. I can't afford to lose you, which is why I have to bring up certain matters."

"What matters?" asked Forrest with a frown.

Hampton paused before speaking, as if he found what he was about to say distasteful. "Forrest, you know that our movement has some pretty powerful supporters. So powerful, and so essential to our success, that they . . . get what they want from us."

Forrest did not like the direction this conversation was taking. "I see. Just who are these gentlemen, and what do they want?" Suddenly Forrest noticed that Hampton's face had taken on an unaccustomed expression; with genuine surprise he realized that the expression was one of fear.

"Forrest, believe me when I say that you do not want to know too much about those gentlemen." He paused for a moment, as if reluctant to go on. "At first I thought I was using them; only gradually did I realize they were using me. They are more powerful than you can easily imagine, and utterly ruthless."

Forrest was taken aback. He would have thought anyone else a coward who talked like that, but he knew Wade Hampton's war record too well to think him a coward. "Why do you continue to serve these . . . gentlemen?"

Hampton's face took on a sour expression. "Because without their aid, we have no chance of establishing our independence, and putting the niggers back in their place." Suddenly Hampton smiled bitterly. "Also, I thought I wanted to learn secrets, secrets leading to wealth and power without limit. Well, I have learned those secrets, and wish I had not. Now, it is far too late for regrets. Believe me, Forrest, you are better off not knowing what I know."

"I don't like the sound of what you're saying. You mean we're the niggers of men who don't share our Cause?

"It's not as bad as that, Forrest. They have their goals, we have ours. They will help us gain our independence."

Forrest gave Hampton a long, hard look. "If I've learned one thing in my life, if you let a feller get a hook into you, you can't get it out without spilling a lot of blood."

Hampton's expression turned to one of alarm. "Don't even think about going against the desires of these people, Forrest. You may think you are a hard man, and you are in fact a hard man, but you are nothing next to these people. There is nothing—nothing—they will not do to those who oppose them. For instance, you love that little granddaughter of yours?"

Forrest narrowed his eyes. "Sir, are you threatening my grand-daughter?" he said in a low voice charged with the promise of violence.

"Not I, Forrest. I'm just trying to warn you that if you push these people, they will take from you whatever you value. They know that some will face their own death cheerfully, so their weapons include actions that will be worse than death. It is well known that your only son was paralyzed in the war, that his wife and your wife died, and that the charming little girl is the only close kin you have."

Forrest's eyes unfocused for a few moments, as he thought of the pitiful ruin of his brave son, reduced to a helpless lump of flesh by Union bullets, moaning continuously in the hospital where Forrest paid a small fortune to keep the husk of his only surviving child alive. His wife dead, his son worse than dead, only his darling, precious granddaughter left of those he had loved. He focused his attention back on Hampton.

"So help me God, if you lay a hand on her, I will have you begging for death."

"Let me be even more blunt. I am genuinely warning you of the lengths to which they might go." There was a long pause before he continued. "There was a time when I began to take some objec-tion to their methods, and I nearly lost . . . well, never mind. Just keep your mind focused on our ultimate goal. You are already the secret Grand Wizard of the Klan. When our independence is established, you and I can expect to be the highest in the land. History books will be written about us."

"I'm not doing this for the fame or the power," responded Forrest coldly. "And there are some things I will not countenance, even for the success of our Cause. I hear that nigger women and children are still being chased, even killed, especially in your part of the Carolinas. I will not have it, sir. You need to make that plain to those . . . gentlemen, sir."

Wade Hampton spoke slowly, softly. "I will relay your message. More than that, I cannot do. Just concentrate on your work in the Mississippi Valley. My people will handle the rest. The day is coming, sooner than I thought possible; in fact, probably in a matter of weeks. When the word comes down, we must all spring into action if our Cause is to triumph." He stood up quickly. "Now, I must get to Memphis for the first train east. The longer I am here, the more likely I am to be recognized, and uncomfortable questions asked as to why I am here."

Forrest nodded his head. "Best be off, then. You will just make the six-twenty train if you leave now."

"I thank you for your hospitality, sir. When next we meet, the South will be on its way to becoming a nation." With an answering nod from Forrest, Hampton left the library and exited the silent mansion, taking his hat from the table by the door.

After mounting his horse and turning its face toward Memphis, Hampton reflected uneasily on his conversation with Forrest. He had always considered Forrest to be a hard man, willing to do whatever it took to succeed; had considered the massacre at Fort Pillow to be proof of that. Much to Hampton's surprise, he now realized that Forrest was going soft. He clearly did not approve of the deaths of nigger women and children, nor of the possibility of . . . removing Grant, much as Forrest must despise the Yankee President.

Hampton realized that he, himself, was beginning to have a few doubts as to the methods recommended by his masters. This surprised Hampton, who had no regrets about having killed a number of slaves in pursuit of certain knowledge, which he had sought for years. Starry Wisdom intended to use methods much more extensive that Hampton had ever considered, and, moreover, to use such methods against the white race. If thwarted, they would not hesitate to use such methods on the few people that Hampton loved. So, Hampton believed, he had no choice. He would take action to remove certain obstacles without informing Forrest. *A good, brave man, Forrest,* thought Hampton, *but no matter how vital his energy and organization and bravery in battle, he lacked the belly to do some of the things it would take for the Cause to succeed, the kind of things that would provoke the North into retaliation, which would in turn enrage the South. Let Forrest keep what passes for his conscience clean.* Hampton knew that he himself would have no problem doing what needed to be done.

With the first glimmers of sunrise at his back, Wade Hampton rode on toward Memphis.

Alphonso Clay burst into the suite at Willard's, angry disappointment obvious on his normally expressionless face. Duval had preceded him by only a few minutes, and was in front of the mirror atop the bureau, in the act of removing her bonnet and inspecting her luxuriant black hair.

"You found nothing derogatory to Colonel Buchanan at the War Department," she said without looking at her lover.

"I did not," fumed Clay. "According to the files, his performance before, during, and after the War was unexceptionable. Some complaints by subordinates over the years about harsh punishments, but in every case there seemed to be some actual offense against the Army, no matter how excessive the punishments.

Judging by his official files, he is a humorless martinet, possessing neither genius nor incompetence, nothing more."

"From what you have told me, Grant does not deny being repeatedly drunk on duty, back when he was under Buchanan's command," replied Duval. "It would seem then that Buchanan's actions against our current President might have been justified, if harsh."

"It pains me to say so, but you are right. Were you able to discover anything derogatory about Buchanan's private life in Baltimore?"

Having finished primping her hair, Duval sat in one of suite's two wingchairs and smiled ruefully at Clay. "Nothing useful, I am sorry to say. The Baltimore house is quite modest, in a neighborhood that is far from choice. Talking to idlers and housewives, I learned that he is a childless widower who is letting his spinster sister live in the house when he is on assignment. No gambling, fancy women, expensive parties. During his infrequent visits, he lives very quietly, seldom going out, and when he does go out, it is usually to the cemetery where his wife is buried." Her smile acquired a tinge of melancholy. "My experience is that men are seldom faithful to women, especially dead ones. Frankly, given what he showed us of his character in New Orleans, it surprises me."

"Motive," Clay muttered. "What could be his motive?"

Duval shrugged negligently. "Perhaps revenge? Given his seniority and record of service, he could reasonably have expected to be a brigadier general by now. It is obvious that Grant has held up his career. People do occasionally commit acts of revenge that benefit them in no material way." She thought briefly of the neighbors who had informed on her parents to the English, back in Ireland, and what she had done to them before she sailed to New York. Oh, yes; revenge is motive enough, she thought.

"You have a point. The trouble is, much as I personally dislike the man, he seems to be no more than a rigid disciplinarian, unwilling to deviate one particle from regulations. The complaints against him lodged in his files originated without exception in his enforcement of regulations and awarding of punishments, no matter how small or inadvertent the violation. I am not sure that such a man would go outside regulations, even to obtain revenge."

"It is possible," commented Duval.

"Of course it is possible, but is it likely? Fear not, we will keep him in the backs of our minds. It would be remiss to not consider other possibilities as to the attempts on our lives. The Klan could have been disturbed by our inquiries, and suborned the lieutenant to . . . remove us."

"In that case, the order almost certainly came from Nathan Forrest," commented Duval. "Prove it, and his life is forfeit to you. Isn't that what you want?"

"More than anything on this Earth," responded Clay in a voice scarcely above a whisper. "The issue remains proof. I must have proof to lay before the President. Then he will be forced to acknowledge his promise, and give me Forrest."

"So, what is the next step?"

Clay drew a crumpled telegram from the side pocket of his frock coat. "I checked at the front desk on my way here, and found that Ambrose had sent a message. Our friend seems to have come up trumps." Clay read the short message aloud.

MY DRINKING COMPANIONS INDICATE NO ONE KNOWS TOP PEOPLE FOR SURE STOP THERE ARE RUMORS THAT OUR FRIEND IN MEMPHIS IS IMPORTANT STOP ALSO W.H. IN SOUTH CAROLINA STOP HOPE YOU ARE HAVING GOOD TIME STOP

Duval frowned slightly. "Ambrose is being cryptic. Still, considering his message was going over a public telegraph, he felt he must be so, and trusted to our intelligence to make sense of it. He is clearly referring to Forrest in Memphis. Who is 'W.H.'?"

"It must be Wade Hampton," replied Clay thoughtfully. "He is bitter die-hard, with great wealth and influence among other die-hards in the Carolinas."

"Didn't you burn one of his mansions down, during Sherman's March?"

A thin smile graced Clay's face. "Indeed I did, and would do it again." His expression turned somber. "I have confided in you some of the things my grandfather, Friedrich von Juntz, had done. Terrible, inhuman things, seeking to gain power and knowledge that no one should have. Things that have caused me to be . . . what I am."

Clay averted his eyes from Duval, and walked over to the window, staring into the darkness, seeing only that which was inside his head. "At Wade's mansion, I discovered that copy of **Unausprecklikien Kulten** which my grandfather wrote, and John Dee's translation of the **Necromonicon**, books that proved beyond doubt that Hampton belonged to Starry Wisdom, a group that for centuries has sought wealth and power through . . . unorthodox means. Wade Hampton is connected with them, and according to Bierce with the Klan as well."

Duval smiled at him. "So, I suppose we will be on our way to South Carolina."

Clay sighed resignedly. "I don't suppose it would do any good to attempt to dissuade you from coming with me?"

"None whatever."

President Grant was at his desk, reading the morning paper. He frowned at an article concerning the frantic gold trading on Wall Street, with the price of the precious metal going up disturbingly. He then remembered how both General Butterfield and his brother-in-law Corbin had assured him this was a normal thing in the fall season, given the heavy international transactions in American grain. A powerful knock at the frame of his door drew his attention to a visitor, and Grant smiled with genuine pleasure. "Phil! What are you doing here? Come in and sit yourself down."

"Don't mind if I do," responded Lieutenant General Phillip Sheridan. The short, round general strode into the room, and sat with a bounce in the wing-chair to the side of the President's desk. Grant looked fondly at his old friend and protégé. Sheridan had picked up considerable weight since the end of the war, but his short frame seemed to carry it well, and the aggressive twinkle was still in his eye.

"Phil, what brings you to Washington? Last I heard, you were crowding the Sioux onto reservations."

"Just a short visit, Mr. President. I needed to kick some asses in the Quartermaster Bureau, pardon my French. The supplies we get are piss-poor, when we get them at all. Thank God for railroads! I can get here, straighten things out, and get back to the boys on the Plains before things start to go to Hell." Sheridan paused, and the smile left his face, to be replaced by a fierce frown.

"Mr. President, the God-damned Klan outrages are getting out of control. You know that as well as I do."

Inwardly, Grant shuddered, knowing where this was going; but his face remained impassive. "Yes, Phil, we are going to have to take some decisive action soon. We simply do not have enough troops in the peacetime army to garrison the entire South and keep the Rebel die-hards under control."

Sheridan looked shrewdly at his commander-in-chief. "I'm not talking garrisoning, and neither are you. We both know it takes far fewer troops to destroy rather than occupy."

"Yes, during the War you and Sherman became authorities on that subject."

"And that was how we won the war, against organized Rebel armies. Now, they may have a lot of trained soldiers hanging around down South, but they lost their best in the War, and what is left will need time to organize and rearm. Give me twenty thousand troops, just twenty thousand, and they won't get that time. My boys will sweep the deep South from end to end, burning anything of any use to the Klan and other die-hards. Then, we'll put some teeth into the Military Districts, suspend habeas corpus, and start having ourselves some hangings. A few thousand should do the trick."

Grant stared at Sheridan for a long moment. If he had been anyone else, Grant would have dismissed Sheridan's bombastic promises as wild posturing. Grant remembered how during the war he had ordered Sheridan to destroy the crops and food in the Shenandoah Valley so that a crow could not live there, and the vindictive Irishman had done exactly that.

"Phil, it may very well come to that. However, let's let things slide for a few months. I've got some irons in the fire that may make that unnecessary."

Sheridan frowned. "Wouldn't happen to be that your Alphonso Clay is looking into the Klan?"

Grant was hard to surprise, but this surprised him. "How did you figure that?"

Sheridan gave a grim chuckle. "There're rumors in the army that reach clear out on the plains. Rumors that this Clay fellow does things for you that you would rather not have seen done."

"What do you think?"

"You are my commander in chief. I trusted your judgment in the war. I guess I'll trust it now. Just remember, if Clay doesn't come up aces, call on me. I'll create a vast silence and call it peace."

For a moment, Grant remembered riding through the Shenandoah Valley, a beautiful agricultural paradise turned into a wasteland. He had wished it hadn't come to that, and he wished it would not be necessary to unleash Sheridan again. But doggone it, he would do it, if that was what was necessary to preserve the Union.

Sheridan had an uncanny way of knowing when his friend would like to be alone. He stood, saying, "Anyway, Sir, I best get over to the War Department and kick those asses."

Grant himself stood, and favored Sheridan with a melancholy smile. "Phil, come tonight at eight o'clock for dinner. I know that you won't be riding the cars until tomorrow morning, and Julia will be so pleased to see you."

Sheridan laughed, and patted his prominent stomach. "I never refuse a free meal. See you at eight o'clock." The two men shook hands, then Sheridan formally saluted, spun around, and marched quickly out of Grant's office.

Grant sat down heavily in his chair, the melancholic smile still on his lips. *Good old Sheridan,* he thought. *Always could count on him during the war. Aside from Sherman, there was no other General of which I could say as much. I just pray that I don't have to count on him to do this thing.* With a sigh, Grant turned his attention back to his newspaper and the article about the increasing speculation on gold. *This is really beginning to worry me. I need to talk to Brother Corbin soon; perhaps have that Gould fellow come down for another chat.*

Dr. Crawford Tillinghast looked on approvingly as the white-haired mongrel dog on the table spasmed and died. *As sudden as a massive heart attack,* he thought. *The prussic acid had probably been smelled by the sensitive animal, but the not-unpleasant odor of almonds had not aroused the animal's suspicions. Now, to see if my own little contribution has worked . . .* He leaned over the table and ruffled the dead animal's fur, inspecting the underlying skin carefully. With satisfaction he observed that there had been no bright pink coloration to the skin; the only obvious sign of prussic acid poisoning.

A grim smile touched Tillinghast's lips. Grant was an aging, somewhat overweight man; no one would question a determination that his death was natural. The only problem was that of how to deliver the poison into the President's food. Yes, Tillinghast had a solution to the problem already in hand. He smiled, thinking of how pleased Starry Wisdom would be, and the access to knowledge and power that would soon be his.

"It's time, Gould. Time to give the orders to straw men to start buying on our behalf. By a week from today we will control the gold market, and hence the economy of the United States."

Jay Gould did not appear to be paying attention to Jim Fisk, who sat facing him in one of the library's matching wing chairs. Instead, he appeared to be staring out the bay window into the drizzly gloom of a Manhattan autumn day. Gould found himself consumed by hesitancy and doubt, sensations new to him. "Today is Friday, the 17th of September," Gould murmured as much to himself as to Fisk. "By next Friday we will either be in control of Wall Street, or utterly ruined."

Fisk frowned, then forced out a hearty laugh. "Too late to be having second thoughts, Gould. Too much of our money has already been spent on gold for us to turn back now. You know as well as I that if we lose our nerve now, eventually the whole plan will become known to the public. We'll have lawsuits without end, never mind what Grant would do. We need to have control of the gold supply so that we can hold off Grant, convince him that we'll crash the price if he tries to prosecute us."

"I never left myself without a bolt-hole to safety before this," muttered Gould uncertainly.

"And you've never had an opportunity for wealth and power like this before."

Gould sighed, then looked directly at Fisk. "You are right, of course. It is too late for second thoughts. Let us send messengers to our buyers, and start our final run on gold. I only wish we could be certain that between them Butterfield and Corbin will persuade Grant not to intervene with Government gold."

Jim Fisk took another long pull on his cigar. "Oh, you can count on that, Gould." Fisk then emitted a hearty chuckle that disturbed Gould for no reason he could easily name.

"So this is where a traitor gets to spend his remaining days," commented Duval bitterly as Clay deftly drove the buggy up the graveled driveway before Wade Hampton's mansion, a sprawling structure in the Greek revival style. "He should be on the business end of a gibbet."

"I would not dispute that," replied Clay as he stopped the buggy before a hitching post, vaulted out, and secured the horse. As he handed down Duval he added, "I understand Grant's position that massive reprisals against the traitors would place the South into a permanent state of insurrection. Alas, there is that in me that would dearly love to see such leaders of the Rebellion as Hampton in Hell." A grim smiled touched his face as he took Duval's arm and escorted her up the marble steps. "Note, we must behave ourselves until we have proof that his treason continues."

"Then we will indeed be able to . . . behave ourselves," replied Duval sweetly.

A knock at the door swiftly brought an elderly, elegantly-dressed black man to the door. "Major Alphonso Clay and Miss Teresa Duval, to see Mr. Wade Hampton," Clay announced in a peremptory manner as he handed the servant his card.

The elderly man stared hard at the card, then harder at Clay. "The General didn't say nothin' about visitors today. He don't see people as a rule without an appointment."

"He will see us," Clay announced as he led Duval past the astonished servant and into the hallway. "Ah, this room to the left seems to be the parlor. Please be so good as to ask Mr. Hampton to joins us here." Clay assisted Duval in settling into the most comfortable-looking chair, then positioned himself directly in front of the mantelpiece.

A touch of fear was visible on the elderly man's face. "It be worth my hide to let someone in here what don't belong. Don't make me bring in some young boys to trow you and the lady out the front door."

Clay waived a hand dismissively at the old man. "I will make it very clear to Mr. Hampton that you had no choice. Now, please summon him." The old man hesitated, then withdrew from the parlor.

In the ensuing silence, Duval murmured, "This should be fun."

"You have a funny idea of fun," responded Clay.

A stocky, fully-bearded man erupted into the room. "Just who the Hell are you people, and what gives you the right to come into my home unannounced?"

Clay gave the enraged Hampton the shallowest of bows. "I am Major Alphonso Clay, on special assignment from the Bureau of the Inspector General. This is my associate, Miss Teresa Duval, who, among other things, has a relationship with the Pinkerton Agency. As she is a lady, I would appreciate it if you would refrain from strong language in her presence." Duval smiled at the last comment; she could swear like a teamster, and Clay knew it.

Hampton's anger had disappeared, to be replaced by amazement. "If you are here in an official capacity, then why didn't you wire ahead?"

"Our schedule was crowded, and we did not have the time, Mr. Hampton. We would appreciate you telling us what connections you have with the Ku Klux Klan."

Hampton kept his face from showing any obvious shock, but the old Rebel's almost imperceptible paling told Clay and Duval all that they needed to know. Duval decided to interrupt Clay, in order to keep Hampton off balance.

"Come, Mr. Hampton, let us not play games. Your leadership in the Klan is known to anyone with the motive to inquire. After all, who better to lead the Klan? You were one of the most rabid of the English-loving traitors, one of those least likely to accept as final the results of 1865. Furthermore, your vast fortune would allow you to fund the Klan lavishly." She smiled sweetly at Hampton, further disorienting the old Confederate.

Hampton frowned, and hesitated slightly before responding to her; he was unused to addressing women on serious matters. "Miss . . . Duval, is it? Miss Duval, I have no idea where you got your information, but I assure you that you are in error. If nothing else, I am not as rich as rumor would have it. Sherman's bummers destroyed my Georgia holdings, burning my favorite home, a truly magnificent mansion, to the ground. The land is only just beginning to become productive again, and nothing could ever replace my home, and the unique library it contained."

"Ah, yes that 'unique' library," said Clay. "You must truly miss those extremely rare volumes, such as Dr. Dee's translation of the *Necromonicom*, and *Unausprechliken Kulten* by my maternal grandfather, Friedrich von Juntz.

Hampton seemed to turn rigid with surprise. "Clay. Alphonso Clay. I thought your name was familiar. Son of Cicero Clay and . . . an unusual mother."

"Yes, I imagine your friends in Starry Wisdom have told you how important I might be to their plans."

Hampton paled. "Do not mention that name aloud," he said in a near whisper. "They prefer anonymity, and do not take kindly to being discussed in front of outsiders." He glanced meaningfully at Duval.

"I have no secrets from Miss Duval; she is under my protection." Duval bristled at this, but Clay continued without appearing to notice. "That is why I am certain you will take no . . . extreme actions against us. Even when you learn that it was I that burned your mansion in Georgia."

Hampton's complexion had gone from pale to beet red. "You are the one who committed that outrage?" he growled.

Clay favored Hampton with a tight smile. "It was done at my command. The home, and its magnificent library—all ash. All save the Dee book and the volume by my grandfather, which I retained as the spoils of war."

"I should kill you on the spot!" shouted Hampton.

"You will not do so. Not without the approval of the Council."

"What do you know of the Council?" asked Hampton, rage turning to amazement in a single moment.

"Not as much as I would like, but enough to know that if you take action against me without their consent, the law would be the least of your worries. They still hope to make use of my rather unusual ancestry, and until they are convinced that will never happen, their operatives will not be allowed to touch a hair on my head."

"Maybe not on *your* head," said Hampton with a nasty grin, looking meaningfully at Duval.

Before an outraged Clay could reply, Duval smoothly rose from her chair, glided slowly over to Hampton, and then in a sudden blur of motion almost too fast for the eye to see got behind him, wrapped her left arm tightly around his throat, placing a gleaming straight-razor lightly on his skin just above the carotid artery with her right hand.

"I can take care of myself, Mr. Hampton," she said in a soft, seductive voice. "Never assume for one minute that an agent sent by you can get the better of me." She moved the razor slightly, and a drop of blood appeared on Hampton's neck. "Now, you will tell us of your involvement in the Ku Klux Klan, who the leading members are, and what their immediate plans are."

Hampton did not struggle, realizing how easily the sharp razor could take away his life. Yet, he was not a coward. Through gritted teeth he said "Do what you will. I have nothing to say to you or your Yankee bastard friend."

Before Duval could act, Clay commanded in a surprisingly deep voice, "Release him unharmed! Unpredictable consequences could flow from his being . . . injured."

After an agonizingly long moment, Wade Hampton felt himself being released, heard the snick of a straight razor being closed. He saw Duval glide over to Clay, a disappointed expression on her face. Gathering his courage, Hampton announced, "Now, leave my house this instant! If you ever return here, I will have the sheriff arrest you and charge you with trespass!"

Clay looked at the old Rebel, and then shrugged slightly. "It will be on your head then. Come, Miss Duval. We have learned enough for today." With the shallowest of bows and a click of his heels, Clay took Duval's arm and led her through the parlor door and out the front entrance without another word; neither of them spared a single backward glance to the red-faced, heavily breathing Hampton, who had a trickle of blood running down his neck.

It took only moments for Clay to hand Duval up into the buggy, unhitch the horse, and climb up beside his lover. With a light flick of the reins, Clay urged the horse into a trot. The still tight-lipped Duval finally spoke.

"You should have let me bleed out that English-loving bastard. It's clear he is up to his neck with the Klan."

"I would not have shed a tear if you had done so. But think, it is *just* possible we may have use for him later on."

Duval hesitated slightly, and then said "That bastard knew of you. He must hate your guts, yet he seemed fearful of that Starry

Wisdom crowd. Just what are they, and why would they want you alive?"

The buggy went on for so long in silence that Duval thought that Clay was ignoring her. Abruptly he began to speak.

"You heard something of Starry Wisdom in '63 during that . . . unpleasant scene in the cabin outside Knoxville. They are an organization that goes back as far as I am able to tell to Roman times, and perhaps even before. They seek wealth and power through means that, shall we say, would have had them burned at the stake in olden days, and today would have them thrown into a lunatic hospital by narrow-minded pendants that would refuse to believe the means they are using. They have had surprising success, in various times and places. And yet, unbelievable as it is, no degree of wealth, no degree of power, is enough for them."

Duval emitted one of her silvery laughs. "What do you mean, the crazy bastards want to take over the country?

"Oh, no," replied Clay quietly, seriously. "Not the country. The world, and perhaps more besides. And they are prepared to call upon the help of . . . beings that are not human. These beings are largely indifferent, capricious in their actions, and even if disposed to give help, demand . . . sacrifice. It has therefore been Starry Wisdom's goal for many years to obtain the services of someone—something that is part of both worlds, something they can control."

Duval examined her lover through narrowed eyes. "You're not joking, are you?"

"No, I am not joking. They believe . . . for reasons I choose to keep to myself . . . that I am some such a man. I have discussed this with you before; the . . . unique ancestry of my mother, von Juntz's child by an unknown mate. So long as they believe that they might be able to make me use that ancestry on their behalf, my life is safe from them, though perhaps not from their minions who are not wholly inducted into Starry Wisdom's mysteries."

"Why would they believe such craziness?"

Clay refused to answer, simply keeping his eyes on the road ahead of them, jaw clenched tightly. Realizing that she would hear no more on this subject from Clay, Duval changed the conversation.

"So where to now?"

Clay was perfectly prepared to speak on other subjects. "New Orleans, I think. If what Bierce hinted is correct, I believe Nathan Bedford Forrest is the weak link in the Klan's organization. We will discuss matters more fully with Bierce, and then apply pressure to that weak link. With luck, we will break the back of Klan power, and at the same time obtain evidence that will persuade Grant to give me Forrest."

Duval rested her head on Clay's shoulder. Smiling, she said. "We will greatly enjoy that, will we not?"

Clay did not smile in return.

President Grant arrived at the breakfast table in a foul mood, sitting at the head of the table without so much as a word to his family. He had studied the morning papers, and found two unrelated causes for concern. Klan outrages were apparently on the rise, especially in the Carolinas, Virginia, and Florida. For some reason, not so much in Tennessee and points south, but in all conscience bad enough. Black churches were being burned, black politicians harassed and even lynched, officers of the Freedman's Bureau shot. On top of that, the gold market on Wall Street seemed to be continuously rising, causing concern near to panic among the investors and businessmen. It wasn't too bad yet, but he feared that something needed to be done to stabilize the gold market, despite his reluctance to interfere with the free market.

Julia turned her cross-eyed gaze on her adored husband and said, "Sam, what is the matter? I haven't seen you look so down in years. What is troubling you?"

"Sister Julia is right," added Virginia, pausing in the act of passing a plate of bacon to her husband Abel Corbin.

"Don't fidget the President," said Jesse Grant cheerfully, snatching some pieces of bacon from the momentarily motion-less plate held by his daughter.

Grant had no intention of sharing his concerns about the Klan, and his reluctant plan to re-subdue the South with fire and sword. Instead, he decided to speak on the gold market, which was serious enough by itself.

"I didn't mean to bother any of you. It's simply something is going wrong with the doggone gold market. The price of gold keeps climbing, and it is causing the business community to get skittish."

"Damn greedy Yankee merchants," grumbled Old Man Dent between mouthfuls of oatmeal. "Speculating on gold instead actually making or growing something. Never saw gold sprout."

"Country is changing, Father Dent," replied Grant moodily. "Big deals are taking place with Europe; big factories requiring lots of capital are opening all the time. Price of gold needs to be stable so businessmen can make long term plans; so the country can grow." After a pause, Grant added, "I'm of a mind to tell General Butterfield up at the New York Subtreasury to release some of the Government's gold, to drive down the price and steady the market. But I don't want to go too far the other way; I need some good advice on exactly how much gold to release. Abel, I want you to get in touch with your friends, Jay Gould and Jim Fisk."

Abel Corbin nearly choked on a mouthful of egg. Carefully swal-lowing his food, surprising himself with his calm self-control, he replied, "Certainly, Mr. President. I will go to the telegraph office immediately and wire them." He patted his lips with his napkin, and rose unsteadily to his feet.

"Don't use the wires for the details," Grant responded. "Just let them know you are coming up on business for me. Take the cars up to New York, and return as soon as you can. If they can spare the time, tell them I would really appreciate it if they could come down and advise me in person. I really do appreciate this, Abel."

"It is my pleasure to be of service," he responded gravely. He then kissed his wife's hand, murmuring "I will be back as soon as I can." Then, with a slow and measured gate that belied the horrified panic that he felt, he left the dining room and exited the Executive Mansion.

A quarter of an hour later, he was in a suite at the National Hotel. No longer needing to control his emotions, he was blubbering like a child. "Good God, what will I do? We are all ruined!"

"Calm down, Corbin," responded his host. "We have prepared for this eventuality."

"Don't tell me to calm down! He's not a fool, no matter what the Democrats think. Sooner or later he will tumble to the fact that he's been cozened, and he will order a flood of Government gold onto the market."

"General Butterfield will talk him out of that."

"Don't be a fool! Butterfield is weak, and will turn on us in a moment in exchange for a pardon."

Corbin's host frowned for a moment, but then his face broke into a broad smile. "Well, I had given thought some time ago about a plan to handle such a contingency. I suspect we may need to act upon that plan. You will have nothing to worry about."

At the hint of salvation, Corbin steadied himself. "Just what is this plan?"

"The less you know, the better. I can assure you that when the plan is implemented, we will have absolutely nothing to worry about." Corbin's host smiled genially.

Having telegraphed ahead the time of their arrival, Clay and Duval were met at the New Orleans train station by Ambrose Bierce. As he watched them disembark, Bierce was surprised to see how fresh they looked from their thirty hours on the rails. Then he realized that he should not be surprised; he knew all too well that they both contained endless reserves of energy. Smilingly, he advanced to shake Clay's hand, and give Duval an elaborate bow.

"Things are coming together," announced Bierce without preamble. "Come into the waiting room and I'll tell you all about it."

The lobby of the station had already disgorged the other arriving passengers, leaving only a few railway employees at the far end, out of earshot. Clay and Duval seated themselves on an elaborate iron-work bench, while Bierce, full of nervous energy of his own, paced back and forth before them. Abruptly he launched into speech.

"When you were last here, some petty criminal connected with the Klan met with a bad end; I am sure neither of you knew anything about the matter at the time." Sparing his audience a grim smirk, he continued. "The man's body was found in a condition that indicated that before death he had been ill used, very ill used indeed. By making myself a regular fixture at several waterfront bars, uttering vile imprecations against Yankees in general and darkies in particular, and paying for a number of rounds on the house, I was able to pick up much gossip. The barflies were uneasy, even afraid. It seems that someone higher up in the Klan is very irritated by the death of that petty criminal, and has offered $1,000 to anyone who can name the person or persons who killed him."

Duval gave off one of her chilling laughs. "I've never had a price on my head before. Have you, Alphonso?"

Clay did not deign to answer her. Instead, he asked Bierce, "And do you know the name and the address of the . . . gentleman who has dared to put a bounty on a Clay?"

"No, but I do know one of the barflies who has been told to place him in contact with whoever has earned the bounty. In return for a gratuity, he gave me a name: Gaston LaPlace."

Clay stood up, and then offered an arm to help Duval rise. "I believe you have just become a successful bounty hunter, Ambrose. Do you feel up to claiming the reward?

Bierce emitted one of his barking laughs. "Of course. Let's just get a good night's sleep first. The meeting with this gentleman may be, ah, taxing, and we should be fresh and with our wits about us."

Clay needed no rest, but he nodded his agreement. He reminded himself that very few had his stamina. Very few indeed. They starting walking toward Bierce's nearby hotel.

Bierce strolled into the offices of Gaston LaPlace, one of the wealthiest cotton factors in New Orleans. Breezing past an astonished male secretary, he entered the owner's inner office, firmly shutting the door behind him, and planted himself in a wing-chair in front of the room's massive desk. Behind that desk, a puffy, middle-aged man with a cruel face stared at the intruder with a combination of surprise and anger.

"Just who are you, and what do you mean barging in here without an appointment?"

Tenting his fingers before him, Bierce replied, "I am here to claim the $1,000 that you have promised for information leading to the murderers of Hiram Needham."

LaPlace tried to control his expression. Nevertheless, his voice quavered slightly when he replied "What do I have to do with ah, Hiram Needham?"

Bierce smirked. "Come, Mr. LaPlace, let us not waste time. I do not deal with middlemen, especially as the killers are truly dangerous. I know where the killers will be tonight; haste is necessary, as they are leaving the city tomorrow morning. Now, I want the thousand dollars that you have had your minions offer, through their contact with waterfront riff-raff, and you want the killers.

In return for a $500 advance, I will take you and your men to where the killers are staying. When you are satisfied that they are who I represent, you will pay me the rest of the money, and I will leave you to take whatever revenge you think appropriate. Do we have a deal?"

LaPlace was taken aback by the breezy confidence of the young man before him. At first LaPlace was inclined to suspect either a trap or a confidence trick. His suspicions were calmed by the young man's assumption that LaPlace would take his own men along with him, and by the demand for only half the reward before the killers were in LaPlace's hands. "Very well, Mr.—what is your name?"

Bierce smiled. "No names, please. I intend to disappear utterly when you do whatever you intend to do to these people."

LaPlace stared at his visitor for a long moment. Then, he opened a door of his desk, removed a wad of currency, and counted out $500. "When shall we go?"

"No time like the present," responded Bierce.

An hour later, Bierce, LaPlace and two of the latter's massive plug-uglies stood in front of a run-down warehouse on one of the least used parts of the New Orleans waterfront. Bierce looked about him; aside from themselves, the only people in sight were tiny figures on the distant, more busy wharfs.

"See here, what game are you at?" asked an angry LaPlace. "This is my warehouse!" LaPlace's two thugs moved closer to Bierce, each removing a bulldog revolver from a pocket.

"Of course it is your warehouse," replied an unconcerned Bierce. "Mr. Needham's killers knew that there is little activity in your warehouse this time of year, and probably did not know Needham worked for you. I was able to suggest that they hide out here. This is all for the best, is it not? You can deal with them and dispose of the remains with no interference from passers-by, much less the law."

A frowning LaPlace addressed his two plug-uglies. "Boys, keep your revolvers out. If there is trouble, be sure to kill our friend here first." Then turning his attention back to Bierce, he said "All right, you go in first. Remember, we will be right behind you, with two pistols aimed at your head."

"Suspicious, aren't we?" replied Bierce, who casually walked to a side door of the warehouse and stepped inside.

"Don't let him get too far ahead of us!" exclaimed LaPlace. His two bully-boys lunged into the darkness, revolvers held stiffly before them. LaPlace heard the sounds of scuffling and a distinct grunt, and dashed into the darkness that had swallowed his men. Temporarily blinded by the transition from bright sunlight to gloomy darkness, LaPlace stumbled. As he righted himself, he felt an entirely unexpected spurt of warm liquid wash the right side of his face. Behind him, the warehouse door slammed shut, making the darkness complete. The flare of a friction match suddenly appeared; it was applied to a previously invisible oil lamp perched on a table not far from the door.

Blinking his eyes, LaPlace saw on the far side of the table the man who had led him here, accompanied by a small, clean shaven man with long blonde hair and spectacles. The small man restored a blackjack to his inner coat pocket, while the larger man pointed at LaPlace a bulldog revolver just like the ones his men had carried. A slight moaning from the side of the table attracted LaPlace's attention, and he saw one of his men, blood trickling from a wound on the side of his head, his hands shackled by heavy iron handcuffs.

LaPlace brought his hand up to the wet side of his face, nervously wishing to wipe away whatever water was on it. He brought away his hand and involuntarily screamed when he saw it covered with bright red blood. He turned to his right and saw his other plug-ugly on the floor, deader than Caesar, an expanding fan of crimson trickling from a throat slashed to the bone. Terrified, it took him a moment to notice the beautiful raven-haired woman leaning over the body, carefully cleaning a straight razor on the dead man's coat.

"Damnation!" the small blonde man thundered with a voice that seemed far too deep for his slight frame. "I said disable his men, not kill them!"

"Sorry," replied Duval. "He was going for his gun a little too fast, and I had to put him down immediately. Only way I know to do that for sure is to kill."

"What is done is done," muttered Clay. "Bring LaPlace over here."

Duval picked up the dead man's revolver, and jammed it into the stunned LaPlace's back. "Walk over to the table, Mr. LaPlace. And no sudden moves or other trickery. I would rather not anger my friend twice in the same day." LaPlace staggered over to the table, vigorously rubbing his blood-stained hand on his linen coat. Bierce was still in shock from the casualness with which Duval had killed the henchman, and left the talking to Clay.

"You are offering $1,000 for the killer of your man Hiram Needham," began Clay conversationally. "Well, here I am. I dispatched his soul to Hell. Now, what is it you wish of me? Nothing to say? Well, let me hazard a guess. You had some notion of obtaining vengeance on whoever deprived you of Mr. Needham's dubious services. Well, you can see that our situations are now reversed. Mr. Needham did not possess certain information that we needed. As his master, I believe that you may have that information."

"What information?" responded LaPlace in a hoarse whisper.

"The names of the principal leaders of the Klan. I am especially interested in any Federal officials that you may have suborned into the service of the Klan. I am also interested in the dates and places where the Klan is planning to launch major attacks against Federal authority."

"How the Hell should I know," responded LaPLace in a voice that was somewhat stronger than before. "I know nothing of the KKK."

Clay shook his head, a faint smile on his lips. "That will not do, Mr. LaPlace. Before he departed this life, we questioned Mr. Needham, very vigorously, I'm afraid. He was quite incoherent toward the end, but he was emphatic that you were the only Klan leader of whom he was aware in New Orleans. Therefore, we terminated our discussions with Mr. Needham, and now turn to you."

LaPlace felt a chill go through him at the mere thought of what the Klan would do if they even suspected he had informed to the Federal authorities. "I know nothing about the Klan, nothing more than can be read in the newpapers."

Clay wagged a finger at LaPlace, as if he were a misbehaving child. "This wastes everyone's time, Mr. LaPlace. When we spoke to Mr. Needham, he was in no condition to invent lies. Now, I have an excellent offer for you, one-time only, and when it is withdrawn, it is withdrawn for good. I want the name of every official of the Klan known to you, along with their address and positions within the Klan. I also want the times and places of upcoming planned Klan atrocities. You will give this information to us in writing, along with a brief discussion of your personal role in the Klan, and sign it."

Terror had worked itself into LaPlace's soul. He had no doubt that these people would kill him if he failed to co-operate. The trouble was that the Klan would kill him if he did co-operate. Gathering the tattered remnants of his courage, he answered the small man standing by the table.

"I fail to see how such a deal would benefit me. It seems I am destined to die no matter which course I choose."

Suddenly he felt the raven-haired woman press her shapely body against his back, and saw a delicate arm encircle his throat, the arm ending in a gleaming straight-razor. Moist lips seemed to press against his left ear, and soft words were murmured while the point of the razor tickled his throat.

"If you do as he asks, you will be given time to grab your portable wealth, change your name, and flee the country. If you do not, your last sight will be that of your life's blood shooting onto the floor in front of you."

Out of the corner of his eye, LaPlace could see his dead henchman. Swallowing, he croaked, "I'll do it." The razor disappeared from his throat, and he staggered forward to the table. Clay produced a chair; as LaPlace sat down heavily, Bierce set paper, pen and a bottle of ink in front of him. Slowly at first, then with greater speed, he began to scrawl names.

"Please add their addresses," commented Clay. "We would not like to seize the wrong man because of an unfortunate similarity in names."

LaPlace quickly filled the paper. He seemed to hesitate over the last two names, then wrote them with a look one would have expected to see on a criminal's face as he approached the gallows. With a hand now visibly trembling, he scribbled a few additional lines, then signed and dated the document at the bottom. Flinging the pen away, he said "This is all I know. Even at my level, the Klan compartmentalizes itself; no one save those at the very top knows all the players. If you don't believe me, kill me now."

Clay took the paper, and held it close to the lamp. As he read the last two names LaPlace had appended, a smile spread across Clay's face. At least, it might have been a smile; it might equally have been a feral snarl. "Wade Hampton . . . and Nathan Bedford Forrest," commented Clay in a voice that seemed to have dropped an octave below his normal speaking voice. "I have Forrest at last," he continued as if murmuring to himself. "Finally, he is mine. Grant will honor his promise; he is that kind of man. Forrest is mine, and he will pay for what happened to Arabella. Oh, how he will pay." Clay's unusually thin tongue darted from his mouth and licked his lips in a surprisingly reptilian gesture. All watching him were deeply disturbed by the gesture—except for Teresa Duval, who found it positively arousing.

Then Clay frowned. "There are two things that still interest me. You indicate that a series of attacks on black politicians and Federal officials are planned for a week from today, on the 24th. What is significant about that date?"

"I don't know. All I know is that the word is the attacks must happen on that day, not one day earlier or later, and that all our members are to be used, for maximum effect."

"I repeat. What is the significance of that date?"

LaPlace shrugged. "I don't know and didn't ask. General Forrest says do something, you do it."

Clay smiled slightly. "I imagine so. Now, as to my second question. Why is Colonel Buchanan not on this list?"

LaPlace looked genuinely startled. "The Yankee garrison commander? Why in the Hell would you think him one of us? He's been a real burr under our saddle."

"I suspect a high-ranking Federal officer has been suborned by the Klan." Clay's eyes narrowed, and his voice became dangerously soft. "Are you certain you have not been holding out on us?"

"Why would I do that?" LaPlace responded desperately. "Giving you Hampton and Forrest is my death warrant, unless I disappear into Mexico or Europe. Why would I risk my neck for some damn Yankee colonel? It might be possible he's with us; I've already told you I don't know everyone in the Klan. But I've no knowledge that he is loyal to our Cause."

Clay stared into LaPlace's eyes for a long time, then nodded slightly to himself.

Suddenly, LaPlace felt his head jerked back by his hair. Simultaneously, he heard Clay bellow "NO!" in an impossibly deep baritone that left his ears ringing. Shaking his head, he saw that the lithe woman had frozen in the act of bringing her straight-razor down on his throat with her right hand, while her left hand held his head back by the hair.

Clay's voice was suddenly back to its soft normality. "I promised this creature his life in return for his information. I believe him to have told us everything that he knows. I will not have you make a liar of a Clay. Is that understood?"

The woman cast the small man a venomous look, but after a moment's hesitation she released LaPlace, flipped the razor closed, and made it somehow disappear. Clay now directed his attention to LaPlace. Gesturing to the surviving henchman, who was groggily returning to consciousness, he said, "Take your minion and leave. Leave the state, leave the country. Your signed statement will be sufficient for our purposes, and you are quite right that when its existence becomes public knowledge, the Klan will not rest until you are dead. Now go!"

A terrified Gaston LaPlace went over to the plug-ugly, dragged the stunned man to his feet by his handcuffed wrists, and led him out of the warehouse in a wobbly-legged crab walk. After they were gone, Clay picked up the paper from the table and studied it intently.

"What next?" asked Duval brusquely, still angry at Clay for depriving her of the pleasure of killing another "English-loving bastard". "Do we go for Forrest?"

"A week is not a long time," said Bierce. "Forget personal vengeance for a moment. We need to stop these upcoming atrocities. We need to get this information to Washington as soon as may be."

"We cannot send this by wire," mused Clay. "Too many telegraph operators in the South are die-hard Confederates; there is too great a chance that an operator would stop this at one of the repeater stations. No, this must be delivered in person."

Bierce shook his head. "We have a mere week. It would take us at least three days to get to Washington by rail. That would leave Grant and the War Department too little time to organize a response."

"A special," responded Clay suddenly, "a hired locomotive with a single Pullman car, and orders to clear the tracks ahead and go at maximum speed. Even with a detour to South Carolina, we should make it to Washington in sufficient time."

"Why the Hell South Carolina?" blurted Bierce.

"Because I think the President's task will be made easier if we bring him something additional from that state."

Bierce mulled that statement over for a few moments, and then said "Anyway, do you have any idea how expensive it will be to rent a private train and clear the tracks?"

A ghost of a smile flitted across Clay's face. "Do you have any idea how wealthy I am?"

The prospect of such an experience had restored Duval to good humor. "It sounds exciting. Let's get moving and go see the elephant!"

Jay Gould and Jim Fisk stepped down from the first-class compartment of the New York to Washington overnight. At their heels was a visibly apprehensive Abel Corbin. They advanced to the entrance of the station, where Fisk hailed a cab. He held the door open for his companions. "This is where I leave you," said Fisk after they were seated.

Gould felt as if the bottom had dropped out of his stomach; he glanced at the President's brother-in-law, and saw that Corbin looked on the verge of fainting. Returning his attention to his partner, Gould blurted "Fisk, what the Hell are you about? We need you to help calm the President, to persuade him to leave the Government's gold in the Subtreasury. He and his wife obviously like you better than me; your famous charm will be vital!"

Fisk laughed genially, but his eyes narrowed with a hardness Gould could not recall having seen before. "You will have to calm the President by yourselves. I have more important fish to fry. We

will meet here in twelve hours for the night train to New York."
Fisk raised his voice and addressed the cabbie. "Take my friends
to the Executive Mansion!" Fisk slammed the door, the cabbie
flicked his whip, and the abrupt start of the horses threw both
Gould and Corbin back into the cushions of the cab. Fisk watched
them go, and then hailed a second cab. He had two vital calls to
make, calls which he wished to conceal from his partners in crime.

In the first cab, Corbin was beginning to blubber. "Fisk is abandoning us! Everything is falling to pieces! We need to take ship
to Europe . . ."

Jay Gould was not himself a man of violence, preferring to
hire violence done when he deemed it necessary; but these were
exceptional times. He slapped Corbin across the face twice, as hard
as his thin arms allowed. The shock rendered Corbin instantly
silent. He looked at Gould in amazement as his partner spoke
with a venomous hiss.

"Speak softly you fool! The cabbie might hear. Fisk is not abandoning us. I know this if for no other reason than all his liquid
wealth is tied up in this operation, and he would never risk losing
that kind of money."

"Then where is he going?" asked the apprehensive Corbin.

"I do not know," answered Gould truthfully. "He has always
had some interests on the side that he does not share with me. You
can count on this: he will never abandon a scheme that involves
controlling the entire economy of this country. Keep your mind
focused on that."

"Won't Grant be expecting Fisk?" asked Corbin in a small
voice.

"We will simply tell him Mrs. Fisk is ill. Grant is a family man,
and will not question that. Now, pull yourself together. We are
at the Executive Mansion, and we must show confidence and
unconcern about the chaos in the gold market."

The cab had pulled into the grounds of the Executive Mansion, and rolled with a sound of crunching gravel up to the South Entrance. An energetic doorman open the cab door; he recognized Corbin, and then confirmed Gould's name on a list of expected visitors before escorting them up the steps of the Mansion and to the study where Ulysses Grant sat, working over the morning documents.

"Mr. Jay Gould and Mr. Corbin," announced the doorman, who without further ado left the room, closing the door behind him.

"Mr. Gould, Brother Corbin, thank you for coming," said Grant between puffs on his cigar. He gestured at two comfortable chairs near his cluttered desk. "Please make yourselves comfortable. Where is Mr. Fisk?"

"He sends his deepest regrets," said Gould smoothly as he settled into one of the comfortable armchairs. "His wife is quite ill with the grippe, and he is reluctant to leave her side. Rest assured, I am sure that I can speak for him on any issue that may concern you. Now, how may I be of help, Mr. President?"

Grant gestured impatiently at the newspapers that cluttered his desk. "I'm getting concerned about the gold market. Doggone newspapers say the price of an ounce of gold may go up thirty percent this week, perhaps even higher. I'm not an expert in such things, but if gold gets up to that level, it seems to me that folks might start taking it out of the market and hording it, burying it in their backyard, that kind of thing. And since the Europeans want transactions paid in gold, it seems to me our international trade could be affected. I have half a mind to tell Butterfield to sell a few million in Government gold on the market; that extra supply should drive the price down. Trouble is, I'm not sure what other effects putting all that gold into the market would have. Mr. Gould, you know more about Wall Street than anyone I know. What do you think I should do?

Jay Gould's heart missed a beat, although his face showed none of the panic that he was feeling. He glanced at Corbin, and was glad that Grant was concentrating on his New York visitor; the President's brother-in-law looked as if he were about to have a stroke.

"Mr. President, I urge you not to be hasty," said Gould in a mellow, reasonable voice. "It is true that the current fluctuations in gold prices are somewhat greater than is typical. I believe they will even out after the fall harvests have shipped and the international banks have balanced their accounts. The merchants expect these fluctuations, and are used to them. At this point, if the Government were to intervene, the merchants would not know what to expect, could not plan. They would be paralyzed; trade would fall, and the stock market could very well collapse."

Grant's cigar had gone out; he did not seem to notice. "Do you agree with Mr. Gould's assessment, Brother Corbin?" The husband of the President's sister had only partly regained his composure, and so only silently nodded.

Grant threw the stub of his cigar into a spittoon, and then stood up. "Gentlemen, you've given me much to think upon. I have to make the final decision, and I may not do exactly what you would like, but I am deeply obliged for the advice. Now, please join Mrs. Grant and me for lunch. We can talk further on the matter."

Gould did not like how Grant would not commit to following his 'advice'. Then an idea occurred to him, and he smiled ever so slightly.

After lunch the President had gone back to his office to continue working on the never-ending stream of paperwork while Corbin had gone to join the President's sister, and it was left it to Julia Grant to escort Gould to his waiting cab. At the top of the steps, she stopped, placing her hand on Jay Gould's arm.

"Mr. Gould, I want to thank you again for coming down to

advise Mr. Grant. He is a soldier, not a banker, and needs all the help he can get in these difficult times."

Jay Gould kept himself from smiling only with difficulty. He had been thinking how to broach a certain subject with the President's wife, and she had just handed that opportunity to him.

"Mrs. Grant, I am always at the President's disposal. I do have one concern."

"What is that?" asked Julia Grant with a frown.

"Your husband has listened to me, but I am not certain he has truly heard. I fear that he may still be influenced by less knowledgeable men, and decide to interfere in the gold market, to its detriment. If you learn of anything along that line, I would like you to telegraph me in New York immediately."

Julia Grant's frown deepened. "I don't like the idea of spying on my husband."

"It is not spying. It is looking after him, preventing him from making a mistake that could harm the country, and his chances for re-election."

"Since you put it that way, I suppose no harm is done," she replied slowly.

Gould started, as if something had just occurred to him. "I just remembered, Mrs. Grant. My partner Mr. Fisk and I have long felt the country has not properly recognized your husband for his services."

"The country has been generous, Mr. Jay. They have made him President; admirers have built him a fine house in Galena."

"Ah, but gratitude has a way of fading after time. There is no pension for former Presidents, yet they are still expected to keep up a certain position in society. We understand that you and your husband went through a period when money was not as plentiful as it should have been."

With a jolt Julia Grant's mind was jerked back to the time in the late '50s, when her husband could not seem to hold a job, but seemed all too proficient in holding a bottle. When there were times when they had been uncertain whether they and the children would be able to eat the following day. The War had provided her husband a second chance, and he won not only his battle with the Rebels but with the bottle. The bad times were gone; gone, but not forgotten. She felt a shudder of fear at the prospect of ever returning to those days.

"Mr. Fisk and I have determined that we should show gratitude for your husband's accomplishments, gratitude on behalf of the entire country," continued Gould. He reached into an inner pocket of his frock coat, and produced a neatly folded document, which he handed to the President's wife. "This is for you. Your husband's political enemies might twist things if we gave it directly to him."

"What is it?" Julia Grant asked, focusing her crossed eyes on the document with some difficulty.

"Technically it is a loan, but only technically. It indicates that we have lent you a certain amount of gold futures at par value. Gold is already trading at a premium of thirty-six percent. All you need do is sell these gold futures at market price per ounce, pay us back at par per ounce, and pocket the difference. With the quantity we have assigned you, that would give you a profit of about $125,000. And if the price of gold continues to climb, your profits will go up; if it goes to, let us say, a sixty percent premium, you will clear a quarter of a million dollars."

Julia Grant stood in stunned silence. $250,000 for doing nothing; all fears about the future banished forever. Gould underestimated her; she was not a stupid woman. Julia Grant was beginning to realize what Mr. Gould expected of her, and it deeply troubled her.

Gould made a show of checking his pocket watch. "My, look at the time. I must hurry if I am to complete certain other business before my train leaves. My thanks again for your hospitality." The slightly-built Gould swung himself into the cab, and the driver flicked his whip, urging the horse into a fast trot. Julia Grant looked at the retreating cab, then down at the document; her hands began to slightly shake.

Wade Hampton stood on his veranda, contentedly smoking a cigar and watching a glorious sunset to the west. Just four days to go, he reflected; four days until the dogs of war were released, and the South would rise to victory.

Suddenly he noticed a carriage drawn by two horses on the road from town. It made a turn off the pike and entered his grounds. Hampton frowned and squinted; his vision was not perfect, yet he was too vain to use spectacles except for reading. The vehicle was almost to his porch before he recognized the driver on the box as that damn Yankee Clay. Clay brought the carriage smoothly to a stop, jumped to the ground, and secured the reins at a hitching post. From inside the carriage came that damn woman Duval, along with a tall, thin man who Hampton did not recognize. Hampton could barely contain his rage.

"Just what are you people doing trespassing on my property?" roared Hampton. "Remove yourselves before I send one of the servants to the Sheriff! I will not have my family home polluted by damn Yankees!"

"Yes, your family," commented Clay. "That might have been a complication. Fortunately, a gratuity to the station master revealed that by happy accident your wife, Mary, and the children are in Charleston visiting cousins, and are not expected back until tomorrow."

The elderly butler and two younger blacks had gathered at the front door, watching what was transpiring with expressionless faces. Hampton turned to them and said, "You three! I want you to throw these trespassers . . ."

Hampton did not finish what he intended to say. Almost casually, Clay struck the old Rebel general in the face. Hampton staggered, as blood flew from his nose. Duval stepped forward, an angelic smile on her face, and produced a small bottle and a cloth. Wetting the cloth with the contents of the bottle, she placed it over Hampton's face; after a few choking sounds, Hampton suddenly collapsed. Before he hit the ground, Duval and Clay smoothly caught him, and bundled him into the carriage. Clay turned to Hampton's three black servants, who had made no motion to protect their master. Clay bowed slightly to them, and then untied the reins, leaped onto the box, and rapidly set the carriage in motion toward the road leading toward town. The servants continued to watch the carriage dwindle, saying and doing nothing.

Wade Hampton gradually became aware of a noisy clacking, and a swaying back and forth. He opened his eyes, and blinked repeatedly until his vision cleared somewhat. He realized a stout rope anchored his chest and arms to a plush arm chair. Facing him in similar chairs were the three people who had assaulted him at his plantation. Looking about him, he realized he was in a luxurious Pullman car in motion; moreover, a Pullman car whose motion indicated it was moving at a dangerously high speed.

"Ah, you are back with us," commented the short, blonde man who Hampton now recognized as Alphonso Clay. "My apologies for the crudity of my methods. We have good reason to believe you and Forrest have directed a series of terror attacks across the South, to commence four days hence. Freedmen and supporters of the Union would be slaughtered by the hundreds. Furthermore, judging by past experience, your minions will not take especial care in avoiding injury to women and children. Churches will burn, schools will burn. All of this simply cannot be allowed to happen."

"You're crazy. I have no idea what you're talking about. I was regularly paroled at the end of the War, and you have no grounds for holding me!"

Duval smoothly rose to her feet and glided over to the Pullman's small but efficient stove, picked up a short iron poker, and began to prod the dying embers back to life. Clay shook his head in an appearance of exasperation at Hampton, and then spoke.

"Mr. Hampton, do not suppose for one moment that I will not resort to extreme measures to obtain the information you possess. I know what you did to your slaves, before and during the War, and I have a fair idea how many died in agony for your support of Starry Wisdom's goals. Now I am giving you one last chance . . ."

With astonishing speed Duval leaped from the stove to the chair where Hampton was confined, and brought the poker down on his right kneecap. Hampton screamed like a hog being gelded, while Bierce blurted out one of his creative obscenities. The writer glanced over to Clay to see if this was part of his friend's plan; the look of shock on the small man's face indicated he was as surprised as Bierce.

As Hampton's screams subsided into agonized whimpers, Duval said in a conversational voice, "Now Mr. Hampton, we would like the names of your major henchmen in the Klan, and their assignments this Friday. Or would you prefer to lose your other kneecap?"

Through tears and slobbery mucous, Hampton replied, "You will get nothing, you God-damned Yankee bitch!"

Duval raised the poker, but felt her arm arrested in a grip of iron. She turned to see that Clay had immobilized her arm with his surprising strength. In a voice seemingly octaves below his normal voice, he said "This was not part of our plan. We were not to escalate the violence . . . so quickly . . ."

Duval kneed Clay viciously in the groin. He did not go down, but he did release his hold on her arm, stagger back a few steps, and then look at her with an inhuman ferocity. All the muscles in his body began to tremble, and Bierce stared in open-jawed amazement as he saw his friend's body appear to start rearranging itself into something impossible.

Duval saw what Bierce saw, but it did not seem to concern her in the slightest. Instead she whirled on Hampton and jammed the point of the poker into his already shattered right knee. As the old Confederate howled like a steam whistle, she ground the poker deeper and deeper into the shattered joint, twisting the iron gleefully.

"Now you English-loving bastard! Names and places, names and places, or I will do this all night, then start in the morning on your other knee!"

All Hampton could choke out between screams was "Stop! I'll tell! For the love of God stop!" Duval withdrew the poker from the obscene wound just as both Bierce and Clay grabbed one of her shoulders each and dragged her away from the mutilated old Rebel. Bierce glanced at Clay and was relieved to see him looking perfectly normal, physically, deciding that the uncertain light from the swaying coach lanterns must have deceived his eyes. Clay casually shoved Bierce aside, and spoke to Duval in a low whisper.

"You defy my instructions like that again, assault me like that again, and I will kill you."

Duval glared at Clay with an expression that seemed to Bierce to indicate utter madness. "You are welcome to try, any time, any where. It would be interesting to see the outcome." She held the poker like a short sword. Bierce feared she would launch herself at Clay, and moved to defuse a situation that had long since spiraled out of control.

"Calm down, both of you," said Bierce in the softest of voices that barely carried over the sound of Hampton crying. "Hampton is broken. We can get what we need from him right now, if we do not give him a chance to recover. Teresa, stand over there by the divan, where Hampton can see you; make sure you hold the bloody poker so he can see, and remain terrified. Clay, start asking your questions; I'll get paper and pen and write down his responses."

Two very strange beings stared at Bierce for a very long moment; then simultaneously broke into laughter. Then with a faint smile, Clay said to Duval, "It would appear that Ambrose remains focused on the mission; that should shame us both. Let us do as he says." Duval's agreement was signaled by one of her silvery, chilling laughs.

A quarter of an hour later, Bierce handed the finished document to Hampton, who scrawled his signature at the bottom. As Bierce waved the paper to dry it, Hampton rasped, "You won't be able to stop them all. Even those you arrest will quickly go free; no Southern jury will convict them."

"You have not been following the papers," responded Clay. "Congress has passed a bill suspending habeas corpus in the South, and the President signed it yesterday. Your colleagues will be subject to the tender mercies of courts martial, manned by officers who spent four years fighting traitors just like yourself."

Hampton's tear-stained face twisted itself into a mask of hate. "At least you three will go to prison for what you did to me tonight."

"I rather doubt it," replied Clay. "We are operating at the direction of President Grant. He proved during the War that there was little he would not countenance if it worked toward saving the Union. If it comes to that, he will pardon us."

"Not after Friday," murmured Hampton to himself. He had spoken so softly he was certain Clay could not hear him. He did not know Clay had surprisingly acute hearing.

"What do you mean, 'Not after Friday'?"

"Nothing. Pain has made me light-headed."

"Do not insult my intelligence. I said that we could count on a pardon from the President, and you said 'Not after Friday.' You expect the President to die on Friday, the 24th of September."

"You're crazy," replied Hampton, fear now added to his pain-distorted features. "How could I possibly know that?"

For a long moment Clay was frozen like a statue, his mind on an April evening in 1865. In his mind's eye he saw himself rushing up the stairs inside Ford's Theater, hurling himself at a closed door only to hear a single gunshot ring out, realizing that he was too late. He knew that in his mind he would always see that moment when he was too late to save the President's life. Clay's mind returned itself to the present, and he looked down at Hampton with an expression that frightened him more than he was frightened of the crazy woman.

"You are arranging for the murder of Grant on the same day you planned to launch your orgy of terrorism," said Clay in his soft, cultured voice. "Of course. The Government decapitated at the same moment civil order disappears in the South. The leaderless army would be slow to respond; the U. S. Attorneys would be paralyzed with fear, for the most part."

"That is a lie!" blurted Hampton.

"I want the name of the assassin, and any information you may have on him."

Duval glided up beside Clay, bloody poker in her hand, an eager look on her face.

"Need we go through this again?" Clay asked Hampton. "You know you will speak at the end, so tell us now."

Hampton looked just once at the inhuman woman behind Clay, closed his eyes, and said, "Crawford Tillinghast. He is a doctor who specializes in . . . removals which do not raise suspicion. I know nothing more, I swear. Not where to find him, not what his exact plans might be."

"Can we really be sure this English-loving bastard has told all he knows?" asked Duval of Clay. "Consider what is at stake."

Clay seemed to consider the matter, then slowly nodded his head. "Procede. However, when I say halt, you will halt. He does us no good as a body."

Hampton began to scream as the beautiful, terrible woman approached him with a look of positively erotic pleasure on her face. A disgusted Bierce turned away. Clay watched impassively.

An unconscious Hampton lay on the floor of the Pullman, bleeding steadily from the mass of flesh and gore that had once been his right knee. Duval daintily wiped blood from her hands with a scrap of cloth; Bierce stared out a window at the sunrise, seeing nothing, tears brimming in his eyes. Clay stared thoughtfully at the unconscious Klansman, then spoke.

"It seems that was indeed all he knew about Dr. Tillinghast. On top of everything else, we must make sure that Grant is protected from whatever the assassin has planned." Clay then glanced over to Duval. "Hampton will bleed to death shortly if his wounds are not attended to. Bandage him up."

Duval smiled angelically. "There is little point. After the fun I had with his kneecap and connecting bones, infection and death by gangrene are almost certain. Best let the English-loving bastard bleed out, then throw his body off the train before we get to Washington."

Clay shook his head. "He still may be of use. Can you amputate his leg without killing him?"

"If I must," she replied negligently.

"Bierce, please assist Miss Duval in the operation."

Bierce did not turn from the window. "If you will excuse me, I fear I will not be of service at this moment."

Clay shrugged his narrow shoulders, and turned to Duval.

"Then I will assist you. Do you have sufficient instruments for an operation?

"Enough for him," Duval said with a smile as she reached for her carpetbag.

Monsieur Lafitte (born Joe Schultz in Albany, New York) was manager of Willard's, and took neurotic pride in assuring that his hotel was the best in the nation's capital, especially when it came to the kitchens. He had felt for a long time that Willard's had been living on its reputation, especially when it came to food, and had frantically searched for a new chef that could take over the kitchens and once again make Willard's cuisine the talk of the town. He had looked high and low for months, but could not locate a candidate that was anything better than mediocre. Then out of the blue, like a miracle, a chef had approached him, asking for a position at what seemed to be a ridiculously low salary. Lafitte had doubted that anyone capable could come to him under such circumstances, but in desperation he had given the man a try. To Lafitte's amazement, the man was brilliant, turning out dishes of astonishing taste and delicacy, and developing a line of deserts superior to any other in Washington.

Now Lafitte was sampling his new head chef's latest creation, a variation on the simple German sauerbraten that had somehow become a dish of infinite delicacy, the meat seeming to literally melt in his mouth.

"Do you like it?" asked the chef.

"It is magnificent! You are literally the finest chef I have ever encountered."

"Thank you," replied Crawford Tillinghast.

CHAPTER 5

"AND EVERY SCHEME OF BONDAGE FAIL . . ."

"You didn't finish your dinner, Granda," said the thin, smiling girl who sat at one end of the table. "You're always telling me how important it is to eat right."

At the other end of the table, Nathan Bedford Forrest stopped drumming his fingers and smiled at his granddaughter. "You are right, sweetpea. I have some things on my mind that have killed my appetite; nothing for you to worry your pretty little self about. Now, tell me how your lessons with the tutor went today."

The girl made a face of distaste. "He kept me writing all the darn day. Practice, practice, practice he said. Make the letters neat, make them readable. It was so boring."

"I know, darling. It is hard now, but a day will come when you will thank him." Forrest smiled indulgently at the person he loved the most in the world, while inwardly he winced at the thought of his own semi-literacy. *That will not be her lot; she will be a lady, and have a lady's accomplishments.*

The cook appeared in the dining room door. "Gineral Forrest, suh, there be a man waitin' in your library. He be the one you expectin.'"

"Thank you," Forrest said gravely; the cook curtsied and left the room. He then spoke to his granddaughter. "Pumpkin, go upstairs and do your reading. Grandpa will be up just as soon as he's done a little business."

The petite girl flounced over to her grandfather, pecked him on the cheek, and skipped out of the room. The smile slowly left Forrest's face, to be replaced by a grim frown. He rose to his feet. Too quickly, a series of deep coughs tore from his lungs. He swiftly covered his mouth with a large linen handkerchief. When the fit finally subsided, he restored the handkerchief to his side coat pocket, squared his narrow shoulders, and marched from the dining room into the library, where his most trusted courier awaited him standing. Nodding to the man, Forrest went to his desk, opened the top drawer, and drew out about thirty envelopes, all save one addressed to leaders in various chapters of the Klan, all containing letters that he had painstakingly written in his own hand, a task he hating doing because it made his semi-literacy all too obvious. He walked over to the courier and handed all but the one to the man.

"These are all to be delivered posthaste to the men to whom they are addressed," said Forrest. "Use whatever other messengers you can trust to make certain they are delivered in person, and no later than three days from today."

Forrest hesitated, then handed the final envelope over to the courier. "This is addressed to someone who will surprise you. It is not a mistake, and you must deliver this one personally. I will trust no one else with it."

The courier, a man who had handled many delicate matters for Forrest over the past six years, looked at the name and address on the final envelope. His eyes widened, but he displayed no other reaction; he never questioned Nathan Forrest's orders. He said, "Yes, General," stuffed the envelopes into an inner recess of his coat, saluted, and left the room and the house without further ado.

President Ulysses Grant had not slept well; in fact, hardly at all. He had stayed quietly in bed, staring at the ceiling the entire night; Julia was having a rough night as well, and Grant knew that his wife's sleep was always sounder when he was in the bed. Still, Grant could see the first rays of sunlight coming through the window, and felt that he was now justified in getting up and doing something; doing anything useful, not just waiting on events. This was Tuesday; Grant had watched the price of gold climb unbelievably every day of the last two weeks, and despite the protestations of Gould and General Butterfield, Grant could not accept that this was healthy and normal for the American economy.

Quietly, so as not to disturb Julia, he crept into the dressing room, dressed in his traditional black suite and white shirt, then padded down the hall to his study. He sat at his desk, rereading the previous day's newspapers, their descriptions of increasing Klan outrages in the South, of increasing chaos in the stock market. He took out his curious mechanical cigar lighter and ignited the first cigar of his day, the first of about twenty he would smoke before again trying to sleep. He took a long draw, expelled the smoke toward the ceiling, then hunched over his desk, rereading several times the signs of increasing chaos in the nation's financial markets. He massaged his forehead with his free hand, trying to see a clear way to a course of action.

He deeply respected the business acumen of Gould and Fisk, and to a lesser extent his brother-in-law Corbin, and they all advised against releasing Government gold into the commercial markets. Still, his gut seemed to tell him that they were wrong, that the markets were spiraling into chaos, and if he did not act there could be a devastation of the American economy. Suddenly, Grant reached into the upper-right door of his desk and drew out a military telegraph form. He rapidly addressed the form to General Butterfield, care of the New York Subtreasury, and wrote out an instruction to sell $4 million in Government bullion onto the commercial market.

"What are you doing, Sam?"

Grant did not startle easily, but this time he was startled. He turned to find Julia peering over his shoulder, her crossed eyes making focusing difficult.

"I'm not sure Brother Corbin and Mr. Gould gave me the best possible advice. I think I'm going to trust my instincts and order Butterfield to sell gold."

Julia Grant felt her stomach drop. She thought of the paper that Jay Gould had given her, the paper that would secure her future and Sam's, the paper currently in the top drawer of her dressing table. Feeling like a Jezebel, she said to her husband, "Don't do anything rash, love. You know that business is not your strong suit. Remember before the war, how you would work hard, work yourself half to death, and at the end of the day having nothing to show for it? It's not your fault. You know war. Corbin and Gould know business and the stock market. Please promise to talk to them before you do anything on this."

Grant took his wife's hand and kissed it. "I cannot promise that, Julia. No matter how many people give me advice, no matter what that advice is, I must make the final decision. The people of this country expect nothing less." He turned his attention back to the telegraph form. "Please take this to one of my aides. Tell him I have a message to send to New York, and I need it coded so word of its content will not leak to speculators. It should be sent to the fort at Governor's Island, where one of the military telegraphers will decode it and take it to Butterfield." He finished the message and handed her the form, so preoccupied that he did not notice the stunned look on his wife's face. She turned and wordlessly left the room.

Julia stopped at the bedroom she shared with her husband, went to her dressing table, and drew Gould's contract out of the drawer. She looked at the two documents, one representing wealth, one representing the evaporation of that wealth, for a considerable time.

The southeast portion of the District was where Washington's worst slums were to be found. Down one of its miserable unpaved alleys a tired horse drew a furniture wagon. Clay, Bierce and Duval rode on the front bench seat, Clay holding the reins, while the semi-conscious Wade Hampton lay in the back, babbling nonsense quietly. Clay brought the wagon to a halt in front of a small, run-down warehouse, jumped down, and negligently wrapped the reigns around a post. He then marched boldly to the structure's one door, and rapped on it loudly. A greasy, skinny man answered, and started; he obviously recognized the small officer. The two men exchanged some words, so softly that Duval and Bierce could not catch them. Then Clay dropped three gold coins into the skinny man's outstretched hand; the man touched his dirty slouch hat, handed a key to Clay, and then staggered unsteadily down the ally. As he passed the wagon he heard some low, piteous moans from the back. He looked over nervously, then turned his eyes resolutely forward and continued his unsteady way down the ally until he was out of sight.

"Who was that?" asked Duval from her seat on the wagon.

"A man I have used before. He owns these premises, which are located where the neighbors are loathe to question each other's doings, and the police are loathe to patrol save in groups of four. Bierce, help me to move our friend inside."

Bierce jumped down, and then helped Duval to the ground more elegantly. He joined Clay at the rear of the wagon, which contained a ravaged looking Wade Hampton lying on a makeshift stretcher, semi-conscious under the influence of laudanum, his right leg ending in a mass of bandages just above where the knee should have been. Bierce grabbed one end of the stretcher and Clay the other; as they leveraged Hampton out of the bed of the wagon, he began to softly wail. They quickly moved the stretcher through the door and into the darkened interior, then placed it on a long dusty table. A single oil lamp provided dim illumination of the Spartan furnishings, consisting of a few chairs and a disreputable-looking mattress. Duval followed them in demurely, carrying a large carpetbag; she paused only to close the door firmly shut.

Looking with genuine concern at the wreck that was Wade Hampton, Bierce asked, "Do you think he will survive? He has lost much blood, and the shock of the amputation may reduce his will to live."

Duval shrugged negligently. "He will probably survive." She then addressed Clay. "I still do not understand why you want him alive."

"The next step is to deliver the list of names to the President. He in turn will notify the War Department, which will start making arrests. The trials will be by military tribunals, but it is still necessary to present evidence and witnesses. If Hampton's signed statement is not enough, we may have to put him before those tribunals to testify."

Duval frowned. "When they see how we have treated him, won't that cause a reaction in favor of the English-loving Klan bastards?"

Bierce shook his head. "Remember, these will be military tribunals, staffed by veterans of the War. They know Hampton, and his reputation for brutality; their sympathy will be limited."

Clay walked over to Duval and took her, not unkindly, by the shoulders. "Bierce and I must go. You have medical supplies along with some food and drink in the carpetbag. I am trusting you to keep Hampton alive." He paused, and then added, "Please do not betray my trust."

Duval smiled. "Go about your business, and hurry back as soon as possible. I want to spend as little time with this bastard as possible."

"Language, Teresa, language," muttered Clay. Then, to the utter amazement of Bierce, he kissed her passionately. Bierce, the veteran of a number of houses of ill repute, turned away, blushing with unexpected embarrassment. Clay suddenly released Duval, whirled on his heel, and was out the door in an instant. Bierce hurried to follow. Duval went to the door, closed and locked it, and languidly walked over to the table on which the semi-conscious Hampton lay, moaning with pain. She leaned over the old Confederate, frowned, and then forcefully pinched both of his cheeks. The sharp pain brought him mostly out of his delirium.

Duval seated herself elegantly in a chair by the table. Hampton turned his head, recognized her, and seemed to shake with fear. Teresa smiled and uttered one of her chilling, unearthly laughs.

"Awake, are we Mr. Hampton? Good. Now, what shall we talk about while we await the return of Major Clay?"

"I've told you everything I know," replied Hampton in a low, slurred voice.

Still smiling, she shook her head. "My friend Alphonso is a hard man, willing to do hard things if he finds them necessary. Nevertheless, he still suffers from occasional delusions of morality and honor. I do not. I also know that you are a strong man. I congratulate you on that; most men would have died of shock under the treatment I gave you. Strong men like you are proud men. Your pride would have made you hold something back, so that in your own mind you could claim some sort of victory. You did not tell us quite all on the train, did you?"

"I told you all I know about the proposed Klan attacks. I even told you about the attempt to be made on Grant's life." Hampton turned his face away from the woman who had broken him.

Duval smiled, and reached over to the carpet-bag she had left near the table. She extracted a small instrument, stood up, and moved over to where she was sure Hampton could see her. She held out the instrument in her hand.

"I am certain you recognize this tool, Mr. Hampton. I want you to say its name out loud to me."

Hampton's eyes widened with abject terror, and responded in a whisper. "You wouldn't dare. It would kill me, and that crazy major would have your scalp."

Duval clicked the nutcracker open and shut several times, with ominous gusto. "Oh, yes, these will kill you. Can you imagine the pain? Oh, with all the blood you have lost from the amputation, with all the shock you have experienced, once I get your bollocks into these," here she clicked the nutcracker again, "you will die. Alphonso is rather . . . shy in some ways, and it will never occur to him to undo your trousers and look for injuries there. He will simply assume that an old man's heart gave out. Now, is there something you would like to tell me, something more than you told Alphonso? Make it good, as it will be hard to convince me you have told everything."

Wade Hampton closed his eyes, and silently wept. Until the previous day he had thought himself a hard, brave man, unconcerned with dangers and immune to physical threats. In fact, he had thought that way before he had even achieved manhood. He had thought that nothing could induce him to betray the Cause. Incredible as it was, this deceptively attractive woman, this devil incarnate, had broken him—broken him with a piece of iron and a nutcracker. He would have killed himself to protect the Cause; but that was no longer an option. His hands were tied, and besides he had already betrayed his teams of nightriders. He could not endure the pain he knew the woman would deliver. For the first time he began to feel uneasy about the suffering and death he had imposed on his slaves, having never thought that they had feelings worth considering. He had broken them, as he was now broken. Then, he decided that he really owed nothing to certain Yankees, whose god was Mammon, not the Cause. If the Cause went down, then he would take them down as well. Insanely, he resisted a temptation to smile; what he would tell her would be so startling that she would scarce believe it.

"You may want to take out paper and ink," Hampton said in a desolate whisper. "I have a story to tell, a story that you will find incredible." He wheezed a high, almost insane laugh.

"What is it?" growled Colonel Buchanan at the sergeant, irritated at being disturbed at his desk. He had allowed the endless round of War Department paperwork to pile up, and was trying to dispose of all pending items in one long marathon day. He was angered by the fact that his once promising career had been derailed by a drunken former subordinate, and that he would spend the rest of it filling out forms in the humid exile of New Orleans.

The sergeant shuffled his feet nervously; no soldier in the garrison liked to deal with Buchanan when he was in one of his moods. "Colonel, there is a man outside who insists on seeing you. Says he has an important message. Won't tell what it is."

"Tell the bastard to get lost!" snarled Buchanan, and turned his attention back to the despised paperwork.

"Sir, he says he won't leave without seeing you."

"Goddamnit! Must I attend to everything myself?" Sourly, he saw the sergeant was actually trembling before his wrath. *What has the Army come to, to have such whey-faced cowards as noncommissioned officers?* "Very well, Sergeant. If you can't tell the bastard to go to Hell, send him in here and I'll draw him a map!"

The sergeant scurried out the door, and a moment later a thin, bow-legged man walked in and gave Buchanan a surprisingly correct salute.

A soldier, mused Buchanan. *Probably some old Reb bastard.*

"Colonel Buchanan. My commander, Nathan Bedford Forrest, has charged me with delivering an envelope to you."

Buchanan had been about to deliver a fiery string of curses at the unwanted visitor. At the mention of Forrest's name, Buchanan's half-open mouth snapped shut. His visitor advanced, drew the envelope from his inner coat pocket, and placed it carefully on the desk before Buchanan. He then saluted, turned and began to walk through the door.

"Wait," said Buchanan in a raspy voice. "What's in the envelope?"

The visitor stopped, and without turning to face Buchanan said, "General Forrest sealed that letter and addressed it to you. It would never occur to me to inquire as to its contents." The man then resumed his march out of the headquarters building.

Buchanan picked up the envelope and stared at it for a long moment before suddenly tearing it open. He read the contents several times, the color slowly draining from his face. Then he screamed "Sergeant!"

The uneasy subordinate appeared at the door.

"Sir?"

Prepare my horse! I need to get to the train depot immediately!

General Butterfield burst unannounced into Jay Gould's office, waiving a telegram. "Gould, look at this! We are ruined. I am ruined!"

"Calm yourself, Butterfield," replied the saturnine Gould. "Now, what is the matter?"

The Treasury official threw himself into an armchair, and looked close to weeping. "It's here," he whined, waiving the telegram. "An order from Grant, telling me to sell $4 million in Government bullion by the close of business Friday. He demands an acknowledgement, so I can't even claim this got lost in transmission. I've bought gold futures on margin at a high price, but when the market realizes Government gold is flooding the market, futures I paid a thirty percent premium for will be repaid at par or worse. How will I pay off the loans I took out to buy the futures in the first place? I am ruined!"

Gould lost his normally polite manner. "Shut up, you fool! Fisk and I are as deep in this as you. Is there any chance of you getting Grant to change his mind?"

"Me? Hardly. Grant never changes his mind; we saw that in the War. You and Fisk were supposed to set his mind against any gold releases."

"I thought we had," replied Gould mournfully. He considered the disaster from all angles for a long minute, then decided on a desperate course of action.

"Very well. This is how we will proceed. I will get in touch with Fisk, and all three of us will sell our futures positions in the next two days."

Butterfield's horror was stamped on his face. "I can't be seen to be selling! Grant will be on me like a duck on a June bug. Besides, when the market sees all three of us selling at once, it will collapse immediately, before we have a chance to unload even a fraction of our futures."

As usual, Gould's face concealed his feelings; in this case the contempt he felt for Butterfield's lack of intelligence. "I have considered that. Gould and I will continue to very publicly and loudly buy gold. For every ounce we buy, secretly we will be selling three through straw men that cannot be easily traced to us. As for your holdings, I will dispose of them through the straw men as well.

We may end up losing some, but none of us will be wiped out when the crash comes."

Butterfield looked relieved. Then a thought occurred to him. "Just where is Fisk, anyway?"

I wish I knew, thought Gould, who answered Butterfield with an assurance he did not feel. "He is handling affairs with our straw men. Don't worry about him; I have his power of attorney to deal with his holdings in gold." *Strange how he gave me that, now that I think on it,* mused Gould. *Jim Fisk never seemed very trusting; but he gave me control of his gold holdings like it was a minor thing, like he had more important fish to fry.* Gould suddenly acquired a suspicion that there were depths to the run on the gold market that were being hidden from him.

"All that wealth—gone," whined Butterfield to himself.

Gould finally lost his patience—something he very rarely did. "Fool! Now is not the time to mourn what might have been. Now is the time for us to take action to see that we are not actually impoverished. More importantly, that we do not see the inside of Sing-Sing!"

Both men were silent for a moment, contemplating the thick iron doors and high stone walls of the place where they might very well end their days.

Grant was at his desk in the Executive Mansion, finishing his third cigar of the morning as he read a newspaper account about the increasing hysteria on Wall Street. His mind was also on the telegram he had just received, in which his father announced his intention to visit the Executive Mansion yet again, and that he would be arriving this very day. Grant sighed. *He's only been gone two weeks, yet he is coming again. Still, I cannot blame him. Things cannot be that pleasant at home, with Mother so . . . difficult,* thought Grant. He reflected on his own estrangement from the woman who had brought him into this world, a woman who would neither write to him nor visit him, and realized how hard it must be for his father to live with such a strange and unsympathetic woman day after day.

Suddenly he heard the ringing of boots rapidly ascending the stairway. Alphonso Clay and Ambrose Bierce burst into the room, followed by an ineffectually protesting male secretary.

"Mr. President, I told them you were not ready to receive visitors at this time," whined the secretary, literally wringing his hands.

"Never mind," responded Grant. "It's all right. Please leave us, and close the door behind you." He stared at the new arrivals until the secretary had left, then cocked his eyebrow and said a single word: "Well?"

"Sir, you tasked me to find you an alternative to taking . . . extraordinarily harsh action to keep the peace in the South," replied Clay, who then took two sheaves of documents from the inner pockets of his coat and laid them on the desk before Grant. "Here are lists of Klan leaders, their locations, and major Klan outrages scheduled to take place on Friday. If the War Department moves quickly, most of those outrages can be prevented, and the Klan leadership decapitated."

Grant stared at the slight officer for a moment, and then he threw his still smoldering cigar into a spittoon and grabbed the papers. Bierce decided to add a few words of explanation.

"The one set of papers relates to the Klan west of the Appalachians. We obtained it from a gentleman who has now fled the country, rightly fearing murderous retaliation from his former colleagues. The most important thing to note is that he indicates Nathan Bedford Forrest is the leader of the Klan, at least in the West. We have long suspected that, but this is the first documented evidence. Even though the author of that document is long gone, some of the Klan leaders can undoubtedly be persuaded to confirm this, once they are in custody. You will note that the second document contains similar information for the East; signed by Wade Hampton himself, who confesses his own role in Klan leadership."

"Sir, some years ago you made me a promise concerning Nathan Bedford Forrest," said Clay, face and voice equally expressionless. "If he was found to have violated his parole, he was to be mine, to deal with as I wish."

Grant looked up slowly from the papers before him, and locked eyes with Clay. After a few moments, the President spoke.

"I did make such a promise. Never thought Forrest would be fool enough to break his parole, and make me have to live up to it. Very well, he is yours. First you must help me make sure that this co-ordinated series of terrorist attacks does not take place." Grant grabbed a fistful of Army telegraph forms, and began addressing concise orders to various army posts throughout the country, occasionally referring to the documents Clay and Bierce had provided him. As he wrote, he spoke to the two friends.

"As soon as I'm finished with these, I want you to take them to the War Department and have them sent with the highest priority. We should be just in time to stop a number of these horrors from occurring." For some minutes the President scribbled. Then, with a sigh, he put down his pen, picked up the forms, and gave them to Clay. Then, he gave Clay a hard look, saying, "Is that all, Major?"

"One more thing, Mr. President. Mr. Hampton has also confessed to having hired a profession assassin to murder you, one Doctor Crawford Tillinghast. Special precautions must be taken as to your safety until this man is captured."

Grant sighed heavily, shaking his head slowly. "So these fine, honorable Southern 'gentlemen' hire murderers to do their foul work for them. Well, I will not leave the Executive Mansion without you as an escort until this matter is resolved."

"Sir, that is not sufficient!" exclaimed Clay with a force foreign to him.

"It is sufficient for the head of a free Republic. I will not cringe behind a wall of Praetorian guards. I have confidence in you; your discreet efforts will be enough.

"One more thing, Major. I read the newspapers thoroughly every morning. I see that there is some confusion down in South Carolina. It seems Wade Hampton has disappeared. The accounts are not clear; but it is reported that Hampton was kidnapped by two men and a woman off his estate. You will not be surprised to learn that when you told me of Hampton's role in the Klan, and of his willingness to identify major figures in it, I made a connection in my mind."

"I am not surprised at all," replied Clay quietly.

Grant paused, and then asked, "Is Wade Hampton still among the living?"

"Yes, sir."

"Since you would like to keep such a witness close at hand, I suspect he is in Washington. Is that not the case?"

"It is, sir."

Grant suddenly leaned forward across his desk and pointed a finger at Clay. "As soon as you are through sending the telegrams, I want you to bring him here to me. Alive. No accident, no 'shot while trying to escape.' Is that clear, Major?"

"Perfectly." Clay saluted smartly, clicked his heels, and then headed out the door, closely followed by a pale, sweating Bierce.

After the two visitors were gone, Grant leaned back in his chair and closed his eyes. He thought of how he needed to see Hampton in person. Not just to confirm the information provided by Clay, but to see for himself what Clay had done to Hampton in order to obtain said information. Grant was not a fool, regardless of what his political enemies said. He knew Hampton to be a hard, brutal man who would not willingly have given up such knowledge. He needed to see for himself just what Clay had done, not so he could decide how much blame should be apportioned to the young officer. So he would know how much blame he would have to shoulder himself, for having unleashed such a weapon on the country's enemies.

After writing down Hampton's half-coherent ramblings, Duval had given the crippled Rebel a dose of laudanum to keep him quiet, and had attempted to get some badly needed sleep in the worn armchair. Over-anxious, sleep eluded her. What Hampton had said would shake the nation even more than a series of atrocities against freed slaves and an attempt to reignite the war, if that were possible. As she dozed, several times she jerked awake, and half rose, intending to go out on the streets in search of Clay, who must learn of Hampton's further confession as soon as could be. Three times she half-rose from her seat, then settled back in, knowing that she dare not leave Hampton unattended, and that in any event the quickest way to find Clay was to wait for him to return to the warehouse. The fourth time her eyes opened, it was for a different reason. Waves of nausea struck her like a hammer; she shot to her feet and staggered to a bucket near the table, into which she was noisily sick. When the vomiting finally ceased, she shakily removed a handkerchief from a pocket of her frock and wiped her mouth.

Damnation! she thought. *No doubt about it. And after all the precautions I took. Well, some chemist in this damnable town must have extract of the Pennyroyal flower. I better get some, and soon.*

Duval whirled toward the door at the sound of the lock being opened. The door flew open, and in stepped Clay and Bierce, neither of whom seemed particularly pleased to her eye.

"Alphonso, what is the matter?"

"We must pack up Hampton immediately, and take him to the White House. There is a wagon outside. Is he . . ." Clay paused, then swiftly approached Duval, taking her by her hands. His delicate nostrils twitched slightly.

"You have been ill," Clay said softly, not directly referring to the odor of vomit that clung to her. "Please sit down and rest. Bierce and I will handle Hampton by ourselves."

Duval glared at her lover. "I am now fine. A brief reaction to something I ate. You will need me, as he keeps drifting in and out of consciousness, and I can rouse him easier than either of you. And roused you will need Hampton, if you are going to the White House with him." Silently she handed him the notes she had taken, with Wade Hampton's shaky signature at the bottom. Clay read with his usual astonishing speed, and lost the little color that his pale face contained. Wordlessly he handed the papers to Bierce, who in turn read them more slowly. Clay had perused them silently, but not Bierce. A crescendo of vile yet creative obscenities poured from the young reporter.

As Bierce finished, he looked at Duval, who smiled weirdly. "Bottom is out of the tub, right enough," she said, for once not concealing her Irish brogue.

"Do I want to know how you obtained this information from Hampton?" asked Bierce slowly. Duval's only response was one of her hearty, heartless laughs. Bierce looked at the woman with genuine fear. Clay merely favored her with one of his tight smiles.

General Butterfield dashed into Jay Gould's office for the second time that day without so much as a knock, and threw himself into an armchair without being asked. Giving his unanticipated visitor a disdainful glance, Gould returned his attention to the trusted courier who stood before his desk. Silently he handed the young man a sealed, addressed envelope, then dismissed him with a flick of his fingers. The thin young man bowed slightly to Gould, then left the room, closing the door behind him. Butterfield spoke the moment the door was closed.

"The Exchange is closed, Gould. There are some rumors going around the floor, and the price of gold is jittery, but it is holding."

Gould was inwardly exasperated that Butterfield imagined that he, of all people, needed a briefing on the status of the market. Gould looked at the corrupt government official, busy wiping sweat off his face with a large handkerchief, and not for the first time thought that this fool was the weak link that could bring them all down. *Perhaps I should get in touch with Duval, and have her remove Butterfield from the equation. A pity his nerves are failing him, his war record was solid enough. Wait. I better talk to Fisk before I contact Duval. I shouldn't do something so . . . irreversible without talking to Jim Fisk. And just where is Fisk anyway?*

"Just where is Fisk, anyway?" asked Butterfield, echoing Gould's uneasy question.

"I take it your partner does not know you are here," said the distinguished-looking, cheerful man, occupying one of the two comfortable armchairs in the finest suite in Washington's National Hotel.

Jim Fisk chuckled, and took a draw off his impressively-sized cigar. He leaned back in the suite's other armchair and waved the hand holding the cigar airily. "Of course not, he still believes he is calling all of the shots. Let him continue to believe it. By the time he finds out what is really happening, he will be in so deep that it won't matter."

Fisk's host smiled broadly. "The Council will be highly pleased with your work. In fact, you can expect to advance to full membership in the Council. Starry Wisdom needs more men like you, able to think grandly and act upon those thoughts without hesitation."

Then the speaker turned off his wide smile in an instant. "I am still concerned about two loose ends. One is your partner. He could still be an impediment, once he realizes what is really happening. The other is that bastard Clay. My sources inform me he is sniffing around, and may be uncomfortably close to unraveling the complete story. The Council has been divided for too long on him, part feeling that his . . . unique ancestry could provide almost limitless opportunities if properly utilized, part feeling that the same ancestry could make him the greatest possible threat to our plans, even our very existence. This disagreement has been why his removal has not been sanctioned. Having said all that, I am part of the group that believes the risks he poses far outweigh any benefits he could bring to Starry Wisdom. That is why after Grant is removed, I want your man Tillinghast to remove not only Gould, but Clay."

Fisk's perpetual good humor deserted him. "Careful there. Gould is not a problem; but if the Council is divided on how to treat Clay, we could make powerful enemies who would not hesitate to take . . . decisive action, even against you, let alone me."

The wide smile was back on the face of Fisk's host. "Do not concern yourself with that. I am giving the order on this issue, and I would positively delight in knowing exactly who my enemies are on the Council."

Fisk gave a low whistle. "You aim for the Grand Mastership?"

His host shrugged. "The current Grand Master is ill, and not long for this world. Someone must replace him. Why not someone who has shown he can take decisive action, and deliver successes to Starry Wisdom where his predecessor has delivered only failures? And when I am Grand Master, you will be at my side. Money will no longer matter to you, as you will have the power to possess anything you wish on this planet. Now, get back up to New York, and keep your fool of a partner quiet until everything falls into place."

Fisk stood, took a final draw on his cigar, and threw the remnant into a spittoon. He then strolled out of the suite humming a cheerful tune, thinking on a future of limitless possibilities.

The wagon pulling up to the rear entrance to the Executive Mansion attracted no attention; there were always deliveries of various kinds of supplies. Clay leaped from the driver's seat and handed the reins to a puzzled black servant. He went swiftly to the back of the wagon where Duval and Bierce were seated inelegantly on either side of the barely conscious Wade Hampton. Clay handed down Duval, then he and Bierce clumsily maneuvered the stretcher with its moaning burden off the bed of the wagon. Clay took the lead position, while Bierce grasped the handles at the rear. As they began slowly moving Hampton up the steps to the rear entrance, Duval fell into step alongside Clay.

Frowning, Clay said, "You should wait outside; there will be no need for you in here."

Duval did not break her stride. "I disagree. The mere sight of me may help loosen Hampton's tongue, if he should prove reluctant to co-operate."

Bierce looked disgusted, but Clay smiled ever so slightly, and raised no further objection to Duval accompanying them. The group marched boldly past a doorkeeper and began ascending the staircase to the second floor where the President maintained his office. The doorkeeper, an old veteran who had lost a hand at the Battle of the Crater, shouted "One moment! Just where do you boyos think you are going? And just who is that on the stretcher? This is the Executive Mansion, not a hospital!"

"The President is expecting us," replied Clay, not deigning to look back at the crippled veteran. The doorkeeper might only have one hand, but he was game. He charged up the stairs and grabbed Bierce by the shoulder, bringing the procession to an abrupt halt. "No one goes up there to the President until I make sure he is expecting you." At the front of the stretcher, Clay slowly turned his head and looked at the doorman. To someone who did not know Clay, the look appeared mild. Knowing Clay, Bierce feared for the maimed veteran who was simply doing his job.

"Let him do his duty, Clay," Bierce said with more firmness than he felt. Duval shot him a venomous look. Clay seemed to consider what Bierce had said, and finally nodded slightly to the doorman.

"Very well. Go to the President and tell him that Clay and Bierce are here with the . . . individual whom he wished to see."

The man squeezed past Clay's party, reached the second floor landing, and seemed to march rather than walk to the President's office. Some soft murmurs were heard. Then the man appeared at the top of the stairs and announced gravely, "The President will see you now."

With surprisingly little effort, Clay and Bierce maneuvered the stretcher into Grant's office. If the President was surprised at the sight of a semiconscious Wade Hampton on a stretcher, he gave no sign. He was visibly surprised at the sight of a woman. After settling the stretcher to the floor, Clay answered Grant's unspoken question.

"Mr. President, this is Miss Teresa Duval, formerly of the Sanitary Commission, now working for the Pinkerton Agency. She is a trained nurse, and is instrumental to my investigation, and the state of Mr. Hampton's health."

Grant sensed something was amiss, but decided to let it pass. Some inaudible words came from the man on the stretcher. Frowning, Grant took in the bandaged stump of Hampton's leg, and asked, "How is a man in that state going to answer any questions?"

"There will be no problem, Mr. President," replied Duval,

completely unintimidated by the presence of the President of the United States. "Major Clay, your assistance please." They each hooked their arms under a shoulder of the old Rebel and none too gently heaved him into an armchair in the corner of the office. When Hampton's bandaged stump bounced against the seat of the chair, he yelped with pain, and suddenly looked much more alert. Duval made certain that he remained that way by producing a small bottle of smelling salts, which she held under his nose for some time, despite his feeble efforts to waive her hand away. She stood back, faced Grant, and in a cheerful voice announced, "Mr. President, may I present Mr. Wade Hampton."

"What has happened to this man?" asked Grant, a cold touch in his voice.

Duval placed her hand on Hampton's shoulder and smiled. "An unfortunate accident, Mr. President. Mr. Hampton was trying to flee us on horseback. His animal slipped and fell on his leg, hopelessly crushing it. Amputation was the only option. Who would have thought that such a famous cavalryman would have handled his mount so recklessly."

Hampton started to open his mouth, but felt the nails of the awful woman dig into his shoulder with surprising strength, causing him agonizing pain. He saw Duval through his peripheral vision, saw her looking demurely at the President, and thought what she had done to him with a simple poker. He could denounce her, he thought, but who would believe him? Who would believe a modest nurse with the sainted Sanitary Commission would be capable of such barbarity? And then he thought what might be done to him if she ever got her hands on him in private again.

Grant shifted his attention to the crippled prisoner. "Mr. Hampton, is that how you came to lose your leg?"

"Yes," rasped Hampton, knowing he was defeated.

Grant stared at him for a long time, and then looked briefly at

Clay, Duval and Bierce. Shaking his head slightly, the President retreated behind his desk, sat heavily in his leather chair, and drew out one of his seemingly endless supply of cigars. He lit it, and took two lingering draws off of it while he stared at the ceiling. Then he suddenly riveted his eyes on Hampton while grasping the document that the old Rebel had signed.

"This indicates you have planned an unprecedented series of barbaric assaults on freed slaves and Federal officials, to begin Friday. I have dispatched cavalry companies to arrest all the leaders you have named, and protect all of the targets you have listed. This is treason, absolute treason. The second time in your miserable life you have betrayed our country and our Constitution. I personally signed the order that granted you, and those like you, amnesty, from a desire to see the horrors of war finally put to an end. Your life was a gift from me. Now you would use that gift to revisit death and destruction on our poor wounded country."

"Not my country," hissed Hampton.

"Like it or not, it is," responded Grant.

"There is more, Mr. President," interrupted Clay. "My associate has obtained further confession from Mr. Hampton." Clay withdrew the short document that Duval had forced Hampton to sign, and presented it to Grant. "According to Mr. Hampton, he and his Klan entered into an agreement with Messrs. Gould and Fisk. The conspiracy was to acquire control of the United States gold supply, and therefore the United States economy, while you were distracted by Klan terrorism. Their advice to keep your hands off the gold market, combined with anarchy sweeping the South, would prevent any action by you until too late."

Grant looked stunned. "But that wouldn't have worked! My sister's husband would have warned me . . ." The President paled; his cigar dropped from fingers rendered suddenly nerveless onto the top of his desk, where it smoldered harmlessly.

"Corbin," he muttered softly. "My poor sister. This will kill Virginia." Then the sadness left his face, and it hardened into the expression it had habitually worn when he looked at the carnage outside Vicksburg, within the Wilderness, in the depths of the Crater. He looked straight into the eyes of Wade Hampton and softly said, "Is this all true?"

Hampton was tempted to deny everything, to sow confusion. The thought vanished as the woman's nails suddenly dug into his shoulder so strongly he almost cried out. "It is true. I will testify to that effect, in exchange for a pardon."

Grant stared at the old Rebel for a long moment before responding. "Now, you present me with a considerable problem. What to do with you? Grant you amnesty for testimony? Give you a trial and a hanging? Allow you to go back to private life with a pledge of good behavior for the future, whatever that might be worth from a 'gentleman' like yourself?" Grant turned to glare at Clay and added, "Or perhaps another riding accident could save the country a great deal of embarrassment." The President sighed, and suddenly looked old and weary. "Well, there is time to decide. Clay, I want you to keep Mr. Hampton under surveillance until I find out how the arrests of the Klansmen have gone. He may wish to consider turning state's witness, if we require his testimony. In exchange, I would be willing to grant him a free pardon—which is more that he deserves."

"What about the gold conspiracy," asked Bierce

Grant shrugged. "As it happens, I have already instructed General Butterfield to sell $4 million in Government gold tomorrow morning. That should cause a quick fall in the prices. If not, I will order more sold. It will ruin some speculators, I'm afraid, and even some legitimate investors. That can't be helped. The important thing is it will put paid to the scheming of Gould and Fisk." Grant turned his attention back to Clay; his face looked as if he had tasted something sour. "Clay, I want you to keep this man safe; and I do mean safe. No accidents, no falls from a horse. I want him well and able to testify. Take him some place secure, and guard him well. Once you have done that, arrange telegrams to be sent to New York to Gould, Fisk, and . . . my sister's husband. Tell them I want them here by tomorrow afternoon."

"Should they not be arrested, sir?" asked Clay.

"Not yet. That would get into the newspapers and cause even greater panic on the Exchange, perhaps even a run on the banks. Just get them to Washington, and we will consider at our leisure how best to minimize the damage from this mess." Grant stifled a yawn. "I'm going upstairs and catch a few hours sleep. I have a feeling that tomorrow will be a busy day."

The President had no idea.

Friday, September 24, 1869. The dawning sun shown fitfully through the smokes and mists of New York City. A one-horse cab drew up before the steps of the New York Stock Exchange. Out stumbled a bleary-eyed, half-drunk Daniel Butterfield, clutching a bulging briefcase to his chest. He stared up the steps at the still-locked main doors. For a moment losing his nerve, then remembering how he had decided, with the help of considerable whiskey, that the only way he could save himself from Sing-Sing was immediate and total obedience to Grant's orders, money, and Jay Gould, be hanged. He then stumbled determinedly up the steps and began pounding ceaselessly on the door. After a full minute he heard the door unlock, and the neatly frock-coated Vice-Chairman of the Exchange stared angrily at him.

"We are closed until nine o'clock, you pathetic sot! Now be on your . . ." The man abruptly stopped, shocked to recognize Major General Daniel Butterfield, Assistant Secretary of the Treasury and Head of the New York Subtreasury, obviously in a state of inebriation. Butterfield shoved the man aside and staggered into the marble-floored interior.

"General Butterfield, sir, this is, ah, an unexpected honor. However, this morning is not a good one for a social visit." He pointed out to the vast floor, which was beginning to fill with frock-coated men, worry written on their features. "The condition of the gold market is unstable, and worrying everyone. I cannot begin to understand what is driving the price so high."

"Need to talk to you in private," muttered Butterfield, looking around with red-rimmed eyes. He spotted a senior clerk's office that was temporarily unoccupied, and began to lurch over to it, mumbling an order to the Vice-Chairman to follow. Nervously stroking his elaborate muttonchop whiskers, the Vice-Chairman hesitated for a moment, but in the end followed Butterfield into the office. The general kicked the door closed, dumped his bulging briefcase onto the office's desk, and then planted himself heavily in the chair behind that desk.

"General, I do not mean to be disrespectful, but should not you go home and, ah, get some rest? You seem in no condition to transact business."

"Shut up and do as you're told!" grated Butterfield, suddenly seeming quite sober. He opened the briefcase and shook out hundreds of pages, each of them with a signature that was scarcely dry. Even from where he stood, the Vice-Chairman could see that the signatures were Butterfield's.

"These are Treasury warrants, allowing the holder to withdraw a stated amount of gold from the Subtreasury. Each of them indicates the amount in question. You are to sell them, this morning, all of them, at a price of par, whatever the current market is. You are to turn all amounts paid for these warrants over to the Subtreasury, minus your standard commission."

The Vice-Chairman was thunderstruck. "General, yesterday the spot price of gold was over fifty percent above par! Most of the recent purchases have been financed by futures agreements where the borrowers signed the agreements at an assumed price of well above par. If the price goes back to par, those borrowers are ruined men. They could never pay back what they borrowed."

Butterfield reached into the inner pocket of his frock coat, and extracted a flimsy copy of a telegram, which he proceeded to waive at the Vice-Chairman.

"You see this? A telegram from the President of these United States. He says that I am to sell not less than $4 million of Government gold today, at no higher price than par. I will do so!"

"At least let me spread out the sales during the day, to lessen the shock to the gold market . . ."

"I want these warrants sold within one hour of the opening bell, without fail! Is that understood?"

The Vice-Chairman was confused, aware that he was suddenly enmeshed in a situation he did not fully understand. Still, Butterfield had the power to demand what he had asked. Nodding his head slightly, the Vice-Chairman said, "Sir, it shall be done."

"Fine." Butterfield stood, then marched out of the office without another word, leaving the warrants and the briefcase in the care of the New York Stock Exchange.

"Time to greet the day, Mr. Hampton," said Teresa Duval sweetly.

Wade Hampton blinked his eyes, and for a moment forgot where he was. Then he remembered: sleeping on a cot in a large pantry at the rear of the Executive Mansion's kitchen. He now recalled that Clay and that vile woman had discussed where to keep him for the night, and finally decided that the basement of the President's home would be best, especially since Grant might want to see him at short notice. Clay and Bierce had rustled up four army cots. One had been set up actually inside the large pantry, which possessed a door that could be locked. Hampton remembered being slung onto the cot unceremoniously and the door being slammed, leaving him in absolute dark. The scuffing noises outside the door indicated that the other three cots were being set up right against the wall of the pantry. Murmuring voices indicated that Clay, Bierce and Duval would sleep in their clothes on those cots, and would instantly awake should the one-legged Hampton attempt something foolish. With the pain in the stump of his amputated leg and the fear and humiliation he was suffering, he had not expected to sleep a wink. The door had not been shut for five minutes before he dropped into a deep, dreamless slumber.

Now he peered at the outline in the doorway, of the woman Duval, arms akimbo. He heard rather than saw that terrible, terrifying smile in her voice, and shuddered.

"Time to break your fast," she said as he struggled into a sitting position, bolts of pain shooting through his stump. Something struck his chest and fell into his lap; he saw with some surprise that it was a quarter-loaf of bread. He found a mug of tepid water being forced into his left hand.

"Eat, drink and be merry, Mr. Hampton. For today you may die," said Duval in a mocking voice. "Make haste; this is all you are going to get for some considerable time."

To his own surprise Hampton discovered he was ravenous. He tore into the bread, pausing occasionally to gulp a mouthful of water, thinking all the time of how he was used to dining with impeccable manners on elegant foods presented on fine china. The moment the last crumb of bread had disappeared, Duval reached behind her, grabbed a wooden crutch, and slung it at Hampton, who just barely caught it before it smashed into his face.

"No more lollygagging, Mr. Hampton. A trip to the water closet, then up the stairs to the second floor, where we will await the President, Major Clay, and Mr. Bierce."

"Where are they?" groaned Wade Hampton as he painfully wobbled onto his remaining foot.

"Over at the War Department telegraph room, monitoring the arrests. You had better pray to whatever god you worship that the President is satisfied with the progress being made by the army in rounding up your friends."

"You mean if he is not, I will hang."

"Oh, no, Mr. Hampton. Somehow I think it will not come to a hanging." Duval emitted one of her blood-curdling laughs, and Wade Hampton found himself trembling.

As the two-wheeler wove its way through New York traffic, Jay Gould was both angry and concerned. Angry, because his courier, normally so efficient, had burst into Gould's office uttering hysterical nonsense about the bottom going out of the gold market, but had no actual facts and figures to present. He was concerned because he knew something had driven his normally reliable man half out of his wits. As the cab turned onto Wall Street, Gould saw his worst fears realized. Crowds of panic-stricken men were dashing in and out of the front doors of the Stock Exchange, most having crazed looks on their faces. The cab stopped. Gould alighted, tipped the driver generously, and turned his face resolutely toward the scene of panic.

Normally, Wall Street crowds made way respectfully for Jay Gould. Not today; this was not a normal day. The slightly-built Gould had to strike repeatedly with his walking stick until he made an opening in the jostling crowd at the entrance large enough to slip through. Once he was clear of the door and onto the Exchange floor proper, Gould was literally frozen with shock. He was used to the floor of the Exchange being boisterous, even rowdy. He was now totally at a loss for words, he had never witnessed a scene such as he now witnessed. Scores of men were screaming the prices at which they would sell gold futures, scores more were screaming the prices at which they would buy; seldom did the two figures overlap. The clerks responsible for the blackboard recording gold transactions were literally in tears, incapable of keeping up with the frantic transactions, almost inaudible over the horse screams of frightened men.

The Vice Chairmen hustled past Gould, who instinctively grabbed the man's arm and spun him around. The man looked wildly at Gould. Gould in turn looked with shock at the Vice Chairman; the stately, dignified man Gould had known seemed reduced nearly to the level of an animal, frock coat and underlying vest completely unbuttoned, necktie missing, hair seemingly standing on end. Gould shouted to be heard.

"What is going on? This is more than a correction in the gold price!"

The Vice Chairman's mouth worked, but at first no sound emerged. Then he found the words.

"The Treasury's dumping gold at par!"

"How much?"

"$4 million dollars."

"That isn't disastrous. It wouldn't cause a run like this."

"You don't understand, Gould! Butterfield demanded it be sold all at once, this very morning, regardless of price! The market saw that, and figured more was to be dumped later. Everyone holding gold futures requiring payment above a thirty percent premium over par is selling for anything they can get above that amount. No, that's wrong. A lot of people borrowed the money to buy at forty precent to fifty percent over par, and simply cannot pay off their loans if they sell for less. Hundreds are going to be ruined!"

Wordlessly Gould dragged the Vice Chairman into the office Butterfield had used not an hour before; the Exchange official too demoralized to resist. Once Gould had closed the door he addressed the Vice Chairman viciously.

"Get a hold of yourself! This is what you are going to do. You know that Fisk and I have lodged major gold futures with your best brokers. You are to see those futures are sold for whatever they can bring, and that the Exchange does not process any other sales until ours are complete."

The Vice Chairman was aghast. "That would violate every rule of ethics! I cannot agree."

"Listen you fool! You may very well be unemployed by this time tomorrow. Fisk and I will pay you $100,000 cash to do this." The Vice Chairman, normally an honest, God-fearing man, was taken aback at the prospect of such wealth.

"Do we have an arrangement?" asked Gould impatiently.

Thinking he knew how Faust must have felt speaking to the Devil, the Vice Chairman reluctantly said, "Yes."

Without a word, Gould stormed out of the office, through the crowded entrance of the Exchange, and out onto Wall Street. Disdaining the waiting line of cabs, he began walking briskly toward his offices, four blocks away. As he walked, his mind worked furiously. He chuckled mirthlessly as he thought of what his visitor had promised, back in May; a promise that he would become the wealthiest man in the world. Somehow, it had all gone wrong; somehow, the political innocent Grant had intervened decisively to defeat the cornering of the gold market. Now all Gould could think of was preserving his existing fortune—and preserving himself from prison.

As he entered his building and quickly ascended the stairs to his office, he decided that he had to get in immediate contact with Jim Fisk. The two of them were going to have to co-ordinate their stories and present a united front to any Federal investigation. Damn Fisk anyway, thought Gould. Fisk had somehow become impossible to contact these last two days, just when his presence was most needed.

Gould threw open his outer office door, and was greeted by his smiling male secretary, who was holding a telegram.

"Good morning, Mr. Gould," the young man said brightly. "You have some good news! The President has sent a telegram, asking to see you this very day. That is a great honor. I have taken the liberty of reserving you a first-class compartment on the 10:45 train to Washington."

Jay Gould resisted the temptation to knock down his well-meaning secretary.

The commotion of several people walking along the hallway awakened Wade Hampton. Much to his own surprise, he found that he had gone to sleep while sitting in a wing chair in President Grant's office. A glance out the window showed him it was late afternoon. He twisted his head around until he spied Teresa Duval, sitting in a chair across the room from him, perusing a tome that she must have taken off the President's shelves. Seeing that he was awake, she closed the book, put it on an end table, and smiled sweetly at him.

The door swung open, and Ulysses Grant strode into the room, closely followed by Clay and Bierce. Seeing that Hampton was awake, the President asked Duval, "Did he give you any trouble?"

"Not a bit," she replied. "He slept like the dead." Duval gave the final word a peculiar emphasis that caused Hampton to shudder. "Did everything go well at the War Department, sir?"

"Well enough," replied Grant grimly. "It seems that Hampton's information was correct, and the army rounded up most of the night-riders before they could cause mischief. A few groups got away, and there were a couple of shootings and burnings. Tragic, but it signifies little in the grand scheme of things."

"Sir, what comes next?" asked Clay.

"For the Klansman? Trial by military courts martial. Habeas

corpus is suspended in most of the areas affected." Grant paused to light up another of his cigars. After he took a long draw and expelled it, he continued. "Don't like the idea of replacing the civil courts with courts martial, but it has to be done. Doggone southern juries would acquit every man jack of the nightriders. The power of the Klan must be broken, or we are back to civil war."

Bierce looked at the haggard face of Wade Hampton, and asked, "Will we be bringing Hampton before the military courts to testify?"

Grant looked appraisingly at the broken old Rebel, then shook his head. "Only if absolutely necessary. We should have enough evidence to send the nightriders to prison for dozens of years. I want the conspiracy aspect played down. If we show they were involved in a treasonous conspiracy to rekindle the war, then the only penalty would have to be death for each and every one of them. I don't want a couple hundred hangings taking place; that in itself might restart the war. Yes, the Southerners and their Democratic friends will grumble about the courts martial, but if we take the point of view that these arrests were largely unrelated, and if there are no hangings, the grumblings will die down with time."

Duval could not contain herself. With dangerous calmness she asked, "Sir, are you just going to let this English-loving bastard Hampton go free?"

The President did not seem unduly shocked by the profanity spewing from Duval. "No, Miss Duval, we will not be releasing him quite yet. I asked Major Clay to check on the responses to my, let's say, 'invitation' for Gould, Fisk and . . . Corbin, to come here today. Tell Miss Duval what you learned."

"Gould and Corbin should be arriving as we speak. I feared we would not be able to contact Fisk, but finally a telegram to his New York office revealed the surprising fact that he is in Washington now, staying at the National Hotel. I have arranged for a military officer to meet Messrs. Gould and Corbin at the train station, and tell them to go directly to the main banquet hall at Willard's. Another officer will go to the National, and tell the same to Fisk."

"Why Willard's?" asked Duval with amazement.

"To keep from scaring them into running, and to keep them off balance," replied Grant for Clay. "I've already asked Monsieur LaFitte at Willard's to make sure a dining room is reserved for only those we wish admitted. To make it seem less threatening, and less empty, I will invite the Vice President, my wife and her father, and my own father." Grant now looked at Wade Hampton. "We will also have Mr. Hampton brought in, and confront them with his knowledge of the conspiracy to control the gold market, and to aid the Klan in its atrocities solely to distract my attention from their avaricious conspiracy. With such an accusation seeming to come out of no where, one or all of them will panic, and confess in hopes of mercy."

Clay interrupted suddenly. "Sir, once again let me protest against this aspect of your plan. It is impossible to predict how they will respond; you may be in danger."

"I am not a coward, Major Clay. And besides, what danger? From three corrupt speculators who do their stealing with pens? Besides, I would never place my Julia there if I thought there was the slightest chance of violence. No, this will be for the best." He looked meaningfully at Wade Hampton. "I do not want any more extreme measures taken in apprehending these criminals. This will be done in a more civilized manner." Then he directly addressed Hampton. "Remember this: you will co-operate at every stage or you will have a date with the gallows. My mercy only goes so far."

Hampton silently nodded his assent, making himself look fearful, repressing the glimmer of hope that he felt.

Grant consulted his pocket watch. "We must all be at Willard's in about ninety minutes. Let us all quickly wash up and change into fresh clothes." He looked intently at Duval, then added, "Miss Duval, I would appreciate it if you would clean up Mr. Hampton and make him more presentable. He seems about my size; have him dress in one of my spare suits. Julia will show you where they are. Whatever you do, do not tell her what this is all about. That applies to all of you. Don't tell Mr. Dent and my father anything about it either; just tell them that we have scheduled a sudden meal to honor Gould and Fisk. I don't want any of them to seem nervous and give away the game prematurely."

Grant sighed. "And now I better go break the news to Julia and those two . . . old men."

The sun had just set when the Presidential carriage pulled up to Willard's. Not waiting for the driver to open the door, Grant sprang out, then offered his hand to Julia. As the few passers-by gaped, he escorted her into the lobby, where Monsieur Lafitte was waiting for them, a combination of worry and excitement. Bowing deeply, he said, "Mr. President, Mrs. Grant. You do Willard's honor by holding your banquet on our premises. I guarantee you a meal that you will never forget."

Although Grant was well aware Lafitte had been born Joe Shultz in upstate New York, he gravely acknowledged the man with his adoptive name. "Thank you, Mr. Lafitte. I truly appreciate you handling our party on such short notice."

"It is no problem at all. We have a new chef who is far superior to any we have ever employed, good as they were. I am certain you will be delighted with the menu we have prepared."

Grant knew that he was the last to arrive. He and Clay had agreed that the conspirators would be put under more pressure if they were made to wait; Grant and Julia had only left the Executive Mansion when Clay had sent a message that all the figures of interest were there. Nonetheless, he asked, "Are all the guests arrived?"

"All of them, Excellency. The last were Messrs. Gould and Corbin, with Mrs. Corbin. There had been a slight delay on the train from New York. They arrived just after Vice President Colfax, who walked over from his suite at the National."

Grant squared his shoulders. "Let's not keep them waiting. Mr. Lafitte, lead the way."

Lafitte led them into the largest of Willard's private dining rooms; it could easily sit the party of twelve. Grant was reluctantly impressed by the luxury of the room, where seemingly everything was decorated with gilt and velvet, with lush potted plants along the walls. In the center of the room was a single long table, set with gleaming china plates and sterling silver. Spaces had been reserved for the Presidential couple at the head of the table. As they seated themselves, Grant noted that Clay and Bierce had taken the two positions nearest to him and his wife. Wedged between Clay and Duval was Wade Hampton, cleaned up and in elegant clothing, but still looking ghastly pale as he fiddled with a crutch. On the far side of Duval sat Abel and Virginia Corbin, the latter looking happy and excited, the former nervous and gloomy.

On the opposite side of the table, to Bierce's side, sat Vice-President "Smiler" Schuyler Colfax, the man Grant had selected as an unknowing witness as to what was going to transpire. Beyond Colfax were Jim Fisk and Jay Gould, the former looking cheerful and content, the latter utterly expressionless. Finally, beyond them were Jesse Grant and Old Man Dent, muttering angrily back and forth about something. Grant suddenly had the thought that the two old men enjoyed their running feud.

As he had discussed with Clay, Grant opened the banquet in a way that was bound to put pressure on Fisk, Gould and Corbin. "Ladies and gentlemen, thank you for all coming on such short notice. It is rare that so many people of importance to me can meet at the same time, and I appreciate you volunteering to join Mrs. Grant and myself."

"We hardly 'volunteered,'" muttered Abel Corbin. "Your telegram left us little choice."

Grant spared his brother-in-law a look that made him quail, and then said "Be that as it may, there is some business of importance to all of us, that I would like to conduct after this meal is over, away from the prying eyes that always surround the Executive Mansion. Most of you probably do not know four of the guests tonight. Sitting to my right is Major Alphonso Clay of the Army Judge Advocate's Bureau, an investigator in which I have the utmost trust. To my left is his associate, Ambrose Bierce, a brave former officer and currently a representative of the press. To the other side of Major Clay are Miss Teresa Duval, and in a sense our guest of honor tonight, Mr. Wade Hampton, formerly a general in the CSA."

Old Man Dent suddenly piped up cheerfully. "General Wade Hampton. I'll be damned! One of the best cavalrymen the Confederacy produced. Sir, it is a pleasure to meet you. But what happened to your leg? I thought you came through the War without serious injury."

"A recent riding accident, sir," responded Hampton, who said no more.

"In any event, I have kept you from your meal too long," said Grant. "Mr. Lafitte, you can tell your people to begin serving."

Lafitte's well-trained waiters sprung into action. Soups, salads, meat dishes, wines flowed smoothly onto the table. Grant and Clay both noted that although Fisk ate with a gusto that was sometimes auditory, Gould and Corbin only picked at the delicious food, and Hampton did not eat anything.

Clay also noticed something about the President's dining habits. Although Grant ate the soups, salads, and potatoes with

enthusiasm, he quietly pushed away the prime rib, and inverted his wine glass, contenting himself only with water. Clay understood the matter of the wine, given Grant's pre-war history. Clay could not understand his rejection of the prime rib, which was prepared just the way Clay liked, so rare that the taste of blood came through distinctly. *Yes*, thought Clay, *that was the only way to eat meat.*

As Gould picked at his food, he noticed the significant glances Clay was exchanging with the President. He then caught Duval's eye, and nodded slightly toward Clay. He had been surprised, if not shocked, to see her at this banquet; but on reflection realized it could be an extraordinary stroke of fortune. He knew she would remember the discussion that had taken place months ago, the discussion where he promised to make her wealthy if she . . . removed Clay. Gould was not certain what was about to happen, but his gut told him it would be very bad for Jay Gould, and was being driven along by the pipsqueak major. Duval must dispose of Clay, as soon as she could catch him alone, before it was too late—if it were not already too late. He was relieved to see Duval glance at Clay, turn her attention back to Gould, and smile. Good, he thought, she understands.

Clay noticed that Abel Corbin's hands were visibly shaking, and that he was repeatedly wiping sweat from his forehead with his napkin. Clay leaned over and murmured to Grant, "Your brother-in-law is about to have a fit. He will break if he is pushed, I suggest we move to the next stage now, this moment."

Grant locked eyes with Clay, and nodded slightly. Then, as Lafitte started to enter the room, leading waiters with more dishes, he said loudly, "Mr. Lafitte, we have some business to discuss in here. Please take yourself and the waiters out, close the door behind you, and let no one in until we call for you."

Lafitte was flustered. "Mr. President, before the dessert? Our chef has been preparing something extraordinary for your and your guests."

"It can wait. This shouldn't take long; we will have dessert afterwards."

Lafitte bowed apprehensively, then shooed his staff out of the room, closing the door carefully.

Grant automatically started to draw out a cigar; he then remembered that ladies were present, and regretfully returned the stogie to his pocket. He stood up, and looked around the room, his level, expressionless gaze stopping for extra moments on Fisk, Gould and finally Corbin. Taking a deep breath, he began to speak.

"There are matters of serious importance to the well-being of the Republic that need to be discussed. Some of you here know that already; those of you who do not are here to act as witnesses. It has been brought to my attention by Major Clay that . . ."

Suddenly a commotion was heard outside the banquet room's door. With a cracking noise the door was kicked open. In the doorway, a large Colt in his hand, stood Colonel Robert Buchanan.

CHAPTER 6

"FIRM, UNITED LET US BE, RALLYING ROUND OUR LIBERTY . . ."

With shocking speed Clay surged to his feet, drawing his large Smith & Wesson, determined he would not have a second President under his protection suffer assassination; but he held his fire. He had noted in an instant that Buchanan's revolver was pointed at the ceiling, and that the Colonel was scanning the guests frantically, not even looking at Grant. Clay further noticed that behind Buchanan were several cavalrymen armed with Spencer carbines, looking grimly into the room.

Beside Buchanan, Lafitte fluttered in an agony of nervousness, saying, "Mr. President, I told him you were not to be disturbed, but as you can see . . ." He pointed wordlessly at the broken door.

In a cold, quiet voice Grant said, "Clay, put away your weapon. Colonel Buchanan is not here to do me harm. Colonel, I presume you have a reason for this outrageous behavior."

Buchanan did not look at the President, but continued his hard-eyed staring at the various guests. In the most formal of voices, he replied, "Mr. President, I have received information indicating that an attempt on your life is imminent."

"Why are you here personally?" asked Clay, as he reholstered his gun beneath his coat with notable reluctance. "Could you not have telegraphed a warning to the War Department? It would have been much quicker."

Buchanan had stopped scanning the guests, and was looking rigidly at a spot somewhere above the President's head. "Because of the . . . prior history between the President and myself, I feared the warning would not be taken seriously, either by the War Department or by him. I weighed the additional risk of a two-day delay while I rode the cars against a possibly futile series of telegrams between New Orleans and Washington, and decided the risk would be less if I came in person to force him to accept serious protection until the assassin is caught. I stopped at the War Department to dragoon a platoon of soldier boys, giving them orders to defend you with their lives. I then went to the Executive Mansion, where I was told you would be dining here; dining in a public hotel with the constant comings and goings of all kinds of dubious characters."

Grant made a dismissive wave. "I am in no danger of violence here. Holster your Colt, and tell your escort to keep everyone else not only out of this room, but out of the outside lobby; it would appear that Mr. Lafitte's door has lost its ability to keep conversations private. Mr. Lafitte, will you excuse us?"

"Ah, yes sir . . . Mr. President. Ah . . . yes." Bowing almost to the waist, the confused Lafitte backed unsteadily out of the room, while Buchanan issued sharp orders to the soldiers at the door. Soon, the room and the adjoining lobby were free of any prying ears. Grant then addressed Colonel Buchanan.

"Now, Colonel, you will tell us what led you to think there would be an attempt on my life."

The old Colonel stood rigidly at attention, refusing to look his Commander in Chief in the eye. "Sir, two days ago a message was delivered to me indicating that such an attempt would be made. It contained . . . matters which prevented me from doubting its veracity. The message said that the writer did not know the name of the assassin or the exact time and manner in which he would strike, but that the attempt would be made in a matter of days."

Grant frowned. "And just what led you to believe this rather incredible statement."

Still not looking at the President, Buchanan replied, "It was written and signed by Nathan Bedford Forrest."

Several of the guests uttered shocked gasps. Clay, having lost whatever color his pale face possessed, asked, "How could you be sure the message indeed came from Forrest?"

"At the end of the War, I took the parole of Forrest's surviving men, and of Forrest himself. I watched him sign the parole document. His rather . . . childish handwriting is unmistakable."

"How could he know of such an attack and yet not know the name of the attacker?"

"He wrote that the actual hiring of the killer had been handled by Wade Hampton, who had not shared any of the details with Forrest."

All eyes turned toward the shocked Hampton, and angry muttering broke out, rising in intensity until Grant sharply struck the table with his fist. All could see the shock and anger on Hampton's features, which he had been too surprised to conceal.

"It's a lie, a forgery!" spluttered Hampton. "Something this blue belly Colonel has faked in order to arrange for my hanging! Forrest would never write such a thing about an old comrade!"

Buchanan turned his attention to Hampton, with an expression of revulsion upon his face. "Forrest wrote that much as he hated the Union and Grant, he would not murder an unarmed man, nor countenance such a murder. Further, he has said that against his original agreement with you, you have authorized Klansmen to attack women and children, and burn schools and churches, as opposed to attacking soldiers, scalawags and carpetbaggers. As further proof of his truthfulness, in the letter he confesses to being one of the prime movers in the Ku Klux Klan. This has long been suspected. Given the crimes of the Klan, this confession could hang him."

The others around the table turned their attention to Hampton, who desperately wanted to say something in denial, but could not come up with a single word. The old Rebel glanced at Duval, who was staring at him intently, the faintest of smiles upon her lips.

In the lightest of whispers, understandable only by Hampton himself, she said, "Later when we are alone we will discuss this matter further."

Although Clay already knew of Hampton's involvement in a plot to murder the President, this further confirmation enraged him. Clay seemed to be trembling all over; the gas fixtures must have flickered in that moment, as several of the guests uneasily believed they saw Clay's body begin to . . . change. The impression lasted only a moment; Clay resumed his normal, politely controlled appearance.

Now shifting his gaze to Buchanan, Clay asked, "Why did Forrest entrust such a critical document to you?"

Buchanan stared at Clay for a long moment, and then produced a folded document from an inner pocket of his tunic. Advancing to where Clay sat, he carefully laid it between Clay and the President. He stepped back, and said, "Mr. President, I would prefer that you read this yourself. I request that you not share the contents with the other people in this room."

Frowning, Grant picked up the document, which consisted of two pages of a semi-literate scrawl. While tension built in the dining room, it took the President several minutes to digest the contents of Forrest's letter. Towards the end of the letter he discovered that Forrest had anticipated his curiosity. The sardonic Forrest told of how Buchanan had mocked and derided him during the surrender ceremony, and of how much that had galled the old cavalrymen. Forrest then told how when he decided that he could not accept the political murder of his greatest enemy, he considered to whom the warning should be communicated. Remembering the stories of how much Buchanan despised Grant, and of how Buchanan had forced Grant out of the pre-war army and into a decade of poverty and despair, Forrest wrote that he decided it would be just too amusing to make Buchanan the agent of Grant's salvation. Buchanan would be too patriotic to not pass along the warning, but it would humiliate the Colonel to no end to be the instrument by which the life of his despised former subordinate was saved. And Grant would be humiliated to owe his life to the man who had tried to destroy his career.

Grant finished reading and looked at Buchanan sardonically. *Forrest may not approve of political murder, but that does not mean he has forgiven me, or Buchanan,* thought Grant wryly. "Thank you for your attention to duty, Colonel," Grant said in a carefully neutral voice. He then turned his attention to Hampton.

"So, Mr. Hampton, where is this professional assassin that you have paid to perform a cowardly act you hadn't the belly to perform yourself?"

Hampton realized it was hopeless to continue denying to this room the plot he had already confessed to Clay. He kept his voice under control, although his darting eyes betrayed his fear. "Sir, I must withhold the name of that individual from any of the others in this room." He looked at Duval, then thought of Starry Wisdom, and seemed to swallow convulsively before continuing. "I wish to be jailed until a suitable pardon is negotiated for me, and certain assurances given."

Grant's eyes bored into Hampton like the barrels of guns. "I will not spare you from the gallows. Not this time."

Hampton smiled nastily. "You may find catching the assassin easier said than done, without my help. The man is extremely good, and extremely discreet. Besides, I can offer you something else."

"What could you possibly offer the President?" asked Clay, his voice charged with unspeakable violence.

"There is more to this than you supposed, more than the removal of the South's greatest enemy and sowing confusion in the North. You know this; Miss Duval has already . . . persuaded me to give you the details. We intend to establish our independence. How could we do that, even with waves of Klan attacks and the killing of the Yankee President?"

Grant and Clay looked at each other. "In point of fact, that has puzzled me from the beginning of this affair," said Clay slowly. "I could not see how you could accomplish more than visit havoc upon the occupation authorities, who eventually would be reinforced by Federal troops, crushing any attempt to resurrect the demented dream of an independent South."

Hampton smiled wolfishly at Clay. "Tell me, Major Clay, how is the gold market doing these days?

Clay stiffened, while Grant banged the table with his fist. The President took a deep breath, let it out slowly, and slowly addressed the room in general.

"Ladies and gentlemen, let me explain something to you. I have recently been preoccupied with two major issues. One is the increasing wave of violence and terrorism sweeping the South at the hands of the Ku Klux Klan. The other was a wave of panicked buying and selling on Wall Street due to the unexpected rise in the price of gold, rising to a level where it could disrupt our entire monetary system. The price of gold has gone so high that yesterday I ordered General Butterfield to sell Government gold to stabilize the market. Well, that has caused a new, different set of problems. Speculators have been ruined by the hundreds, and are dragging down some banks and brokerage houses. I am being told that legitimate, careful businesses are suddenly afraid of a crash in stock prices and a run on the banks, and the latest word in the newspapers is that everyone is withdrawing what they can from Wall Street. Suddenly, businesses are being starved for cash. They will shortly stop building new factories, constructing new railroads, hiring new workers. And yet, much the same thing would have happened if I had allowed the price of gold to continue to spiral upwards; the devaluation of paper money would have caused businesses to suddenly become afraid of a crash and stop their activities."

All the people in the room were looking with some surprise at Grant who did not have the reputation of a man with a firm grasp on economic issues. Looking especially surprised were Gould, Fisk, and Corbin. Grant saw the surprised expressions of the three financiers, and smiling grimly, addressed them directly.

"Yes, I do know something about how our economic engine runs," said the President. "Still, I know well that I don't know everything about the stock market. That is why I placed my trust in you three, expecting you to give me advice in the best interests of the country. Imagine my shock when I learned from Mr. Hampton that you were not only engaged in a plot to control the gold supply of the country, but that you were directly co-coordinating it with a treasonous attempt by the Klan to split this country apart. Hurting the country to make money is bad enough; hurting it to deliberately destroy it is foul beyond my ability to express." Grant turned his grim stare directly on his brother-in-law.

"I especially trusted you, Abel. You are married to my sister; it seems incomprehensible to me that you would betray not only your country, not only me, but your wife, my dearest sister."

"Abel, what does he mean?" asked the suddenly bewildered Virginia Corbin.

"He means nothing," said Gould, answering for his fellow conspirator. "He has been listening to my enemies on Wall Street, enemies telling the vilest of rumors, and to Klansmen who despise all Northern capitalists."

Virginia had looked at Gould, and then returned her attention to her husband, whom she now saw was quietly crying, having buried his face in his hands. "Abel, what is Hiram saying?"

"It's over," replied Corbin in a low voice. He uncovered his face and looked at his homely wife, tears streaming down his cheeks. "I told Gould and Fisk that everything was falling to pieces, but they wouldn't listen. They forced me to continue . . ."

"SHUT UP!" growled Gould in a voice completely opposite to the soft, controlled tone he always used. Clay decided it was his turn to take part in the conversation.

"We know enough to send you to prison for the rest of your life," he said softly to Corbin. "There is only one way to save yourself. Turn state's evidence, and testify against Gould, Fisk and Hampton. You will get at most a short time in prison."

"Prison?" gasped Virginia Corbin. "Abel, what have you done?" She then turned her attention to her brother. "Hiram, you cannot do this. Not to my husband; not to your own sister's husband!"

An agonized look flitted across Grant's features, so quickly that of all the people in the room only Clay and Duval were certain it had ever been there.

"Virginia, I cannot shield him, even if I wanted to do so. All I can offer him is leniency if he testifies against the more important members of the conspiracy."

Resting his elbows on the table, Corbin had once again buried his face in his hands. Virginia took his head in her hands.

"Please, Abel, you must do what Hiram says. You owe these

other men nothing; you owe the country, you owe Hiram, and above all you owe me!"

Abel Corbin was significantly older than Virginia; but as he raised his tear-stained face and looked at her, he seemed to have aged enough to be her grandfather. "Yes . . . yes, you're right. I'll do what he wants . . ."

Suddenly, the room was filled with booming laughter. Startled, everyone turned their attention to the source of the mirth—James Fisk.

"Enough of this farce, Mr. President," said Fisk in a voice full of genial good humor. "This dog won't hunt sir; it simply won't hunt."

"And why is that, Mr. Fisk?" asked Clay on the President's behalf.

"It would be bad enough for the public to learn of the involvement of Grant's sister and brother-in-law. Imagine the public's reaction if they learned the First Lady was deeply involved in the gold speculation."

Clay was rendered temporarily speechless. Ulysses Grant looked like a man who had just been punched in the stomach. Julia Grant focused her crossed eyes into her lap, and began to quietly cry. The President was the first to break the shocked silence.

"You lying monster!" he boomed. "How dare you tell such a falsehood!"

"Please look at your wife," responded Fisk in a cheerful tone.

Grant looked closely at Julia; her tear-streaked face answered all the questions that he would not have dared to ask himself.

"What is that Yankee scoundrel saying about my daughter?" asked the querulous Old Man Dent. At his side, a grim-faced Jesse Grant replied, "That bastard's saying he's got a hold on my son's wife."

Gould spoke, although he felt an odd hesitation, almost as if he were ashamed of what he was about to say. "We . . . donated to Mrs. Grant a futures contract that would have brought her several hundreds of thousands of dollars, provided we succeeded in cornering the gold market. Unfortunately, it is completely worthless now. We have retained a copy, with Mrs. Grant's signature, stored where no one but us would ever be likely to find it.

Jim Fisk laughed heartily. "So you see, Grant, the extremely delicate position you would find yourself in if you attempted to prosecute Gould, Butterfield and myself." Fisk laughed at the involuntary start of the President, and continued. "Surprised? Yes, your man at the New York Subtreasury has been ours from the beginning. Pity he lost his nerve, and didn't ignore your order to sell Government gold."

"Was it wise to reveal Butterfield's involvement?" asked a frowning Gould of his cheerful partner in crime.

Fisk waved a plump hand dismissively. "Of course it is. It makes the scandal even larger. Imagine the public reaction if it is revealed that the President's appointee, as well as his wife and brother-in-law, were involved in this matter. It would tear the Government, and perhaps the country, apart, especially with what Hampton's friends have been doing in the Klan."

An ashen-faced Grant turned to his wife and said, "Julia, tell me this . . . THING is lying." The President's wife said nothing at first, simply looked at her lap, tears flowing freely. In the lowest of voices, she finally replied to her husband.

"I didn't ask for it. But when Mr. Gould offered it, I thought of those times before the War, when we sometimes didn't know where our next meal was coming from. This politics is grand, but it will come to an end before many years have passed and . . . oh Sam, I know you tried so hard, but you just don't have a head for business."

"I always kept you and the children fed and clothed," muttered Grant. Julia looked up, still crying but with a sad smile on her face, and stroked her husband's stubbly beard.

"I know you did. You worked hard, oh so hard, but somehow the money never came in. I remember that Christmas when you sold your watch so the children would have gifts. You were always working for us; that is why I will always love you. But Daddy lost the plantation, and Father Grant has supported us so much before the War. I just wanted to have something there, so the bad times would never return."

A thought crossed the stricken President's mind. "I gave the order to sell gold to you to send to Butterfield. You sent it, immediately, instead of holding it back until you could cash in the futures contract."

"I simply could not be that disloyal to you. I never could be. If what I did was wrong, it was to protect you."

Grant leaned over, and drew his wife's head onto his chest, gently stroking her hair, to the embarrassment of some around the table. "Julia, you will never want again, as long as I live. I will give my very life if necessary to guarantee that."

Fisk applauded while laughing. "Isn't this sweet? Well, time to leave you lovebirds to yourselves. Gould and I are going to walk out of this hotel and return to New York. If the slightest action is taken by the Federal Government against either of us, the whole entertaining scandal will be revealed to the press. Gould, it is time for us to depart. Are you coming with us, Corbin?"

The President's brother-in-law simply stared at his plate, shaking his head once. Fisk shrugged as if it were of little importance, and stood up with Gould. Meanwhile, Old Man Dent had leveraged himself upright with his heavy cane, and was hobbling around the table toward the pair, a wildly furious look on his face.

"Filthy, thieving Yankee bastards! You've dishonored me by hurting my baby, and the man who has always stood by her. By God, sirs, if I were younger I would have tied you both to a post and flogged you till the bones showed!" He raised his cane as if to strike Fisk, who with a laugh strongly pushed the old man in the chest, causing him to go sprawling on the floor. Dent began to cry tears of impotent rage. Stringy old Jesse Grant sprang from his chair and went to help his old nemesis to his feet while snarling at Fisk, "You bastard!" He turned and almost shouted at his son, "Hiram, arrest these scoundrels. Have them strung up! The people will understand."

Fisk looked at the President and smiled. "I really don't think they will, do you Mr. President?"

Clay had risen to his feet, and was reaching under his coat for his revolver. None paid attention to the fact that Duval had also smoothly risen to her feet. Grant made a calming, weary gesture toward Clay and said, "No, let them go. It would play into their hands."

The President refocused his attention on Fisk. "This was never about the money, was it Fisk? This was about destabilizing the Government."

Fisk's smile now acquired a bitter twist. "Yes, you might as well know. Money was the means, not the end." Involuntarily, Gould looked sharply at his partner. Fisk noticed, and laughed.

"Surprised, Gould? You wouldn't be, if your mind was not so limited. The corner on gold, the assaults by the Klan, they were only a means to our goal."

"Our goal?" repeated Gould.

Fisk patted his smaller companion on the shoulder. "Yes, Gould, you only thought you were a partner in the plan. My group was running its own plan, which you were never meant to notice. We were to do nothing less than take control of this country—lock, stock and barrel. With the Government burdened with a new civil war at the same time the economy is collapsing, we would have been able to move in and take over. We have the resources to do so."

"Just who is this 'we' you are referring to?" asked Jay Gould, shocked at finding himself for once the pawn in someone else's plan.

Fisk's smile had disappeared. "I may have said too much already."

Grant had risen from his chair, and glared at the financier. "You sound awful happy for someone whose plans have come crashing down."

Fisk shrugged. "It is disappointing, it is true, but the disappointment is temporary. As you will come to see, our resources are vaster than you can imagine. This will only be a temporary setback in our ultimate goals."

"Who is this 'we'?" demanded Grant in a voice that was near to a shout.

"Starry Wisdom," said Alphonso Clay quietly.

"Fool!" blurted Fisk, who then spoke to the room as a whole. "This man is spinning tales out of whole cloth. His history shows that he is diseased in the brain; the massacre at the Devereaux plantation during the War shows that."

Clay simply shook his head. "Your masters have tried several times, during the War and thereafter, to make use of my... ancestry. You may tell those masters once and for all that I will never serve them. Never. You may further tell them that as powerful as they consider themselves to be, I will make it my mission in life to thwart, and ultimately destroy, them. This I promise, on the honor of a Clay."

Gould seemed as puzzled as anyone else in the room. Turning to his partner in crime, he asked, "Just what is he talking about? Just what is this Starry Wisdom?"

Fisk looked angrily at Gould, but suddenly his face cleared, and he laughed. He patted Gould on the shoulder, laughed again, and strolled out of the dining room without saying another word.

Gould waited nearly a full minute, looking as if he had something to say. However, in the end he also silently withdrew.

Throughout the tense scenes that had preceded, the normally voluble Vice-President Schuyler Colfax had remained absolutely silent. With a sad look on his face, Colfax rose and bowed toward the President, saying, "This is terrible sir, just terrible. I hardly know what to think. I will withdraw, and allow you and Mrs. Grant to console each other."

"Not quite yet, sir," said Clay as he quickly walked around the dining table until he stood before the Vice-President. "I believe your role in all this should be discussed before the President."

"My role?" exclaimed Colfax in an astonished voice.

"Yes, your role." Clay then addressed his words to Grant, although his eyes remained locked on Colfax.

"The traitor and conspirator, Hampton, has as good as confessed the truth of Forrest's allegation that part of the overall plot was your assassination. Initially, that puzzled me. Yes, your death would result in a day or so of confusion, but then Mr. Colfax would smoothly assume your office. He is a Radical Republican, former Speaker of the House, known to be hostile to the Klan. How could that event be of advantage to the conspirators?" Clay now directly addressed the Vice-President.

"It only made sense if they could be assured that someone sympathetic to their goals would replace the President; someone a party to their conspiracy. Is that not so, Mr. Colfax?"

The Vice-President looked around the room for support, and found none on the faces of the diners. Even Wade Hampton was staring at him with a dawning look of revulsion.

"You bastard," muttered Buchanan quietly, moving his hand to the butt of his revolver.

"Schuyler," said Grant softly. "Schuyler . . ." He trailed off. Clay glanced at the President, and felt pity for the man who had been betrayed by nearly everyone close to him.

The normally articulate Colfax sputtered, then said, "This is absurd, Mr. President. This man, Clay, hasn't one particle of evidence connecting me to this conspiracy."

Grant responded in a mournful voice. "That may be true, but I notice you don't say you're innocent, just that there is no evidence against you."

"I won't stand here and be insulted! If you will excuse me . . ."

"Major Clay, escort the Vice-President to his seat," interrupted Grant, the steel returning to his voice. "We have more to discuss, before this evening is over."

Clay took Colfax by the arm. The Vice-President tried to pull away, but found that the deceptively small officer had a grip of iron. Meanwhile, Colonel Buchanan had walked over, drawing his Colt as he went. Jamming the barrel into Colfax's ear, he snarled, "Give me a reason to blow your brains onto the floor, traitor!"

Colfax immediately ceased resisting, and allowed himself to be led back to his chair. Once Colfax was seated, Clay and Buchanan marched to the end of the table and stood behind the President's chair; their expressions daring anyone to make a commotion.

"This evening did not go as I expected, to say the least," commented Grant to no one in particular. "I expected it to end with the arrest of a trio of scoundrels, not with the attempted destruction of my family, and a scandal of epic proportions in my administration."

"Sir, arrest the traitors Fisk, Gould, and Colfax," responded Clay grimly. "Arrest the coward Hampton as well. Fisk was bluffing; he would not dare to reveal the involvement of General Butterfield and, ah, certain of your relations."

Duval laughed in her silvery, chilling way, then said, "Oh

Alphonso, trust me on this. I can read people like books. Fisk is not bluffing. It would be better if the President announced that without his knowledge, his wife had . . ."

"NO!" bellowed Grant in a parade-ground shout few ever heard. He then turned his hard, melancholic eyes on Clay.

"Major, we need to pick up the pieces of this mess as carefully as we can. Mrs. Grant is not to become involved in any way." He glanced lovingly at Julia, who seemed unable to look into the eyes of the man who loved her more than his life.

Clay nodded agreement. "Let us then concentrate on the positive. The Klan has had its back broken; a few score trials, those convicted quietly sent to various prisons on the frontier, and the threat of the Klansmen to Federal authority is under control. No need to take the . . . other measures we discussed some time ago, sir. In addition, the attempt of Fisk and Gould to gain control of the economy of the North, and hence its government has come to nothing. There will still be echoes of their manipulations causing harm to good businessmen and their employees, but the Government is secure." Clay shifted his unreadable gaze to the Vice-President. "Finally, we have learned something vital about the man who would step into your shoes, should something . . . untoward happen to you. Now, if I may suggest . . ."

Clay was interrupted by a commotion at the entrance to the dining room. A grim-looking soldier was blocking the doorway with his carbine, while beyond him could be glimpsed Lafitte, and behind him a tall, thin man in chef's clothing pushing a dessert tray. Buchanan's face turned beet red.

"Goddamn it, the President has said he did not want to be disturbed, did not even want anyone in the outer room! What the Hell is going on?"

"I tried to stop him, sir," replied the fussing Lafitte. "But the chef . . ."

"I am truly sorry sir, but the dessert cannot wait," interrupted the man in chef's clothes. "It's ice cream, and would melt if not soon served. You cannot believe how much difficulty I have had in making it. It's almond-flavored, a variety I believe you can find no where else."

Grant emitted an exasperated sigh, but then decided to humor the temperamental chef. "I suppose we could all stand a cooling refreshment. Go ahead and serve them out." Grant waived away the guard, then turned back to his wife and comforted her with soft murmurs. The chef swiftly distributed the desserts, already apportioned into twelve china bowls, along the table. The dishes themselves were all identical, save for the one that was placed in front of the President, which was decorated with elaborate gold leaf. The chef frowned and said, "Mr. President, two of your guests are missing."

"That's all right; we've picked up one more in the shape of Colonel Buchanan, so only one serving will go to waste."

"Don't have any taste for fancy treats," snarled Buchanan. "There are important things to be decided."

Grant had a decided weakness for ice cream in all of its forms. He shrugged, and said, "Suit yourself." He nudged his wife, who unenthusiastically took a spoonful without seeming to taste it. Grant noticed that his brother-in-law and the Vice-President were making no effort to eat their own desserts. Grant smiled grimly and said, "Corbin, Schuyler, no appetite? Where are your manners? The chef slaved to provide us with a rare treat. The least you could do is show some appreciation." Grant took his spoon and scooped up a large dollop of the ice cream, the shaved bits of almonds clearly visible.

Alphonso Clay had a peculiar brain; more peculiar than any doctors of the time might imagine. One of its peculiarities was that under stress it operated at incredible speed, a speed that in turn caused Clay to see everything about him moving in slow motion. As he stood behind Grant, his eyes roving about the table, his attention was suddenly drawn to Wade Hampton. Hampton was looking intently at the chef, the slightest of smiles gracing his face. This puzzled Clay, as he had already noticed the aristocratic Hampton seldom even looked at the waiters and servers at Willard's, obviously considering them beneath his notice. In the midst of his puzzlement, Clay became aware of the odor of the ice cream that wafted from the President's elaborately decorated dish. He thought of how laden with almonds the ice cream must be for its odor to be so noticeable; so noticeable in fact that it seemed to carry a hint of bitterness . . .

Clay leapt forward and knocked the spoon from Grant's hand just as it reached his lips, scattering ice cream across the table. At the same time he screamed in a strangely deep baritone "Arrest the chef!"

Crawford Tillinghast realized that something had gone wrong, that the game was up, and bolted for the door. Just as he passed where Old Man Dent sat, the President's father-in-law stuck out his cane, tripping the lean doctor. Tillinghast regained his feet, but only in time to have Colonel Buchanan bring the barrel of his heavy Colt down on his head, stunning him into passivity.

"Tie his hands behind his back," said Clay in his normal voice. With no hesitation, Buchanan tore a long strip off the table cloth, and in a trice had secured Tillinghast's hands.

By now all of the guests except the crippled Hampton had risen to their feet, staring in astonishment at the battered chef.

"What has just happened?" asked the stunned Grant.

The grim Buchanan viciously kicked Tillinghast in the ribs, eliciting a long moan. "Sir, Clay saw it; I did not. It is to him that you owe your life. He somehow figured out this bastard had poisoned your dessert. When Clay shouted to arrest the man, it struck me instantly like a ton of bricks. That Rebel bastard Hampton had hired a professional killer. Unlike Booth, an amateur who wanted world fame, such a man wants anonymity, so he can spend his blood money in peace. I apologize for not seeing it until that instant; the threat to you was not to come from a fanatic with a gun, but in some sly manner. Besides, when Clay shouted to arrest him, the chef didn't act surprised or confused; he instantly bolted for the door. His actions shout his guilt."

"That's why I tripped him," added Old Man Dent in his quavering voice. "I didn't know what was going on, but only a guilty man runs like that." His old adversary Jesse Grant looked at Dent with something that looked like, for the moment at least, respect.

"What made you suspicious? asked Grant of Clay.

"Several things, sir. The first was the way that Hampton kept staring at the chef. I had noticed he normally acts as if menials do not exist. This made me think that he recognized the man. Then that raised another question. How could a man like Hampton have come to know the chef? Finally, I noticed the smell of the ice cream. Of course, we were told that this was almond-flavored ice cream, but even so, the smell seemed intense, even having a trace of bitterness. Then I remembered something from my studies of chemistry at Miskatonic College, before the War. At one point my class was being instructed on the uses of prussic acid, a chemical useful both in mining and the textile industries. The professor insisted that the chemical be handled with utmost care. It is immediately deadly, yet colorless and tasteless. The only warning would be its odor, which is that of almonds that have gone bitter. Given that I knew the President's life was at risk, I drew the logical conclusion."

Clay glanced over toward Wade Hampton, who was now sweating profusely, and saw that Duval had put herself behind the old traitor and was placing her hands lightly on his shoulders.

She locked eyes with Clay, and raised one eyebrow in an inquiring manner. Clay shook his head emphatically, and she visibly sighed in disappointment.

"This is nonsense," said Schuyler Colfax. "There's not the slightest proof that there is any poison in that dessert."

Clay gestured dismissively at the Vice-President. "This is easy enough to determine. Mr. Lafitte, it is my understanding that even the best restaurants have occasional problems with mice and other such vermin, and keep one or more cats on hand to control the problem. Please go to the kitchen and bring us one of the animals. Mention to none of your staff what is occurring in here."

An expression of indignation replaced the one of apprehension that Laffite that had been on his face. "Monsieur Clay, I assure you that Willard's has never had a problem with vermin . . ." He trailed off at the expression on Clay's face, and without another word hurried out of the dining room. In less than a minute, Lafitte had returned with a sleek, cross-looking tabby.

Clay took the cat from Lafitte gently, and stroking the animal, walked over to where the President sat. He placed the cat upon the table, and controlling it firmly with one hand, drew the dish containing Grant's dessert in front of the animal's face. The cat sniffed at the ice cream suspiciously; but finally gave in to the temptation of the rich dairy liquid to which the treat was rapidly being reduced by the heat of the room. It took a tentative lick, and then apparently satisfied, it began to lap contentedly at the lique-fying ice cream. Everyone in the room watched intently, waiting to see what would happen.

They did not have to wait long. Suddenly the cat stiffened. Jerking its head back, it emitted one plaintive howl, convulsed and then collapsed, lying inert in front of the horrified President, who was fonder of most animals than most people, if the truth were known.

"I ate some of that!" exclaimed Julia Grant, a hand going to her throat.

"There is no reason for concern, Mrs. Grant," responded Clay soothingly. "The murderer wished for your husband's death to appear to be natural. It would hardly seem natural if all the guests at this table collapsed and died at the same time. That is why the President's dish was different from the others; to assure that the assassin did not accidentally provide the poisoned food to the wrong guest. Besides, as you have just seen, prussic acid operates very quickly; if any had been in your dessert, this conversation would not be taking place." Clay parted the dead animal's fur in various places, and frowned. "Our assassin is a bit more sophisticated that I would have expected. Death by prussic acid results in a bright red tinge to the skin. I can detect no such reddening. I suspect he added some additional substance to prevent such a color change in the skin. That being so, it would have been presumed that the President had died of some seizure or apoplexy; rare in a man of his age, but not unknown."

Clay glanced over to where Buchanan had slammed the semi-conscious Tillinghast into one of the empty chairs. "Whoever he is, this man has some extremely sophisticated knowledge. When he is more himself, I would like to talk to him at length about what found its way into the President's dessert." Clay then directed his attention to the horrified, quaking Lafitte. "Just how did this man find his way into your employ?"

"Sir, I swear I ain't got nothin' to do with this!" exclaimed Lafitte, his faux French accent completely gone. "I just had an opening, an' he took the job at a ridiculously low wage . . ." Lafitte went silent as the implication of what he had just said sank in.

Clay smiled grimly. "I am not surprised. Tell me, what name did he give you?"

"Johannes Schmidt."

Clay barked out one of his unlovely laughs. "Johannes Schmidt. Of course it is. It translates into English as John Smith. He would not use his real name. Naturally, we will have confirmation that he is this Crawford Tillinghast as soon as he is recovered, or if not from him, then from Mr. Hampton."

"Shall I arrest Colfax and Hampton, along with this murdering bastard?" asked Buchanan grimly.

Grant and Clay exchanged looks, and then the President shook his head.

"Why the Hell not?" demanded Buchanan.

"Alphonso, Mr. President, allow me to explain to the Colonel," interrupted Ambrose Bierce. "I think I know how matters must proceed." Clay and Grant looked at the young writer with some surprise, and then glanced at each other. With a hint of a smile, the President nodded his head. Bierce needed no further urging.

"Colonel, a public trial on this mess could be devastating to the Republic," he began. "I do not mean the embarrassment to the President caused by friends and relations, although that is of course a factor. Much more important is the fact that a public trial would reveal that unrepentant Rebels and the Klan are in an unholy alliance together with important Wall Street capitalists to bring fire and destruction to the South, along with economic chaos to the North. We did not realize this connection until today. Not only will knowledge of this trigger demands for bloody revenge against the South in the North, there would also be violent fury against Wall Street and the banking interests. Personally, I care little whether Fisk and Gould are lynched, or for that matter if *every* last millionaire is sent to the gallows; but it is an undeniable fact that without the Wall Street capitalists, business and economic expansion will grind to a halt in the country for want of investment capital. Banks will default, factories will close, railroads will remain unfinished, millions of unemployed workers will starve along with their families.

Officially, the government must be content with having thwarted the aims of Hampton, Gould, and Fisk, and whoever these 'Starry Wisdom' people are behind Fisk. Unofficially, steps will be taken to eliminate their power to cause future mischief." Smiling grimly, Bierce turned to Clay and Grant. "Did I get things right?"

Once again, Clay and the President exchanged significant glances. Grant sighed, and then began to speak.

"All right, this is how things will go down. Colfax, leave, right now. Leave Washington. Never come back unless the Senate is in session, and then only to perform your Constitutional duty of presiding over it. When I run for re-election in three years time, you will be replaced. You will never run for public office again. If you ever do, or if you ever mention in public the events of this night, I will have you charged with treason, no matter what the consequences to me or to the nation. Do you think that I am bluffing?"

An uneasy Colfax looked at Grant, and saw the grim determination of a man who had decided to ram his head through a wall and was about to do it. "No, I don't believe that you are."

"Then take your worthless carcass from my sight!"

Without another word, the Vice-President rose and walked through the door; for once "Smiler" Colfax had lost his smile. Grant now turned his attention to his brother-in-law.

"Corbin, you are a miserable rascal, whose betrayal hurt not only me, but poor Virginia. Normally, I would have you prosecuted and sentenced to the Dry Tortugas for the rest of your useless life. It wouldn't matter if you tried to blackmail me by speaking of these horrible events; you are so insignificant that no one would pay attention to you. But seeing as my sister Virginia loves you, Lord knows why, but she does, take yourself and her away from here. Never come near me again, or so help me I will see you jailed. Now go!"

The miserable wreck that was Abel Corbin could only look at the table. Gently his wife took his arm, drew him into a standing position, and led him shuffling from the room, casting a last, agonized look at her brother as she led her husband through the doorway.

"Now we come to Wade Hampton," said the President grimly. He stood up, patted his still sniffling wife on the shoulder, and walked over to where the crippled old Rebel sat. Staring down at Hampton with a look of contempt, Grant said, "I can easily have you tried, prosecuted and hanged for just a fraction of what you have already confessed to. There is no need to even go into your dishonorable attempt to murder me by stealth; Southern chivalry indeed! Your life would end in well-deserved disgrace and agony. There is only one way for you to save your miserable, worthless life—if you care to take it."

Wade Hampton had always imagined he was perfectly willing to give his life for the Cause. Now he knew better. The horrible woman standing behind him had broken him. Now he could visualize the gallows, the rope—the snap of his neck, and found he was willing to do anything to avoid that.

"What is it you want?" he muttered.

"I want you to become the political leader, and ultimately Governor of, South Carolina," replied the President.

It was very, very rarely that Alphonso Clay was surprised by anything. This was one of those times. His eyes widened slightly, in Clay a sign of complete shock.

"Sir! What are you saying? This man is one of the two leaders of the Ku Klux Klan, and a major conspirator in a plan to break up this Republic! Even if you could place him in such a position, he would only betray America again!"

Grant actually favored Clay with a tight smile. "Oh, the governorship's his for the asking; the people of South Carolina regard him as a deity. And when he is governor, he will be our complete tool. Without making it too obvious to the die-hard rebels down there, he will take steps to keep the Klan from resurrecting itself. Remember, we have only captured the leaders; there will be some attempts by various members to move into those leadership positions and keep the Klan a going proposition. This would be hard to stop in South Carolina, much less the rest of the South, with the pitifully small army Congress is allowing me. With the power of the state government deployed by Governor Hampton, it will be much easier. We can use the troops that would have been needed in South Carolina in the other former states of the Confederacy."

A smile slowly crept onto Clay's face. "Sir, that is positively Machiavellian reasoning."

Grant chuckled. "You disapprove then?"

"Far from it, sir. Niccolo Machiavelli was always a clear-sighted, practical philosopher."

A frowning Duval could not restrain herself. "You mean this English-loving bastard is going to go Scot-free?"

"Hardly, Miss Duval," replied the President, apparently not shocked to hear such crude language coming from such an elegant-appearing lady. "He is going to be the minion, the slave, of the Federal government, for the rest of his life. For a man like Hampton, that may be a fate worse than death."

"What if I won't go along with your little scheme?" muttered a surly Hampton.

"Forget for a moment the fact that I could have you prosecuted and sent to the gallows," responded Grant in an amused voice. "Have you forgotten that we have your signed confession, identifying the major leaders of the Klan and giving the locations of their planned attacks? I wonder what would happen to you if that confession became known to your old associates."

Hampton knew only too well. He glanced at Duval, saw her

sparkling, predatory smile, and shuddered. "I suppose I must. What exactly do you wish me to do as governor?"

"It will have to be subtle; you're no good to the country or to me if it suspected you are working for Washington. Clay, I want you to listen closely, and tell me if I miss anything."

As Grant began to speak, Clay stepped alongside him, eyes riveted on Hampton in a way that added to the broken old traitor's uneasiness. Duval and Julia Grant watched with rapt attention as the President smoothly set forth, off the top of his head, a brilliant and subtle course of action for Hampton to follow. Even Buchanan was mesmerized by the performance of the man whom fifteen years previously he had dismissed as a worthless drunk.

Sitting far apart from the others, Dent and Jesse Grant looked on, not with admiration but with growing anger. Old Man Dent leaned over and whispered to his adversary.

"Grant, you know this only works if they let that murdering bastard who tried to kill my baby's husband go. The moment he is put on trial, he would reveal this whole God-damned mess. Your boy is a cold one; he will let that monster go, for the greater good of his precious Union. He would let go the man who tried to make my Julia a widow."

"Hiram never knew how to take care of himself," whispered Jesse Grant back. "Could take care of others, take care of the army, take care of the country, but couldn't take care of himself. To him, it won't seem important to punish the man who tried to murder him; the man who tried to murder my boy."

The two elderly men looked over to where the President stood, giving Hampton his orders. From where they sat, they could see that not only were the others intently focused on the President, but that the ornate dish containing the poisoned dessert was blocked from their view by the President's sturdy frame. They looked over toward Tillinghast, who was still reeling from the pistol-whipping Buchanan had given him. Jesse Grant then turned his attention back to Dent and nodded his head toward the dazed assassin. Old Man Dent in turn nodded in agreement, and then ostentatiously stretching his aged frame, he leveraged himself out of his chair with his heavy cane and began to walk in the general direction of the prisoner, taking small steps as if he was trying to loosen his stiff, arthritic joints.

Quietly, Jesse Grant himself rose, and began to walk slowly toward his son; if any of the group saw him, to them it did not seem worthy of comment. When the old man was within reach of the dessert dish, he suddenly snatched it with both hands, whirled, and bounded over to Tillinghast. At the same instant, Old Man Dent dropped his cane and with hands surprisingly strong for a man of his age pried Tillinghast's jaws apart; with his hands tied behind his back, the assassin was unable to make any resistance.

As the President and those in front of him turned there attention in astonishment to the two old men, Jesse Grant slopped the mostly-liquid contents of the dish into Tillinghast's open mouth. The man gagged and tried to spit up the lethal confection, but a grim Jesse Grant pinched the man's nostril's shut with one hand while with the other assisted Dent in wrestling the assassin's mouth shut. Involuntarily, Tillinghast took one large gulp, then another, at which point the two old men released him and stood back.

The President and his wife simultaneously shouted "FATHER!" At the same time, Clay and Duval leapt over the table with seemingly impossible agility, while the more elderly Colonel Buchanan ran around the edge of the table with scarcely less speed. They all came to sudden stops, shocked by the scene before them.

Crawford Tillinghast was gasping for air like a stranded fish, his eyes bulging nearly out of his head, his body arched with the unconscious effort to free his hands from behind him. Spittle came out the right corner of his mouth, while his bladder obviously voided itself. Gagging sounds emerged from his mouth, as incomprehensible as the croaking of a frog. His body stiffened even further, creating an outward bow like the victim of lockjaw. Then his body sagged, and with a last exhalation of air, he died.

Colonel Buchanan advanced slowly and touched the assassin's throat, to confirm that he was dead. He then stood back, and with genuine reverence softly said, "Jesus Christ."

Recovering quickly from the shock he felt, the President looked angrily at Jesse Grant and said, "Father, what have you done? You and Mr. Dent have committed murder in front of a roomful of witnesses. There is no way this can be concealed."

"Don't care about that," replied Jesse Grant. "You were going to let this bastard go; no way your plan would work if he were brought to trial. No one trying to murder my boy lives, no one. If you feel I need to be tried for this, go on ahead; I think Dent feels the same." He looked at Julia Grant's sour old father, who nodded once. Then he turned back to his son.

"Doesn't matter if you hang us, we'll say nothing about what happened here; both of us have one foot in the grave as it is. I just want you to know that whatever you need to do, I'll understand. You're my boy, and I love you more than my life."

Clay strode over to where the corpse was rapidly cooling, drawing a Bowie knife from beneath his coat. With one stroke he severed the bonds on Tillinghast's hands; they fell to the floor, and Clay swiftly kicked them far under the table. Restoring the Bowie to its place under his coat, he turned to the President and said, "Sir, I saw this man drink from the poisoned dish of his own free will. He obviously preferred suicide to the hangman's noose. I cannot swear for what others may have seen; but that is what I saw."

"I saw the same thing," said Duval immediately.

"So did I," added Buchanan, with considerably more hesitation.

Lafitte looked at the others, licked his lips, then chimed in. "Me too."

Clay turned his attention to Hampton, who felt increasingly uneasy under the scrutiny of those weird sky-blue eyes. After a long hesitation, he said, "Didn't get a clear view myself; but if that's what you say happened, then I won't say otherwise."

Clay looked at the old Rebel for a long time, then slowly nodded his head. He then turned his attention to the President.

"Sir, if you have finished giving Mr. Hampton his instructions, I suggest you and Mrs. Grant return to the Executive Mansion and get some rest. Miss Duval will escort Mr. Hampton to the station and put him on the next train South. Meanwhile, Mr. Lafitte and I will attend to matters here. With any luck, there will be no mention of this evening's events in the newspapers.

"Thank you, Major," responded Grant, who then gently helped his still-stunned wife out of the chair. He started to lead her out of the dining room, but suddenly stopped and addressed Buchanan.

"Colonel Buchanan, I want to thank you for the extraordinary measures you have taken to protect me. Given our . . . previous history, I would not have expected it."

"There is no need," replied Buchanan grimly. "What I did was not for the worthless drunk I drove out of the army. What I did was for the savior of the Union and the President of these United States." He then slowly and correctly saluted Grant. A puzzled Grant absently returned the salute, and then helped guide his wife out of the dining room.

Lafitte turned and nervously said to Clay, "What are we to do with this body."

Clay nodded negligently. "Wait until after midnight, then load it in a wagon, drive it to the Potomac, and dump it in the river."

Later that night, Wade Hampton stumped along the platform to his assigned car in the last train South, aided in equal degrees by his heavy crutch and the arm of Teresa Duval. When they reached the assigned compartment, Hampton stopped to catch his breath, while an amused Duval open the door for him.

"Here you are, Mr. Hampton. My apologies that we had no time to acquire some toiletries for you. I think you agree that we would all feel better if you were in South Carolina as soon as possible."

Hampton maneuvered himself clumsily toward the door. Before he could manage the hop over the short distance between the platform and the train, Duval grabbed his arm, leaned in, and whispered fiercely into his ear.

"You are very lucky that the President needs you, very lucky indeed. Perhaps Grant doesn't know; but Alphonso and I know about those dozens of slaves you used in your little rites, trying to call upon things to give you and your worthless friends more power than they already possessed. I know what things you did to them. You have good reason to know I'm not squeamish, but even I'm revolted by what Alphonso told me you and your friends must have done.

"Worse than that, you made a fool of me. You led me to believe you had surrendered up all you information, while you withheld your recognition of the chef as Crawford Tillinghast. Frankly, I feel no great obligation to Grant; but Alphonso would have blamed himself if the President had come to grief, and I do feel the greatest obligation to Major Clay. I am very, very . . . disappointed in you, Mr. Hampton."

Trying to conceal the terror he had of this woman, Hampton said gruffly, "Just why are you telling me all this?"

Duval smiled sweetly at Hampton; almost a lover's smile. "Because I want you to understand that if you double-cross Grant in any way, you need have no fear of him. I will be coming for you, and I will keep you a week dying." She leaned forward and kissed him on the mouth, and then with a whirl of skirts, she was gone.

Hampton hopped quickly into the compartment, slammed shut the door, and pulled the shade. Then he gingerly sat down on the hard seat. His fresh stump still pained him, yet he was not thinking of the pain in the remains of his right leg; he was thinking of just how vital it was that he follow Grant's instructions to the letter.

Grant gently led his still sobbing wife into their bedroom in the Executive Mansion. "It's cold," he muttered, letting her go. "Lie down and rest. I'll get the fire going." Grant went to the fireplace, went down on his haunches, and began to arrange the wood and kindling.

Meanwhile, Julia dried her eyes with a lace handkerchief, and then went over to her dressing table. She drew open the drawer, extracted the document, and looked at it for a long moment. It was worthless monetarily, now that the price of gold had crashed. Regardless, it was still a powerful document, symbolizing her weakness and avarice. She walked over to where her husband was still hunched over, frowning; he was having trouble kindling the fire.

"Sam, here is that document that Mr. Gould gave to me. I wish to God I had never touched it."

Grant looked up at his wife, frowned, and took the paper. He glanced at it briefly, and then quickly shredded it into a dozen strips, which he scattered strategically on the kindling. He ignited his curious cigar-lighter again, applied it to the shreds of the document, and the paper began to flame immediately. With a groan he rose to his feet, restoring the lighter to his coat pocket.

"There Julia, that's done the trick. Some good has come out of that paper after all. We will never speak of this again. Now let's get ready for bed."

Julia Grant focused her cross-eyed stare on her husband, and smiled.

Jim Fisk was having a very good time indeed. He had rented out the largest of Delmonico's private dining rooms for the evening, and had invited his half-dozen best drinking buddies—and of course the delicious Miss Josie Mansfield. He felt not the slightest guilt about partying with the uninhibited, curvaceous Josie, while leaving his wife at home; after all, he made sure that his wife had every conceivable material comfort. Besides, she had never enjoyed these sorts of parties, no matter how much Fisk wanted them. And now, he *needed* a party such as this. Despite the brave front he had put on before Grant the previous week, he had been deeply depressed by the failure of his plan. Success would have guaranteed him the Grand Mastership of Starry Wisdom, once the ailing incumbent finally shuffled off this mortal coil. Now, that was completely out of the question. The Grandmastership would probably go to Schuyler Colfax, who had always made it clear to the Council that he thought Fisk was moving too far, too fast. It was even possible that the Council might decide that . . . discipline was in order for Fisk's failure. He was reasonably sure that he had enough credit with the Council for them to forgive him this one major failure, but he was not absolutely sure, and fears nagged at him uneasily. Hence the need for an evening of garish pleasures, to take his mind off his concerns.

He looked around the gaudily decorated dining room, and smiled at his friends as they chattered among themselves, stopping only to guzzle the champagne that flowed like water or to stuff their mouths with foie gras and other exotic victuals. A quite competent pianist sat at the stand-up instrument in one corner of the room, playing an endless series of light-hearted music hall tunes.

The buxom Josie leaned over to kiss him on the cheek, and Fisk was rewarded with a spectacular view of that ample bosom. "I feel like singing a song, Jim. Would you mind?"

"Of course not, Josie. Tell the piano-player what tune you want, and I'll get these rowdy dogs to quiet down and give you all their attention." As Josie bustled up to the where the pianist sat, Fisk started pounding with a meaty fist on the table, until his cronies had quieted and given him their full attention.

"All right, boys, Miss Mansfield feels like exercising her pipes. I want you to all give her your full attention. Josie, what treat do you have for us?"

The curvaceous songbird simpered and replied, "I feel patriotic tonight. I shall present 'Hail Columbia.'"

Fisk frowned slightly as his friends applauded and cheered. He had not a particle of patriotic feeling; indeed, the plans of his shadowy associates called for the destruction of America as a prelude to their even more audacious goals. Still, this is what Josie wanted, and it hurt nothing. He nodded to the pianist, who started off with some flowery introductory scales. Then Josie began to sing in her weak but serviceable soprano.

> "Hail Columbia, happy land!
> Hail, ye heroes, heav'n-born band,
> Who fought and bled in freedom's cause,
> Who fought and bled in freedom's cause,
> And when the storm of war was gone
> Enjoy'd the peace your valor won.
> Let independence be our boast,
> Ever mindful what it cost;
> Ever grateful for the prize,
> Let its altar reach the skies."

In through the entrance to Delmonico's strode the lean, haggard-looking Edward Stokes, a former partner of Jim Fisk's. Stokes had been involved in several speculations with Fisk when he had met Josie Mansfield and had fallen madly in love with her. He abandoned his wife and did not contest it when the heart-broken mother of his children divorced him and took much of his modest fortune. Josie always had her eye on the main chance, and had quickly abandoned him for the much more successful Jim Fisk. Stokes could not, would not, accept that she had not loved him, but had only regarded him as a stepping stone in her own advancement. He had begged her tearfully to take him back; she had laughed at him. He doggedly kept trying to see her; an irritated Fisk had taken actions to render Stokes' few remaining investments worthless. Stokes persisted, and finally Fisk ran out of patience and had hired plug-uglies to beat Stokes to within an inch of his life, while Josie watched, laughing at his humiliation and pain. Yet still he loved her madly.

Stokes looked angrily around the main dining room, until suddenly he heard a familiar voice wafting through the entrance to one of the private rooms. He recognized Josie's voice as she began the second verse of "Hail Columbia."

> *"Immortal patriots, rise once more,*
> *Defend your rights, defend your shore!*
> *Let no rude foe, with impious hand,*
> *Let no rude foe, with impious hand,*
> *Invade the shrine where sacred lies*
> *Of toil and blood, the well-earned prize,*
> *While off'ring peace, sincere and just,*
> *In Heaven's we place a manly trust,*
> *That truth and justice will prevail,*
> *And every scheme of bondage fail."*

Not an hour before, a telegram had reached him at the run-down boarding house that his new poverty required him to call his home. The telegram said that the sender had observed Jim Fisk and Josie Mansfield at Delmonico's, regaling a group of cronies with how they had humiliated Stokes, and even sharing indelicate details concerning his inadequacy as a lover. Something had snapped inside Stokes, and he had rushed out of the boardinghouse with no clear plans save that he must confront Jim Fisk over the humiliations, disgrace, and mockery that had been heaped on his head.

Now hearing Josie's voice, he began striding straight as a bullet toward the doorway from which it emerged, shoving a startled waiter out of the way without even looking at the man. As he neared the door, a woman who had apparently been dining alone suddenly shoved back her chair and rose to her feet, right in front of the charging Stokes. Without intending to, Stokes ran into her hard, knocking her off balance. She instinctively grabbed his shoulders to keep from falling; but Stokes was off balance as well, and they half fell onto her small table, scattering glass and cutlery. Stokes immediately helped her to her feet, his face beet-red with embarrassment and shame.

"Madame, my very deepest apologies. Are you hurt.?"

"No harm done," replied the lithe, raven-haired beauty with a silvery laugh.

"At least let me pay for your meal."

"No need," she replied. "I have already paid, and I am late for an appointment."

She snatched at her reticule and without another word glided away and disappeared into the crowd. Stokes had heard a small thud as the woman had grabbed her small handbag, as if something had fallen out of it onto the table. He glanced down at the table, and to his surprise saw a Remington two-shot derringer, the kind favored by gamblers and ladies that were no better than they should be. It was small and inaccurate; but at close range the .41 caliber bullets it fired could be quite deadly. It was surprising to see a respectable-looking woman carrying one in her reticule, but, he considered, after all this was New

York. Obviously in her haste she had not noticed it fall from her bag. He picked it up, intending to restore the weapon to its rightful owner; but as he scanned the main room, he could see no trace of her. Just then, his attention was seized by Josie Mansfield beginning the third verse of her song.

"Behold the chief who now commands,
Once more to serve his country stands.
The rock on which the storm will break,
The rock on which the storm will break,
But armed in virtue, firm, and true,
His hopes are fixed on Heav'n and you.
When hope was sinking in dismay,
When glooms obscured Columbia's day,
His steady mind, from changes free,
Resolved on death or liberty."

He stepped into the room, but no one noticed him; every eye was focused on the beautiful singer. The gun clutched in his hand forgotten for the moment, he stared adoringly at the woman for whom he had given up his family, his fortune, his self-respect. Entranced, he listened to her bring the song to its conclusion.

"Sound, sound the trump of fame,
Let Washington's great name
Ring through the world with loud applause,
Ring through the world with loud applause,
Let ev'ry clime to freedom dear,
Listen with a joyful ear,
With equal skill, with God-like pow'r
He governs in the fearful hour

Of horrid war, or guides with ease
The happier time of honest peace.
Firm, united let us be,
Rallying round our liberty,
As a band of brothers joined,
Peace and safety we shall find!"

The roomful of partiers broke into wild cheers and loud applause. Then, still not noticing her former lover standing in the doorway, Josie went over to Jim Fisk, planted her ample bottom into his lap, and gave him the kind of kiss that was seldom seen in public.

Everything seemed to go red before the eyes of Edward Stokes. He strode over to the affectionate couple, and stood before them, saying nothing. Fisk broke off the kiss, and then noticed Stokes; his smile turned into a sneer.

"Well, well, well, Stokes. Come to go crawling to Miss Josie? Well, she isn't going back to you; she's now with a man who can actually satisfy her."

Fisk had not noticed the small Remington derringer, almost concealed within Stokes' hand. Not saying a word, Stokes cocked the hammer of the gun and fired a .41 caliber slug into the center of Fisk's chest. Fisk looked down at his shirtfront which was beginning to leak blood, his expression more amazement than pain. Stokes cocked the hammer again, and sent a second bullet into Fisk's massive frame.

For a few moments after the two shots, the dining room was so silent one could have literally heard a pin drop. Then the shouting and screaming began. Josie Mansfield rolled off Fisk's lap, hiked her skirts, and sprinted for the door, ignoring her current lover, fearing the vengeance of her former lover. Some of the guests and waiters followed her in flight; but four of them clumsily tackled Stokes, driving him to the ground, and began to pummel the unresisting gunman senseless. Neglected for a moment, his mouth making gasping motions like a fish out of water, James Fisk slipped slowly out of the chair to the floor, blood from his two wounds gushing onto his expensive, hand-tailored clothes. In the main dining room, the fleeing guests were screaming for help, for police, for doctors—some were just screaming inarticulately. The entrance to the dining room became crowded with ghoulish diners, anxious to feast their eyes on an act of violence.

Among the spectators was a short, blonde man with spectacles, dressed in a somber yet expensive frock coat; beside him stood a tall, lithe beauty, whose eyes avidly drank in the scene of violence and blood. She touched the arm of the man next to her, and softly said, "Come, it is time to go."

Alphonso Clay nodded, offered his arm to Teresa Duval, and led her with difficulty through the rapidly-growing crowd until they exited Delmonico's. They walked silently until they reached a quiet-looking side street, and turned down it.

"You are certain he is dead?" asked Clay.

Duval laughed one of her silvery, chilling laughs. "Oh, he is still alive. But I saw where the bullets hit him, and the volume of blood. He will soon die of shock, or if not that, of infection."

His sky-blue eyes focused somewhere in the distance, Clay responded, "Then James Fisk will never again threaten the Republic; never again further the hellish goals of Starry Wisdom."

Eyes sparkling with malicious amusement, Duval said, "I must hand it to you, Alphonso. I didn't believe you when you said all we needed to do was to bring Stokes into the presence of Fisk and Mansfield enjoying each other, and let him 'accidentally' come upon a gun, and the rest would follow. But that is exactly what happened."

Clay gave his lover the thinnest of smiles. "Once I had observed him for a day or two, it was clear that the man was a bomb, primed and ready to blow. All that was needed was to place him in the right place at the right time. Of course, he might not have acted on his murderous impulse, after all. If that had happened, then more direct action would have been taken."

"I don't understand why you didn't simply slit Fisk's throat in the middle of the night, rather than implement such an elaborate plan that could have gone wrong at any one of several places."

Clay gave vent to a melancholy sigh. "I could not. President Grant made me promise not to touch Fisk and Gould. As I told you, he instructed me to come up to New York and 'persuade' them to co-operate in with the Government by using their influence behind the scenes to support certain Government financial actions. He was convinced that fear of exposing their role in the Black Friday Crash and the attempt on his life would make them willing to agree. I could not convince him that Fisk would never co-operate; his connections with Starry Wisdom made him too confident that he was invulnerable to any pressure the Government could bring. I could not convince him that only by Fisk's death could Starry Wisdom be made to reconsider its plots against our Government. Since I promised him that I would not kill Fisk, and since I am loath to break my word to him, I needed to maneuver someone else into doing the deed. A little investigation was all that was required to find Stokes, and to determine how Josie's abandonment of him had rendered him violently unstable. Technically, I have not broken my word to the President."

Duval gave vent to another of her chilling laughs. "Why, you hypocrite! You and I have killed Jim Fisk, just as surely as if we had shot him ourselves. Besides, now you leave that pathetic madman Stokes to hang for what you planned! I've been hearing of your precious Clay honor for years. Just how do you reconcile all this with that honor?"

Clay's normally expressionless face took on a look of infinite sadness. "Perhaps you are right in saying that I am a hypocrite. It was essential to the future of this country that Fisk die, if for no other reason than it will give his masters in Starry Wisdom pause. I am sick unto death of merely responding to Starry Wisdom. From now on, I will be taking the battle to them. Besides, Fisk intended to murder Grant to put his fellow conspirator Schuyler Colfax in the Executive Mansion; there is no reason to think that he would not try again, and soon. I could not make Grant see this. Therefore, I had to take this dishonorable burden on myself.

"As for using Stokes, I feel no guilt whatsoever. The man abandoned his wife and children to go mooning after a cheap, grasping whore, and deserves to be punished for that. Oh, he will not hang; I have already anonymously and discretely hired for him New York's best criminal defense attorney, Grover Cleveland, who I am certain will be able to get Stokes off with a manslaughter conviction. Five years in Sing-Sing should be appropriate punishment for the pain he caused his blameless family."

Duval laughed again. "It amuses me the convoluted way your brain works. I wouldn't have your scruples for all of Jay Gould's money. Speaking of which, when do we pay him our little visit?"

"Later tonight. In the meantime, dinner is in order; anywhere but Delmonico's."

Jay Gould sat at his expensive yet functional desk, reviewing the late edition of *The World.* He had not wanted to read this before his wife and children were safely in bed and asleep; he was a good husband and father, and tried to shield them from the nastiness of the world that was outside of the luxurious cocoon of privilege that he had constructed for them as well as himself. He finished reading the article on Jim Fisk's murder for the second time, then leaned back in his leather chair and sighed. *Fool! How many times had I told him to get his private life in order? How many times!* He looked at the clock softly ticking over the mantelpiece, and saw that it was after midnight. He knew that he should be going to bed, that the last few weeks had left him so drained of energy that, given his poor health, it would take months before he was anything like normal. However, he needed the hours around midnight, with his family and servants sleeping and the mansion as quiet as a tomb, to do his best thinking.

Tonight his thoughts revolved around the murder of Jim Fisk. In one sense, Gould was glad it had happened. The confrontation in Willard's dining room had made Gould aware that Fisk had drawn him into a conspiracy deeper and more sinister than he had originally imagined. Fisk's death at the hands of a jealous rival had freed Gould from a connection with Starry Wisdom. Gould had not in fact heard of Starry Wisdom until that night at Willard's; but what Clay and Fisk had said had been enough to convince Jay Gould to stay very far away from involvement in such a shadowy organization.

Gould was suddenly aware of a slight, chill night breeze sweeping across him. He frowned; his lungs were weak, and he was always very careful to secure the library's windows before the cold night air could invade his favorite room. Frowning, he rose from his chair and turned toward the windows—to see Alphonso Clay and Teresa Duval step lightly from behind the luxurious curtains.

Recovering from his initial shock, he sternly asked, "What are you doing in my home at this hour, uninvited? Leave instantly, or I will summon the police!"

"I rather doubt that," responded Clay mildly. He gestured toward the newspaper on Gould's desk. "You have seen how Mr. Stokes has killed your erstwhile partner James Fisk. One word from me, and the police will find a telegram that has been carefully hidden in his boarding house room. It described some unfortunate comments Mr. Fisk had made about Stokes, especially his inability to meet the . . . needs of Miss Josie Mansfield, and went on to describe how Fisk was that very evening regaling a party at Delmonico's with tales of Stokes' inadequacies as a man. That telegram was sent by one Jay Gould."

Gould almost never allowed his emotions to show to anyone outside his immediate family; this was one of those rare occasions when he did. In a shocked voice he blurted, "I sent no such telegram!"

Clay shrugged negligently. "The records of the telegraph office will show otherwise. Oh, it is doubtful that any criminal charges could be made to stick, but imagine the scandal. Contemplating the fate of James Fisk, what financier would enter into any dealings with you? And of course, what would be the reaction of Mrs. Gould, and of your children?"

Glaring at Clay, Gould asked, "What is it that you want from me?"

"Ideally, I want to see you hanging from a gallows; it is no less than you deserve. However, the President would prefer for you to be alive, to do some good for the country. His experience with your schemes has convinced him that he must play a more active role in regulating unpatriotic practices on Wall Street. Congress and the people would not support direct, public intervention by the Federal government, at least not at this time in our nation's history. Therefore, he will find it useful to have a wealthy, influential man on Wall Street to discreetly take economic actions he deems best for the Republic. You will perform those actions, without question or delay. I will make that telegram disappear from Stokes' room. Mark my word, if at any time you balk at following the President's directions, that telegram will find its way to a major newspaper."

Gould glared hatred at Clay. How dare this little man attempt to make me Grant's puppet, he thought. I am the master of Wall Street, and will serve only myself! And then he remembered that he had a way out of this. Standing beside Clay was Teresa Duval, an accomplished killer and Gould's tool; one to whom he had promised the small fortune of $50,000 if she would obey an order to kill Alphonso Clay. The body of an intruder on the floor of his library was something with which he could deal; he had enough influence with Tammany Hall for that.

He looked directly at Duval and mouthed the words, "Do it." He felt relief as a straight razor appeared in her right hand as if by magic, and as a smile graced her lips. With no warning, she leaped.

Gould felt Duval crash into him with surprising force. He rolled on the thick carpet, gasping for air, and ended up on his stomach, the wind knocked out of him. He attempted to rise, but was knocked back down, a knee planted in his back. A deceptively small hand grabbed a hank of his hair and jerked his head backward. With surprise he realized what was about to happen to him.

"DO NOT KILL HIM!" thundered Clay in a hellishly low voice. With amazement Gould realized that the windows were still rattling in the aftermath of that titanic sound. He carefully looked down past his beard, and saw the gleaming razor poised less than an inch from his neck.

"Please Alphonso, grant me this," said Duval, her voice almost a whine. "You have no idea how much I've longed to do this over the past few years. Besides, this bastard offered me $50,000 to murder you whenever he said."

"I am disappointed," replied Clay, a hint of a smile on his lips. "I would have thought my life worth considerably more. In any event, he is needed by Grant. Help him to his feet."

Duval paused for a long moment, and then drew the razor across Gould's throat. For a horrific moment Gould thought he was a dead man; but he quickly realized Duval had only nicked him, to enjoy a sadistic moment as Gould panicked. The razor disappeared, and Duval helped the financier to his feet. Gould was now shaking visibly, a delayed reaction to his close encounter with death.

"Now, Mr. Gould, no more of this foolishness. You are to do exactly what President Grant requests in times of economic strain. In addition, I am adding my own condition: that you no longer employ illegal acts of violence in your pursuit of money. If you fail the President, the telegram concerning Mr. Stokes will be made very, very public. And if you are found to be engaged in felonious practices, I believe I will let Miss Duval have her way with you. Do we have an agreement?"

Gould looked at his former employee, who smiled at him. Shivering, he replied, "Yes."

Clay nodded. "One final thing. We will require your copy of the options contract you had with Mrs. Grant."

"I, ah, do not have it here."

Clay's eyes glittered dangerously. "Please, Mr. Gould, no games. You would keep it close, so it could be used immediately in time of need. Did you put it in a private safe? Most mansions of this sort have one. Though, I rather think you did not. Safecracking is becoming a common crime, and you would not want to take such a chance. Certainly you would not place such a document in your office."

Clay scanned the volumes that lined the walls of Gould's library. "Quite a collection you have here. I also appreciate books." He walked over to one section, seemingly devoted to fiction, care-fully alphabetized; after a moment, he snatched out a volume and examined it closely. "Edgar A. Poe. And well worn; obviously read it a number of times."

"So?" responded Gould shakily.

"It is just that I recall one of his stories, "The Purloined Letter," where a disreputable man needed to hide an important document where even a careful search would never find it." Clay restored the book to its place, and then walked over to Gould's desk. He examined the cluttered papers on the desk; then noted one covered with figures that seemed to deal with tradesmen's bills. "In that story, Poe's character hid the document in plain sight, by writing mundane household details on its back, and leaving it exposed for all to see." Clay turned over the paper, and saw that the reverse was a copy of an options contract. Folding it carefully, and placing it into an inner coat pocket, Clay said, "We will be taking this with us."

He then offered Duval his arm, and led her to the door of the library. There they stopped. Duval turned, smiled sweetly at Gould, and said, "You may consider this my two week notice." Then the pair glided out of the room. Gould collapsed into his desk chair, and buried his face in his hands, shaking uncontrollably.

After they had gained the street and were walking toward a busier thoroughfare, where a cab could be found at this late hour, Clay glanced at Duval and asked, "I am curious; what would you have done if the offer from Gould for my life had been $100,000 instead of $50,000?"

Duval laughed her silvery, chilling laugh, and took Clay's arm possessively. "I suppose we will never know, will we?"

Around eight in the morning, Teresa Duval was suddenly awakened by a spasm of nausea that hit her like a sledgehammer. "Alphonso," she moaned, but there was no reply. Naked, she staggered from the bed she had been sharing with Clay to the hotel suite's water closet, and violently vomited. When the wave of nausea had finally passed, she looked at herself in the mirror, and was shocked at how haggard she appeared. *I must take the extract of Pennyroyal flower soon,* she thought. *The longer I wait, the more dangerous it becomes. But first I must talk to Alphonso.*

She gingerly re-entered the suite, and noticed that the clothes-press was open, and that a carpetbag and most of Clay's things were missing. She was seized by panic, a very uncharacteristic emotion for her. Then she remembered that Ambrose Bierce occupied a room down the hall; the young writer might know what had become of her lover. Dressing hurriedly, she strode quickly down the hall to Bierce's room. She was about to knock when she noticed that the door was slightly ajar. Pushing the door fully open and entering the room, she found Bierce fully dressed, and in the act of stuffing some articles of clothing into an already bulging carpetbag.

"Where are you going, Ambrose?" she asked. Bierce started violently and turned to face her; he had not heard her enter the room. Recovering quickly from his surprise, he smiled ironically and clicked his heels.

"Good morning, Miss Duval. I intended to pay my respects before I actually left. I received a telegram from my employer late last night, demanding my immediate return. I cannot continue to live on Clay's charity, so I must comply. It is a good thing the transcontinental railway is finally complete. I can be in San Francisco in less than a week."

"I wish you well in your career," replied Duval, not caring one way or the other about what happened to Ambrose Bierce. "But before you take leave, perhaps you can help me on another matter. By the time I awoke, Alphonso was gone, along with his clothes and travelling bag. Do you have any idea where he has gone?"

The ironic smile deserted Bierce's face. "I did see him this morning, but he did not see fit to tell me his destination when I asked. He did request that I give this to you." He handed her an envelope. She tore it open, expecting to find some sort of letter, some kind of explanation. All the envelope contained was a check for $50,000 made out in her name.

There had been a time when she would have been ecstatic at receiving such a check. Yet, to her own amazement, all she felt was hollowness, and a sense of terrible loss. Bierce noted the expression on her face, and did something very uncharacteristic for him; he offered her consolation.

"Teresa, I am truly sorry. He is gone, and you will not be seeing him again. Take the money, and try to forget him. It would not have worked in the long run. You know as well as I that there is something . . . inhuman about him."

She looked into Bierce's eyes. "Where has he gone?" she said in a voice that pleaded rather than threatened.

Bierce hesitated a long moment before replying. "He did not tell me, but I know. You know, too, if you only think upon it." He grabbed his carpetbag, then impulsively leaned over and kissed her gently on the cheek. Then he was gone.

The devastated Duval stood still as a statue for nearly a minute, then suddenly cursed aloud. The check fell from her hands and fluttered to the carpet; she did not seem to notice.

"Granda, tell me another story," said the girl tucked under the comforter of her small bed. "Tell me one about the War."

"Now pumpkin, stories about the War are not what good little girls should hear just before they go to sleep," answered Nathan Bedford Forrest, looking down with adoration at his granddaughter.

"I am not little!" she announced with charming petulance. "I have just turned ten."

"Have you now?" he announced with mock severity. "All the more reason to follow orders like a good little soldier. Go to sleep tonight without any fuss, and I will tell you a war story tomorrow morning."

"All right, Granda," she said grudgingly, eyelids already heavy with sleep.

Forrest leaned forward to kiss the child's forehead. As he drew away, he saw that she was already asleep. With a melancholy smile, he departed the room to go down to the library to take care of estate paperwork. He preferred to do such work late at night, with his granddaughter and the servants in their rooms, like now. His semi-literacy caused him to sometimes struggle over the simplest matters, and he did not wish them to witness that struggle. Quietly, he descended the stairs and entered the library, sighing at the sight of the pile of unanswered business correspondence.

"Mr. Forrest, I have waited years for this interview."

Forrest whirled to face the voice, instantly regretting that he had ceased to carry a pistol while inside his own home. In a leather wingchair in a far corner of the room, he spotted the intruder; a small man dressed in a black frockcoat, with straight blonde hair falling to his shoulders, blue eyes shining weirdly behind wire-rimmed spectacles. In the darkness, Forrest did not recognize Clay.

"Sir, what are you doing in my home," snarled Forrest, genuinely unafraid of the intruder.

Alphonso Clay stood up. "There must be a reckoning, sir. I have come to see that reckoning is made."

Forrest misunderstood Clay. "I am not ashamed in the slightest for having given the nightriders over to the blue-bellies. It is one thing to kill carpetbaggers and scalawags; I would do that with joy. But the thing was getting out of hand. I won't have the blood of women and children on my hands. Even nigger women and children."

There was a long pause, and then Clay spoke, almost unwillingly. "That is to your credit sir, although you must still bear the guilt of getting the Klan started in the first place. In any event, the reckoning to which I refer has nothing to do with your actions in the Klan, or even in the War."

"What then?" the old Rebel demanded.

"Just as the War was breaking out, you made some final trans-actions in human flesh, some final dispositions of black human beings."

"And what of it?" countered Forrest. "Slaving was legal, and I, and others like me, provided the service that kept the planta-tion system going."

"Provided the service," echoed Clay with wonder. "In any event, I am not here to discuss the general, but the specific." Clay stepped fully into the light; Forrest recognized him with a shock. "My father was Cicero Clay. He asked a service of you in the last days of peace."

Forrest looked thoughtful for a moment. "Yes, I remember. Some nigger wench he wanted sold south . . ."

"DO NOT SPEAK OF HER IN THAT WAY!" thundered Clay in that impossibly deep, resonating voice, so different from his normal, cultivated speech. He took several steps forward, and Forrest could now see him even more clearly. Or, he thought, not so clearly; Clay seemed to be trembling all over and his body appeared to expand and retract in the most impossible of ways. An uneasy Forrest decided that this was an illusion caused by a badly flickering fire.

Clay seemed to make a supreme effort to calm himself; the odd distortions of his figure were now no longer apparent. "Her name was Arabella Lot, and she was a lady of cultivation and education. You were told to place her with a family that would respect that. Instead, you placed her with a family that hounded and abused her until she took her own life!"

Forrest shrugged. "That was nothing to do with me. The Devereaux family seemed decent enough." Suddenly his eyes narrowed. "I remember. You're the one who massacred the Devereaux family. You did that over a nigger woman? Good God, you must have loved her. Have you no shame, mixing white with black blood?"

Clay shot forward and grabbed the old cavalryman around the throat; his deceptively small yet powerful hands instantly cut off air to the lungs, blood to the brain. As Forrest felt consciousness slipping away, he clawed ineffectively at Clay's hands.

"Stop hurting my granda!"

With shock, Clay glanced at the open library door, and saw a girl of about ten, dressed in a frilly nightshirt, eyes wide with horror. Reflexively, Clay released his hold on Forrest's throat; the semiconscious old cavalryman slipped to the floor, gagging for air. His gagging became loud coughs, wet and rasping. After an especially vicious cough, Forrest spat bloody phlegm onto the elegant carpet. The girl screamed and ran over to her grandfather. Cradling the old man's head in her arms, she shouted at Clay, "What have you done to granda, you . . . you mean man?"

Through the library's open window Teresa Duval vaulted effort-lessly. Landing on the balls of her feet, a small Remington derringer appeared in her right hand. She took in the scene in a moment, including Clay's look of utter astonishment, an expression she had hardly ever seen. Clay spoke first.

"How did you know where to find me?"

"Stop thinking I'm a stupid woman. You left me a check for the value Gould placed on your life. That meant you were about to throw your life away; that could only mean you intended to kill Forrest."

"But how did you get here so soon?"

"I was one train behind you. While you took your time and waited for night to fall, I got off the train at sunset, rented a horse, and about killed the nag galloping out here." She glanced down at Forrest, who was still coughing and who gagged up another wad of bloody phlegm, to the horror of his granddaughter. "There is no point, Alphonso. The man is dying by inches. If you killed him, you would hang, unless all the witnesses were gone." Her small pistol swiveled toward the child, who in terror buried her face in her grandfather's shoulder. Forrest looked at Duval with white-hot fury and tried to surge to his feet, only to be seized by another horrific fit of coughing, which left him weak and helpless on the carpet. Duval laughed heartily, heartlessly, and looked at Clay, a questioning expression on her face.

"No," said Clay quietly. "I find now I could not do it in front of his granddaughter, even if Forrest were in good health." He looked down at his hands as if he had never seen them before, and continued to himself. "It would not make any difference, would it? He would never understand what he did was wrong." Clay then looked at the coughing Forrest and said, "My apologies for interrupting your evening, sir. I will not be bothering you again." He then went to the door of the library, passed into the short hallway, and was out the front door.

Duval looked at Forrest; his coughing spasm was over for the time being. The old Rebel looked daggers of hatred at her. Duval smiled, blew him a kiss, and followed Clay out into the night.

She found Clay standing beside the horse he had rented from a Memphis livery stable. As he absently stroked its mane in the dim light of the quarter moon, she could see that he was crying. Duval was not introspective, but she knew Clay well enough to know he felt the meaning had gone out of his life. He had lived for eight years on his white-hot hatred of Nathan Bedford Forrest and his determination to kill him, and now he had a vast emptiness inside himself. She knew he needed something to fill that emptiness. Impulsively, decisively, she made a decision on a matter she had been contemplating for some weeks. She walked up to Clay and took his arm.

"Alphonso, I am carrying your child. I know this is not your responsibility, and I do not expect you to . . ."

He had turned his face to her at her first words, and she trailed off at the look on that face. The normally expressionless Clay now indeed showed expression: surprise, wonder, utmost joy . . . love. He instantly took both of her hands in hers, and dropped to one knee.

"Miss Teresa Duval, will you consent to be my wife?"

All kinds of thoughts, schemes, plans buzzed around inside her brain, but for once in her life they did not control her words or actions. With no conscious thought, she said, "Of course I will, you stupid bastard!" Then she leaned down, and to her own amazement kissed him with the gentlest tenderness.

As the kiss broke off, Clay murmured, "Language, Teresa, language."

Alphonso Clay paced the hall outside the master bedroom of his mansion at the family estate of *Dignitas;* the mellow sunlight of a Kentucky spring day slanting in through the windows, illuminating his features which now showed signs of tension and worry that had never before graced those features. He had spent much of the last few hours trying to work in the library, but not even the arrival of his commission as Lieutenant Colonel, complete with a personal note of congratulations from President Grant, could distract him or ease his worry. In the note Grant had mentioned that Gould and Hampton were doing as instructed, the former stabilizing the financial markets, the latter subtly restraining the worse bigotries of the die-hards in South Carolina.

No matter what he did to distract himself, his mind kept coming back to his wife's difficult delivery. He kept telling himself that old Doctor West knew his business; he was the most famous doctor in this part of Kentucky, and certainly the most expensive. Still, Teresa had been in labor for over eight hours, and Clay knew that there was only so much that even the best of doctors could do.

Oddly enough, it was the silence behind the bedroom door that

Clay found most disturbing. He understood that women always screamed with the pain of childbirth. Yet, despite the length of the delivery, Clay had heard no screaming, no crying—only the occasional grunt. Illogical as it might seem, Clay would have felt more assured if he had heard Teresa screaming in agony.

Suddenly the door was flung open, and one of Clay's maids came rushing out with a basin filled with bloody water and bloodier towels. Clay's heart leapt into his mouth at the sight of the servant's eyes; round and staring, giving an impression of fright. The way that she ran past him without so much as a sketch of a curtsy caused Clay's right hand to go to his throat and start pulling at his collar. Then Dr. West appeared at the door, iron-grey hair mussed, vest unbuttoned, walking unsteadily, like a man who had just received a tremendous shock. He looked at Clay and answered Clay's unspoken question.

"Colonel Clay, Mrs. Clay will live, and so will the twins."

"Twins?" asked Clay blankly.

"A healthy boy and a healthy girl. The . . . children are fine. I have left instructions on the care of all of them with your house-keeper, who is still with Mrs. Clay. The delivery or . . . something before the delivery has caused significant damage to Mrs. Clay. She must not attempt another pregnancy. Given the injuries she has suffered, another birth would almost certainly prove fatal.

"There is one further thing, Colonel Clay. I wish nothing further to do with you or your family. You will receive my bill for today's services in the mail. Please go to another physician in the future." The doctor bowed slightly, and turned to go.

Clay was utterly shocked by Dr. West's statements, and felt rage building in his breast. Staying his temper, he realized that West was terrified, not of Clay but of something he had seen in the bedroom. As West rapidly retreated down the stairs and toward the front door, Clay entered the bedroom quietly.

In the room he saw his wife propped into a half-sitting position, her lustrous black hair damp with sweat, her beautiful face haggard from hours of suffering. Yet she was smiling; not the cynical, vaguely predatory smile she usually wore, but a smile of the purest joy. Her breasts were exposed, and at each one she held a tiny figure wrapped in swaddling clothes, each sucking greedily.

Beside her stood Clay's housekeeper, an elderly black woman he had known all of his life, who had looked after him ever since he could remember. Clay looked at her, and realized with a start that his old nurse looked worried, almost frightened. Clay nodded to her, and asked, "Hannah, what is wrong? Is Mrs. Clay all right?"

"She had a rough time of it, but be in no danger of dying, Master Clay," said the old woman to the man who had freed her within hours of his father's death. "If you can excuse me, I need to go tell that worthless maid to get herself back up here. She ran out, swearing under her breath she would be quitting. She ain't quitting, not so long as your wife and children need help."

Wordlessly, Clay waived to Hannah to indicate she was dismissed. The old retainer swiftly left the room, sparing one backward glance at the bed, a glance that Clay would have sworn contained an element of terror. Clay sat on the bed and gently placed his hand alongside her cheek.

"I will not insult your intelligence by asking how you are. Dr. West indicated you will recover. He also said that the . . . injuries you have sustained will prevent us from having more children. I want you to know that matters not to me. I will make no demands on your body, but will still love you with all the intensity I possess."

Teresa Clay laughed, not her usual silvery, ominous laugh, but a warm chuckle. "Oh Alphonso, I am sorry there will be no more children. But, you are not getting off so lightly; there are a number of ways we can please each other without risking pregnancy, and when I am better we will explore them all."

Clay blushed, and quickly changed the subject. "Dr. West departed rather abruptly, and did not explain the nature of your injuries. Did he indicate them to you?"

She laughed again, this time her regular, chilling laugh. "Right after the babies came, he started to say something like it looked as if some of my female parts had been chewed. Then he got this scared look, and clammed right up. He quickly cleaned the babies off, handed them to me, and almost bolted out of the room. I have been thinking of names. What do you think of Cato Alphonso Clay for your son, and Brigid Doyle Clay for your daughter?"

"They sound perfect," replied Clay with sincerity. "May I see them?"

"Of course, silly," she responded with a smile. She disengaged the two infants from her breasts, and turned them to face their father.

Clay stared for a moment, and then hissed as he drew in air in surprise. Both children had open, bright, alert blue eyes, focused intently on him, something that was simply not possible in a newborn. Their mouths were surrounded by a revolting mixture of mother's milk and blood. Visible in their partly open mouths were a row of tiny, sharp teeth, not the red gums to be expected in a newborn. Clay glanced at his wife's exposed breasts, and saw tiny wounds around each nipple, oozing red. He looked up at his wife and children.

Teresa smiled lovingly at him. After a moment, both of the children followed suit.

AFTERWORD

This is a work of fiction. For reasons of plot, massive liberties have been taken with the historical record. Still, I have tried to stay close to the spirit of the events. For instance, Ulysses Grant did indeed wage a successful war to break the back of the original Ku Klux Klan (the KKK we think of today was resurrected in the time of Woodrow Wilson, who was a staunch supporter of its racist goals). Grant's crusade was much more complicated than indicated here, and peaked around 1871, not 1869; I moved it forward two years to make it coincide with Jay Gould and Jim Fisk's attempt to corner the gold market. Similarly, Jim Fisk was indeed shot to death during a dinner at Delmonico's by a spurned lover of his mistress; but this happened nearly three years after the attempt to corner the gold market. Although my main goal is to provide the reader with an entertaining work of fiction, my secondary goal is to give the reader of feel for those long ago days, so very important to making our country what it is today, so inadequately taught by our public schools.

The following gives the reader some background on the historical characters who appear in *Hail, Columbia!*:

AFTERWORD

AMBROSE G. BIERCE
WRITER & JOURNALIST

Ambrose G. Bierce (1842–1914?) Bierce had been a scout with the Army of the Cumberland, and performed numerous acts of lunatic bravery. His commanders thought so highly of him that although he enlisted as a private, he ended the war as a major of volunteers by brevet. He miraculously survived being shot through the head during the Atlanta campaign. Within two months he had returned to combat, despite being plagued by blinding headaches and vertigo that would be with him on and off for the rest of his life. Some people attribute his black view of life to damage from this head wound, but the evidence was abundant that he was a strange and difficult personality long before a Confederate bullet injured his brain.

After the war he earned his living as a journalist, working much of the time for the young William Randolph Hearst. On the side, he wrote fiction on the supernatural and the all-too real horrors of the Civil War. His greatest moment of glory, aside from the Civil War, was when he directed for Hearst the public relations campaign against the Southern Pacific Railway's attempt to sneak through Congress a bill forgiving some $70 million in back taxes owed to the Federal Government. The then-head of Southern Pacific, the old robber baron Collis Huntington, was nothing if not direct. He personally accosted Bierce on a street, informing him that every man had his price, and bluntly asked what Bierce's price would be. Bierce's reply is reputed to have been: "A check for $70 million, made payable to my good friend, the Treasurer of the United States"; eventually, that check was written.

From this point, his life slid downhill, due as much to his own flawed character as anything else. By 1913, he was seventy-one years old, in constant pain, and divorced by a wife he had genuinely loved, who could no longer tolerate his repeated infidelities. One beloved son had murdered a friend in a sordid fight over a girl, before turning the weapon on himself. Another had quietly drank himself into an early grave. His daughter wanted nothing to do with him. Telling some people he intended to go to Mexico to join a revolution, and others that he intended to throw himself into the Grand Canyon, he disappeared. No trace of his fate has ever been found. He would have undoubtedly been amused by the mystery he left behind.

ROBERT BUCHANAN
COLONEL, U.S. ARMY COMMANDER,
MILITARY OF LOUISIANA

Robert C. Buchanan (1811–1878) A nephew of President John Quincy Adams, Buchanan graduated West Point in 1830 and served in the Army continuously for forty years. In 1853, he founded Fort Humboldt on a wild stretch of the Pacific Coast.

Shortly thereafter, he was reinforced by a young, troubled lieutenant named Ulysses Grant. The precise Buchanan was disgusted by Grant's slovenly dress and increasing drinking, and told him to either resign or face court martial; Grant chose the former. Buchanan performed competently if not spectacularly in the Civil War, rising to the rank of Brevet Major General in the volunteer army. After the war, he reverted to his permanent rank of Colonel in the Regular Army, and was assigned command of the Department of Louisiana during Reconstruction. It is probably not a coincidence that Buchanan retired within a year of the man whom he had forced out of the peacetime army assuming the office of President.

DAN BUTTERFIELD
MAJOR GENERAL, ASSISTANT SEC. OF THE TREASURY

Daniel A. Butterfield (1831–1901) A member of the family that founded and owned American Express, Butterfield had no formal military training. Despite that, and to his credit, he joined the Army at the outbreak of the Civil War. Rising rapidly to become chief of staff to General Joe Hooker, he was a willing participant in Hooker's drinking and whoring. He was also wounded twice in battle, and was awarded the Congressional Medal of Honor.

Appointed Assistant Secretary of the Treasury by Grant in 1869, he took a $10,000 bribe to warn Jay Gould and Jim Fisk of any transactions Grant might take to frustrate their attempt to corner the gold market. Suspecting something, Grant bypassed Butterfield to frustrate the gold conspiracy, and shortly thereafter demanded Butterfield's resignation. Today, if Butterfield is remembered at all, it is as the composer of the army bugle call of "Taps."

SCHUYLER COLFAX
VICE-PRESIDENT OF THE UNITED STATES

Schuyler Colfax (1823–1885) Colfax was first elected to congress in 1855, and became Speaker of the House of Representatives in 1863. His cheerful geniality earned him the nickname of "Smiler." He was elected Vice-President on Grant's ticket in 1868. His apparent involvement in a railroad scandal soured both Grant and the GOP on Colfax, and he was not renominated in 1872. In 1885 he died of a heart attack, apparently induced by his effort to fight his way through a blizzard from a railway station to his hotel. Although he was corrupt, there is absolutely no indication that he ever participated in any sort of treason.

AFTERWORD

FREDERICK F. DENT
FATHER-IN-LAW TO ULYSSES S. GRANT

Frederick F. Dent (1786–1873) Before the Civil War, Dent was a wealthy, slave owning planter in Missouri. He doted on his daughter Julia, and was less than thrilled when she fell in love with an impecunious northern army officer named Sam Grant. Openly sympathizing with the South during the Civil War, he viewed with bitterness the rise of his son-in-law. The collapse of his fortune in the aftermath of emancipation only increased his bitterness. Utterly impoverished, he suffered the final humiliation of being invited to spend his final years in the White House by his son-in-law, President Grant.

JAMES FISK
WALL STREET SPECULATOR & FINANCIER

James Fisk (1835–1872) Fisk was a robber baron whose methods were extreme even for robber barons. In partnership with Jay Gould, he used fraudulent practices to gain control of the Erie Railroad, and went on to gain ever increasing wealth through shady practices, leading up to his attempt to corner the gold market with Gould. Interestingly, by the standards of the time Fisk was a friend of labor, and was genuinely liked by the employees of the firms he controlled. Although married, he publicly flaunted his affair with a beautiful performer, Josie Mansfield. A former suitor of Ms. Mansfield's shot Fisk to death while he was dining at Delmonico's.

NATHAN FORREST
FORMERLY LIEUTENANT GENERAL, CSA.
NOW PLANTER & POLITICIAN

Nathan Bedford Forrest (1821–1877) Although born in poverty and semi-literate, by the start of the Civil War, Forrest had made himself rich through planting, real estate speculation, and slave trading. Taking a commission in the Confederate Army, he proved that despite his lack of formal education he was an intuitively brilliant cavalry leader. He ended the war as a Lieutenant General, having had thirty horses shot out from under him, and having killed thirty-three enemy soldiers with his own hands. The major, indelible stain on his record occurred in April 1864 when he overran the Federal position of Fort Pillow, which was manned primarily by poorly trained black soldiers and their white officers.

Attempts to surrender were rejected, and a massacre of the black Federals ensued. To this day, there is debate as to whether Forrest ordered the massacre, or simply allowed it to happen. In either case, he bears responsibility for what was one of the major war crimes of the Civil War. In 1866 he was a major figure in the the formation of the Ku Klux Klan. Given his cold-blooded ruthlessness during the War, it is therefore surprising that he became increasingly disillusioned with the brutality of the Klan's tactics, to the point where by 1869 he had totally withdrawn his support for both their methods and their goals. To general amazement, in his final years he became a public advocate of racial harmony and reconciliation. His complicated family life presented in this novel is entirely fictional.

JAY GOULD
WALL STREET SPECULATOR & FINANCIER

Jay Gould (1836–1892) He was probably the most sinister character of the age of the robber barons; a man who was a model husband and father, but completely devoid of honesty and decency when it came to business transactions.

He gained control of the Erie Railroad through bribery and fraud, and shamelessly looted its assets to finance his further ventures. His supreme effort came in late 1869, when he embarked on a scheme to control all contracts for the future delivery of gold. As the United States was on the gold standard, this would have effectively given him control of America's currency supply. The only thing that could stop him would be a Presidential order to sell government reserves of gold on the open market. Thinking to cover this contingency, one of his henchmen, Abel Corbin, wooed and married the spinster sister of President Grant. Disproving the charges of cronyism, that then and thereafter were levied against him, when Grant learned of the scheme, he ordered the release of Government gold, destroying his beloved sister's husband. Gould managed to get out of the scheme with most of his fortune intact, and left insufficient evidence to support a prosecution.

In later years, Gould acquired control of the Union Pacific and Western Union, treating them as his personal piggy-banks. He died of tuberculosis, having spent his last years with his books and gardens which, aside from his wife and children, seem to have been the only things he ever loved.

JESSE R. GRANT
RETIRED TANNER & LEATHER MERCHANT,
FATHER OF ULYSSES SIMPSON GRANT

Jesse R. Grant (1794–1873) Jesse Grant was a rather unscrupulous businessman, who succeeded in becoming moderately wealthy in the tanning business. He was a loving and indulgent father, who was never known to raise a hand to any of his children; a restraint virtually unknown in that time and place. He undoubtedly loved his son, and unhesitatingly provided for him when Sam was at his lowest ebb. Later, he had no hesitation in attempting to gain lucrative Government contracts for his leather goods by trading on his famous son's name. On two separate occasions during the Civil War, General Grant had his father escorted out of Grant's area of command, upon finding Jesse trying to extort profitable contracts on the basis of his now-famous son's name. This led to no hard feelings; the elder Grant continued to pay cheerful visits to his son for the rest of his life. Incidentally, there was apparently some estrangement between Ulysses Grant and his mother. Despite the fact she outlived him, she never once visited him or set foot in the White House. That might have been one of the reason's for Grant's closeness to his rather unscrupulous, though loving, father.

ULYSSES SIMPSON GRANT
PRESIDENT OF THE UNITED STATES

Ulysses S. Grant (1822–1885) He was born Hiram Ulysses Grant. A clerk at West Point made an error in recording his name as Ulysses S. Grant, and he never bothered to have it corrected. His initials of U. S. Grant led to classmates calling him "Uncle Sam", later shorted to "Sam."

Throughout his career, everyone noted the absence of foul language in Grant, all the more puzzling in that he seems never to have formally joined a church. His foulest epithets really were "darn" and "doggone." Controversy over his political career has obscured the fact that most modern military historians rate him as one of the three greatest American generals (for those who are interested, Winfield Scott and Douglas Macarthur are usually considered the other two). It is clear that he was not happy with his military profession, the only career in which he was completely successful.

Although often denounced by political opponents as a mindless butcher, interested only in attrition, he in fact was supremely skilled. He lost fewer men in completely defeating Robert E. Lee than his predecessors had lost in repeated abject defeats at the hands of the Confederates. His Presidency is usually considered a failure. Recent historians have been revising his political reputation upward, although it will never equal his military reputation. The corruption of his administration was exaggerated by his political enemies. In fact, when he learned of illegal practices, he moved against them relentlessly, even if it involved his own relations.

The group called the "Liberal Republicans" criticized him as incompetent and dictatorial, and since many then-famous writers were members of that group, their hatred has tarnished his political reputation to this day. It should be noted that they meant to be "liberal" to the defeated Confederates, and were angry at Grant for using martial law to put down the Ku Klux Klan and to enforce the political rights of blacks. Although it did not happen as quickly as is indicated in this novel, he did indeed break the power of the Ku Klux Klan in the South. If Grant's successors had continued his policies, the civil rights struggles of the 20th Century would not have been necessary.

In 1884, his savings were completely wiped out by the failure of a fraudulent Wall Street firm in which he had been persuaded to invest. At the same time, he discovered he was dying of throat cancer; a twenty-cigar-a-day habit had caught up with him. His family was still dependent on him for support, and he knew the only thing he had to sell was his memoirs. Racing death, unable to eat solid food, refusing more than low doses of pain killers in order to keep his mind clear, aided by his friend Mark Twain, he finished the book the day before his death, gaining his family $500,000 and winning his last battle.

WADE HAMPTON III
FORMER LIEUTENANT GENERAL, CSA,
NOW PLANTER & POLITICIAN

Wade Hampton III (1818–1902) Hampton was born into one of the wealthiest families in the South. As an adult, he would own more slaves than any other individual in the South. At the outset of the war, he organized his own regiment, paying its expenses out of his own pocket. He demonstrated competent, if unspectacular military ability, and during the war rose steadily from Colonel to Lieutenant General. After the War his fortune was considerably diminished by the loss of his slaves and the destruction that Sherman's army had inflicted on his many estates. He was violently opposed to Republican Reconstruction policy, and for a time was a major figure in the Ku Klux Klan. Nevertheless, over time, his racial views moderated to the point that when he ran for public office, he would actively solicit, and receive, the support of black voters. He served as Governor of South Carolina from 1877 to 1879, and as a United States Senator from 1879 to 1891. He did indeed lose his right leg in a riding accident. Unlike how it was portrayed in this novel, it was during a hunting trip in 1878, not 1869.

ABOUT THE AUTHOR

Tracing his Californian ancestry all the way back to the 1830s, Jack Martin developed a passion for American history and the mystery genre. With encouragement and support from his beloved wife Sonia, he began writing the Alphonso Clay Mysteries. Sonia passed away on Christmas Eve 2009. He promised her he would finish the books and become a published author. The series includes: *John Brown's Body, Battle Cry of Freedom, Marching Through Georgia, Battle Hymn of the Republic, and Hail, Columbia!* Martin is also the author of the Harry Bierce Mysteries.

ALPHONSO CLAY MYSTERIES OF THE CIVIL WAR

FROM OPEN ROAD MEDIA

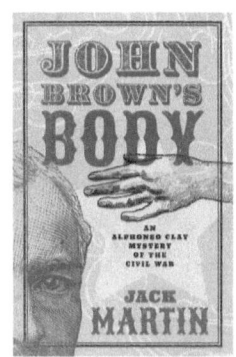

OPEN ROAD
INTEGRATED MEDIA